"Mariah Stewart is fast becoming a brand-name author."

—*Romantic Times*

Praise for Mariah Stewart's Dead Trilogy

DEAD WRONG

"Fast-paced and intricately plotted . . . [a] chilling, creative tale . . . Stewart excels in writing romantic suspense."

—*Library Journal*

"Mystery writer Stewart kicks off her new interconnected trilogy with a bang. Nail-biting suspense and emotional complexity make this launch irresistible."

—*Romantic Times* (☆☆☆☆½)

DEAD CERTAIN

"Stewart's Dead trilogy crackles with danger and suspense. Great characterization and gripping drama make Stewart's books hot tickets."
—*Romantic Times* (☆☆☆☆)

"A stand-alone read, and highly recommended . . . Mariah Stewart is an awesome storyteller, and the Dead trilogy is wholly entertaining and totally outstanding."
—America Online's Romance Fiction Forum

DEAD EVEN

"Get set for an exceptional tale. *Dead Even* is a masterpiece of writing. You will not want to put this book down."
—*Romance Reviews Today*

"Hold onto your seats, because Mariah Stewart will plunge you into a heart-pounding roller-coaster ride. You won't come up for air until the last page has been turned. Excellent!"
—Huntress Reviews

"Well plotted, imaginative and entertaining . . . The race against time is nail-bitingly tense."
—BookLoons Reviews

"An elaborate balance of suspense and outstanding storytelling . . . Ms. Stewart is truly a master of the romantic-suspense genre!"
—Reader to Reader

By Mariah Stewart
(*published by The Random House Publishing Group*)

COLD TRUTH
HARD TRUTH
DEAD END
DEAD CERTAIN
DEAD EVEN
DEAD WRONG
UNTIL DARK
THE PRESIDENT'S DAUGHTER

A Novel

Dark Truth

MARIAH STEWART

BALLANTINE BOOKS • NEW YORK

Dark Truth is a work of fiction. Names, characters, places, and incidents are the products of the author's imagination or are used fictitiously. Any resemblance to actual events, locales, or persons, living or dead, is entirely coincidental.

Ballantine Books Mass Market Original

Copyright © 2005 by Marti Robb

Published in the United States by Ballantine Books, an imprint of The Random House Publishing Group, a division of Random House, Inc., New York.

BALLANTINE and colophon are registered trademarks of Random House, Inc.

ISBN 0-345-47669-7

Cover photographs and design: Tony Greco

Printed in the United States of America

www.ballantinebooks.com

OPM   9   8   7   6   5   4   3   2   1

For Bridget, Marianne, Liz, and Nicole—
with thanks for the warm welcome
to the Meadows

Acknowledgments

Getting a book from the author's hands to the shelves in your local bookstore takes an incredible amount of teamwork. In the case of my Truth series, it took the Herculean efforts of some extraordinary people. My most humble thanks to the talented, dedicated, and hardworking professionals at Random House: Nancy Delia and Caron Harris in production; Carl Galian in the art department; Gilly Hailparn, Tom Perry, and Stacey Witcraft in publicity; Anthony Ziccardi and Kelle Ruden in sales. In editorial, the usual suspects: Signe Pike, Charlotte Herscher, and my new favorite guy, Dan Mallory.

And as always, Kate Collins, Linda Marrow, and Gina Centrello have my love and gratitude.

Prologue

Mounds of dirty snow rose from either side of the walk where the campus maintenance crew had just piled it. An unexpected storm had hit just as students were returning for the second semester. A slick glaze of ice made each step an adventure, but Nina Madden barely noticed. If not for the fact that she'd already slipped several times since she left the student union, she'd have been dancing. As it was, she was dancing on air.

Twenty minutes ago, she'd opened her on-campus mailbox to find the bid letter from the president of Theta Kappa Alpha, the first and only sorority she'd preferenced as the rush season came to a close. In forty minutes, she would walk into the Theta Kappa house and accept their offer of sisterhood. Nina shivered at the thought of it. She had just enough time to stop at her father's office in the liberal arts building and give him the good news.

Her father, American lit professor Stephen Madden, might not be as pleased as Nina was, but that was to be expected. He'd not been keen on her decision to participate in rush, afraid it would take too much time from her studies and result in a lower GPA. Well, she'd just have to prove to him that one could be both brainy and popular. There was no question of her academic ability, and God knew the Thetas were the most popular sorority at St. Ansel's College. Nina couldn't believe *they* thought she was one of them.

And then there was the matter of the Theta house. It was definitely the best house on campus. Every sister was required to live in that house during her sophomore and junior years, and that suited Nina just fine. It was more than just fine. It was a lifeline. With a stepmother who made Cinderella's look like a candidate for Mother of the Year, Nina couldn't wait for the fall semester, when she could move into the house and be out from under Olivia's scrutiny. It seemed no matter what she did—or didn't do—she could not please her father's wife of six years. A little breathing room would be good for everyone, Nina thought. Although Olivia did have her moments, Nina conceded. She had defended Nina's decision to rush.

Probably because she wants me out of the house

and out of her hair. But still, she'd proven to be an ally when Nina had least expected it.

Nina rounded the corner of Celestine Hall, deep in her thoughts, for a moment oblivious to the crowd that was gathering quietly. As she crossed onto the walk that led to Celestine's front steps, she noticed the police cars that lined the narrow drive.

Intent on seeing her father and making it to the Theta house on time, she ran up the front steps of the redbrick building. Several of her father's colleagues stood at the top of the stairs, their arms folded across their chests, their voices low, their expressions somber. Was it her imagination, or was everyone avoiding meeting her eyes?

In her hurried passing, Nina greeted those faculty members she knew, but received only muted responses. A member of the English department stood tall and imposing at the front door.

"Hello, Father Whelan." Nina reached to grab the door handle and attempted to step past him.

"I'm sorry, Nina." Father Whelan blocked her way and stopped her forward motion. "I'm afraid no one's allowed into the building."

"What's happened?" She tried to look past him, into the lobby, but she couldn't see beyond the police officers who were crowded around inside. "What's going on?"

Suddenly realizing her father wasn't outside with

his colleagues, a really bad feeling began to spread through her. For a long minute, she felt as if she were holding her breath. Pushing Father Whelan aside, she ducked into the building, only to be caught inside the door by a young cop who grabbed her by both arms and held her against the wall.

"Let me go." She struggled against him. "I need to see my father. Something's wrong . . ."

In the crowd gathered in the lobby near the elevator, Nina spotted her father's secretary, and called out to her.

"Mrs. Owens, what's happened? Where's my father?"

"Who's your father?" The police officer shook her gently. "What's your father's name?"

"Stephen Madden. Dr. Madden. His office is up there, on the second floor." She tried to calm herself, tried to stop the feeling of panic that was rising within her.

Whatever was happening here, it wasn't good, but maybe she could get this nice young cop to help her find her father.

"Please, if you would just let me go up to my father's . . ."

The elevator doors opened and the crowd fell silent.

Nina's father stepped into the lobby, his head held high, his spine straight as a rod, his gaze straight ahead and unseeing. He was, as always, tall and handsome, and he wore the brown tweed jacket he'd bought the summer before in London, where he'd taught a course on Hawthorne at an English university as part of an exchange program. His prematurely white hair was tucked behind his ears; his beard was neatly trimmed. He walked toward her, his bright blue eyes focused on a spot above the door, his arms held behind his back. A police officer accompanied him on either side, and as he passed Nina, she saw the cuffs that held his hands together.

"Dad?" she said incredulously as soon as she could find her voice. *"Daddy?"*

In the murmur of the crowd, she could make out the words *the Stone River Rapist.*

Nina's knees went weak, and her lungs felt as if all the air had been squeezed out of them. Her head began to spin, and through the blackness that engulfed her, she felt two strong arms catch her on her way down.

That sensation of spinning toward the floor, that loss of control, would be the last thing she'd remember of the day her father was arrested and charged with raping and murdering four of her fellow students over the past eighteen months.

One

November 2005
New York City

At eleven-ten on Tuesday morning, Nina Madden stared at the phone that sat on the corner of her desk, and willed it to ring.

Thirty seconds later, it did.

Finally. She punched the speaker button.

"Nina, we're ready for you in the conference room." The perky voice of the assistant to the marketing director chirped through the speaker.

" 'Bout time. This is *only* the *third* time we've tried to have this meeting." Nina slipped her feet back into the brown suede three-inch heels she'd kicked off the minute she got into her office that morning, and smoothed her newly cut short black hair. Then, papers in hand, she went immediately to the conference room at the end of the hall.

The door stood open, as the other participants in the marketing meeting of Griffin Publishing were already assembled. She closed the door behind her and took the first open chair. The head of the marketing department and her assistant, two copywriters, the art director, the publicist, and two people from sales were gathered around the oval table.

"Okay, next up on the schedule is Regan Landry's *Fallen Angels*." As always, Phoebe Valentine, the marketing director, got right to the point. She was mid-forties and buff as a twenty-year-old, blond and stylish. She was also the granddaughter of the company's founder. "We've all read the blurb—college girls who earned their tuition money dancing in 'gentlemen's clubs,' and who at some point were found murdered. Cases span the country . . ."

"Right." Nina nodded. "Regan went through her dad's files and found twenty-two such cases that remain open after nearly as many years. She selected four she felt were representative of the group as a whole, and concentrated on those."

"Have you seen any of it?" Phoebe asked.

"No, but I'm sure it's terrific," Nina assured her.

"It's her first solo work," Darren Heller, VP of sales, reminded Nina.

"Regan worked with her father on a number of books before his death," she replied calmly. "I have no reason to think this book will be any less wonderful than *In His Shoes,* which—I'm sure I don't need to remind you—she completed after her father's death. She's experienced—"

"She's not her father," Darren interrupted. "Josh Landry was the biggest selling author this company had. Griffin built its reputation on him."

"No, Regan is not her father, but she is a very fine writer, a good investigator. She does have her own style, puts her own spin on things. But that's no reason to assume that her book will be any less riveting than Josh's were." Nina folded her arms and leaned back in her seat. The last thing she'd expected this morning was to have to defend her author, in whom she had complete faith. "I don't think we need to worry about the quality of the book."

"What were the sales on last year's book?" Phoebe asked.

"Huge," Darren admitted. "Almost two million copies."

"Well, it was released not long after Josh's death," Tom DeMarco, the sales assistant and newest member of the staff, reminded them.

"Not so soon," Nina said. "Actually, it was a full year before we released that book."

"You sure?" Tom started searching through a folder.

"Positive." Nina nodded. "Josh died in August of 2004. *In His Shoes* came out in July of 2005. The book was less than a third complete when Josh was murdered. Regan finished it herself, got it in on time, and went on tour to support the book. I don't think we need waste any more time discussing whether or not she can carry this alone."

"I agree." Phoebe jumped in before anyone else could. "She's proven herself. I do, however, think we need to invoke Josh's name as often as possible."

Phoebe pointed to Hollis Behl, one of the copy assistants.

"Make sure the cover reflects that this is Josh Landry's daughter, the same daughter who coauthored his last however-many books." Before the young girl could reply, Phoebe turned to the publicity director. "And Lydia, I think we need to use her father's name in all our ads."

"Of course. We've already worked up some preliminary promotions . . . magazine ads, newspapers, radio." Lydia Post, the senior member of the group, skimmed her notes. In her mid-fifties, with fading strawberry blond hair and a soft waistline, Lydia was always one step ahead. "A shot on *Today* the day the book comes out, *Oprah* the day after."

"How 'bout one of the late-night talk shows?" Darren rubbed his chin thoughtfully.

"I don't think she'd want to do that," Nina told them.

"Why not?" Darren asked.

"I don't think it's her kind of thing. We can ask her, but I don't think she'd go for it. She really likes to keep a pretty low profile."

"How low a profile do you think you can keep with this kind of print run?" Phoebe wondered aloud. "And she'll do *Oprah* and *Today* but not the nighttime talk shows?"

"I can talk to her about it, but she declined to do Leno last time because she feels it is too celebrity driven. That's the best I can do." Nina shrugged.

"When do you think you can do that?"

"Later this week." Nina closed her file. "I've

already made plans to meet with her, since I'll be in Maryland anyway."

"Oh, that's right. Your stepmother." Phoebe nodded. "You have our condolences, Nina."

"Thank you."

"Yeah, sorry to hear about your stepmother," Darren added. "Anything else we need to discuss?"

"Just the cover art." Phoebe turned to the art director, Leo Curran, Nina's deceased stepmother now tidily tucked away with the cover copy and the publicity plans. "What have you got for us?"

Leo held up the poster that had been leaning against the table leg.

"Whoa. That's a strong image." Darren sat up straight in his chair.

"Amazing." Nina nodded, as the others began to murmur. "I love it."

"She's pretty slick, I have to admit." Leo's smile played above his grizzled beard as he turned the poster to the opposite side of the table, so all could admire the shadowy silhouette of the girl poledancing on a deep gold background.

"Leo, it's fabulous," Phoebe told him. "That is simply fabulous."

"I can see that on posters in every bookstore window . . ." Lydia said, scribbling notes. "Every college bookstore . . ."

"What do you think the author will say?" Leo asked Nina.

"She'll say it's outrageous. It *is* outrageous." Nina

grinned. "She's going to love it. May I take that with me to show her?"

"I'll get you a duplicate." Leo beamed, pleased that his efforts were so well received.

"Maybe we ought to look again at that print run," Tom suggested. "How many were we looking at, first printing?"

"Three quarters of a mil," Nina reminded him.

"Maybe we ought to go out with a little more." Phoebe turned to Darren. "Can you sell that many?"

"With that cover?" He laughed. "If you're thinking of eight hundred thousand, I think you ought to be ready to go back to press real soon. That book is going to fly off the shelves, cover like that. Josh Landry's name behind it."

"You're right. We're going to have to come up with something really fresh—marketing-wise, publicity-wise—to really launch this one in a big way," Phoebe agreed. "Ideas, anyone?"

"Ah, actually, Phoebe, I have to catch a plane." Nina checked the time on the wall clock.

"Sorry, my fault," Leo told her. "We spent way too much time on the last book, talking about cover possibilities for Sandra Ingram's next historical romance."

"I should have cut that discussion off sooner," Phoebe said. "I knew Nina had to leave before noon to make her plane. We'll shelve the marketing and publicity plans for now. Everyone, keep it on the front burner. We'll talk again after Nina gets back from meeting with Regan and we'll see what she's comfortable doing."

"Great idea, Phoebe, thanks." Nina rose and pushed the chair back.

"Hey, again, our condolences," Leo called to her as she left the room. "Sorry you lost your stepmother."

Nina nodded her thanks and closed the door behind her. There was no need for her coworkers to know she'd lost her stepmother sixteen long years ago. Right after her father was tried and convicted as a serial killer.

Nina tossed her bag into the backseat of the rented Trailblazer that was waiting for her at the airport, then studied the directions her stepbrother, Kyle Stillman, had given her over the phone when he called on Sunday to let her know that his mother— her late father's wife—had passed away.

"I wasn't sure if you'd want to be notified," he'd said somewhat stiffly. Understandable. Nina hadn't been in close contact with Kyle or his mother, Olivia Madden, in years.

"Yes, of course I'd want to know," she'd assured Kyle. "I appreciate your thinking of me. And of course, I'll be at the funeral. It will be good to see you again."

"You, too, Nina." Kyle relaxed and lowered the shield of attitude with which he'd started off the conversation. "I'm glad you're going to be here. Do you think you'll be able to stay for a few days?"

"I'm not sure." Curious, she asked, "Why?"

"Well, there's a lot of stuff in the house that needs to be dealt with."

"Nothing I want, Kyle," she quickly assured him.

"Well, don't be too hasty. For one thing, before Mom died, she told me that she had some things she'd been meaning to send to you, but never got around to it. She made me promise to get them to you."

"What sort of things?"

"Some things that belonged to you, some to your father. Your things you can just take and sort through later if you like, or throw away now, if you prefer. But I don't want to be put in the position where I'm throwing away someone else's belongings. I was hoping you'd be around long enough to go through his stuff."

"I don't need to go through it. Toss it all out. There's nothing of my father's I would want."

"Well, that's fine, Nina, except that some of his things—and yours, for that matter—are boxed up in the basement, where some of Mom's things are. Which means someone has to go through the boxes to determine whose things are in which." He paused, then added, "I could use a hand sorting through what belongs to whom."

"You're absolutely right, Kyle. You have enough on your plate right now. I'll see if I can swing a few days off, at least long enough to clear out Dad's things." She tapped the fingers of her right hand on her desktop. "It never occurred to me that any of my things would still be in that house. And frankly, I'd assumed Olivia had tossed every trace of my father a long time ago."

"You'll be surprised, then, to see just how much of your father is still in this house. You, too, Nina."

Swell, she'd thought then. Just . . . swell.

Nina read through the directions one more time, then tucked them into the top of her handbag next to her cell phone. She'd made reservations in Stone River at the Cloisters, a motel just outside of town, and if she hurried, she'd beat the rush-hour traffic. Not by much, she conceded as she followed the signs for I-95 and eyed the number of cars already vying for space on the interstate. Well, she'd only be on it briefly. She'd be taking the Bay Bridge across the Chesapeake, then she'd opt for one of the less traveled roads once she got onto the eastern shore. If there were still any less traveled roads, ones that she could find. It had been years since Nina had left Maryland. At the time, she figured she'd never be back. If Kyle hadn't called her, she probably wouldn't have returned at all.

Not quite true, she reminded herself. Regan Landry lived about twenty-five minutes from Stone River, and whether Olivia had passed away last weekend or not, Nina most likely would have been making this trip soon enough. Though visiting Regan didn't cause the lump of anxiety she'd felt the minute she realized she'd be returning to Stone River and the house she'd lived in all those years ago.

She had no interest in looking through any of her

father's belongings. She could barely stomach the thought of touching them.

And what of hers, if anything, could she have left behind that could possibly have a place in the life she'd made for herself far away from Stone River?

Two

"This was a soul that knew sorrow." The priest addressed the small gathering of mourners from the pulpit. "This was a heart that knew heartbreak. But the soul never surrendered, and the heart had faith enough to heal. Olivia never gave in to the sadness, and never permitted the pain to put out the light of her beautiful being."

Nina shifted uneasily in her seat. She hoped the priest wasn't going with this where she thought he was going.

"Olivia was a gallant soul, a generous soul. She was quick to offer a helping hand to those less fortunate than she, quick to offer a shoulder to cry on to the lonely, to the betrayed, to the abandoned. Because she herself knew what it was like to be lonely, to be abandoned, to be betrayed . . ."

Nina stared at the back of the head of the woman who sat directly in front of her. If she looked anywhere else, she'd see the others staring at her, and she wasn't in the mood to deal with that today.

". . . and earned her a place in heaven. To you, Olivia," the priest turned to address the closed coffin, "we say, Godspeed. For you, we pray, and we ask God our heavenly Father to give you the peace in death you could not find in life."

There was some restless shuffling behind her, and several weighty sighs from the end of her row, but Nina's eyes never wavered. When she'd entered the church, she'd seen Olivia's sister, Roseanne, directing her husband, three grown children, and their spouses into the pew behind the one in which Nina sat. Roseanne, who'd never seemed to care much for Nina's father before he was arrested, had made it plain by her loud, exasperated sighs that she and her family—or anyone other than Nina—should have been sitting in the pew directly behind Kyle and his wife, Marcie, their two children, and Marcie's parents. Nina wished she had the nerve to turn around and tell Roseanne that the seating arrangement hadn't been her doing. Kyle had led her up the aisle and guided her into the pew. Moments later she was joined by several of his cousins whom she'd never met before, and who, she assumed—judging by their warm smiles—had no idea who she was.

Nina bit the inside of her lower lip and tried to ignore the whispers behind her. She'd been uncomfortable from the moment she arrived and realized the sedan she'd parked next to in the lot carried several once-familiar faces. She recognized two members of St. Ansel's faculty in the backseat, though she could not recall their names. She'd smiled weakly when she'd met the eyes of the sedan's driver, Professor Overbeck, who'd been an up-and-comer in the American lit department. She tried to remember something her father had said about him back then, but couldn't quite recall what it had been. Something about Overbeck having his eye on the chair that her father occupied. She wondered if he ever attained it. And wasn't that Professor Toomey—Jacqueline Toomey, once known on campus for her wonderful lectures on Shakespearean comedies—in the front passenger seat?

Whatever, she shrugged. It hardly mattered now. While they all stared as she got out of the car—Overbeck had even raised a hand in a sort of startled wave—none made any effort to speak to her.

Just as well, she thought as she'd walked briskly toward the church. *What the hell would we talk about?*

So, what have you been doing with yourself since your dad's conviction?

The gruesome nature of the murders aside, her father had brought infinite shame to the college. She wondered if they still talked about it, there at St. Ansel's.

She knew one thing for certain. They'd all be talking about it today.

* * *

"Nina, wait up," Kyle called to her as she started out of the driveway.

The service had ended minutes ago, but Nina had not waited to follow the coffin before slipping out of her pew and heading for the parking lot. She'd paid her respects to the woman who had once been her father's wife, she'd prayed for her eternal happiness, and now she wanted out and away from here. She felt edgy and conspicuous and the small church had become claustrophobic after a while. She'd been grateful when Father Whelan, a longtime friend from St. Ansel's, had finally concluded the service with his heartfelt comments to Kyle and his family and the pallbearers rose to accompany the coffin out of the church. She'd had almost a full minute to leave by the far end of the pew and slip out a side door while the priest was waiting for the altar boys. She'd gone straight to her car, hoping to escape unseen, but the buses for the parish school across the street blocked her way. The bottleneck was just about to break free when Kyle jogged toward her, calling her name.

Dammit.

"Hey, you're not sneaking out before the luncheon, are you?" He gestured to her to roll down her driver's side window. "And were you skipping the cemetery, too?"

"Actually, I was." She debated which excuse to use, then decided to go with the truth. "I'm really uncomfortable here, Kyle. I know your mother's family must have been shocked, seeing me in the church. And I don't blame them. My father caused your mother a great deal of pain." She smiled wryly. "As Father Whelan reminded us."

Kyle patted her arm, which rested where the window had been. "Father Whelan was a very close friend of my mother's. He stood by her through everything, all those years. He was a good friend, right to the end of her life. I think we have to forgive him if he lost sight of the fact that there was more to my mother than the fact that she was Stephen Madden's widow." Kyle squeezed her arm. "Sorry, I don't mean to sound insensitive. But it seems that that's how my mother was known, these last years. As Stephen Madden's widow."

A grimace marred Kyle's handsome face. "Why she stayed here in Stone River, why she didn't leave and move on with her life . . ." He shook his head. "I tried to convince her to move to Delaware with Marce and me, but she did not want to leave that house. For the life of me, I'll never understand her attachment to it. It was as if she just couldn't let go of that part of her life."

"Kyle, I'm so sorry. I don't know what to say to you."

"Say you'll come to the luncheon with us, say the hell with the rest of them. You were her stepdaughter. She cared about you." He smiled benignly. "You were the daughter she never had."

Nina wisely chose not to debate that particular point with him. Olivia had never given her the warm fuzzies. Most of the time, she tolerated her. No need to get into that with Kyle, though. Perhaps his memory of those years differed from hers. After all, he was already in college when Nina came to live with her father and his new family. Perhaps his mother hadn't shared with him the animosity she'd directed toward Nina.

That was okay. He'd been gracious to her since her arrival this morning, and was going out of his way to make her feel less of a pariah. If his memory of one happy family didn't quite match Nina's, he was welcome to it, as far as she was concerned.

"Kyle, I appreciate your invitation, I really do. But I think it's best that your mother's family have this time with you and Marcie and your children." She looked up at him. "I have an author who lives nearby. I'd planned on seeing her while I was in the area."

"But you're not going back to New York right away, are you? Not without coming by Mom's house."

"I'll be in the area for a few days. I have a room at the Cloisters through at least tomorrow night, so I'll be around."

"I don't know if I trust you not to sneak back to New York while I'm wining and dining the relatives."

"Hey, I promised I'd help out with the house. I wouldn't go back on that." He'd leaned into the window, and she patted his arm.

"Good, good. There's a lot of furniture in that house that belonged to your dad, you know? My mom moved into his house, not the other way around."

"If there's anything there you and Marcie can use, please feel free to take it. I don't have room for another stick in my little apartment, so if you want anything . . ."

"I don't know if I'll pass that on to Marce or not. I want to think on that." He rubbed his chin. "I hate to complicate things right now."

"I'm not following you."

"Oh. Of course. You'd have no way of knowing." He laughed to cover his embarrassment. "Marcie and I are separated. She's here today with me because, well, because of the kids, mostly. She and my mother weren't that close. Not like you and Mom were, back then."

"I'm sorry to hear that, Kyle. Are you trying to work things out?"

He held one hand out, palm down, and wiggled it side to side.

"Touch and go," he told her. "We're putting that on the back burner for now. I told her I couldn't deal with that until we got past Mom's funeral and disposing of her things."

"Do you have to do that all right now? Can't you just close up the house for a while, wait until things settle down a bit, then go back and do what you have to do?"

"Well, I'd thought you'd be wanting us to get her things out of your way as soon as possible," he said.

"I don't understand. Your mother's things aren't in my way."

"They would be if you wanted to sell the house right away."

She stared at him, not comprehending.

"Hasn't Mr. Wexler, the attorney, been in touch with you?" Kyle frowned. "The house belonged to your father. He never added my mother's name to the deed. Under the terms of his will, the house was to pass to you upon her death. Didn't you know?"

Speechless, Nina shook her head from side to side.

He dug in his pocket, and pulled out a single key. He handed it to her, saying, "That's why I was in such a hurry to get Mom's things out of your way. The house belongs to you now, Nina. I thought you knew. It's all yours . . ."

Three

Nina found the house that Regan Landry built at the end of a long drive through a marshy area. Five years ago, when Regan purchased the plot, the entire three acres were covered with reeds and scrub pines. Now, a tall house sided with weathered-gray cedar stood a hundred feet in from the bay that it over-looked. A wooden walk led to a dock where an old boat was tied up, and a hammock swung between two posts. The boat appeared to need a paint job and the hammock looked as if it was hanging over the choppy waves of the bay. Nina parked her car at the end of the drive, which looked out over the dock and offered a wide and glorious view.

"Hey, you're early!" Regan called from the deck at the back of the house. She rose from her chair where she'd been seated next to a small table and looped her thumbs into the pockets of her jeans.

"Oh, I'm sorry. I didn't realize . . ." Nina frowned and looked at her watch. It read one o'clock, the agreed-upon time, but apparently it was running a bit fast. She made a mental note to have it checked.

"Not to worry," Regan assured her as she came down the two steps to ground level. "I was just reading over last night's work."

"Did you want to take a few minutes to finish up?"

"Don't be silly." Regan waved her on. "Close that car door."

Regan greeted her editor with a hug.

"I'm so glad to see you. Did you have a hard time finding me?"

"Not at all. The directions were great."

"Well, come on in, I have lunch all ready." Regan took Nina by the arm. "And then we can get down to business."

"Oh. Right. Business." Nina smiled. "I have something in the car for you. I'll be right back."

Nina returned to the car and opened the trunk. She took out the large envelope she'd carried with her on the plane.

"A gift from Leo." Nina handed the envelope to Regan.

"A gift from Leo? It can only be cover art." She grinned and began to open it.

"What do you think?" Nina asked as Regan removed the wrapping from the poster.

"Oh, wow." Regan's eyes widened. "Wow. Look at that. Oh, wow . . ."

"That's what we all said." Nina grinned. "That's what we were hoping you'd say, too."

"Are you kidding? This is simply . . . awesome. It's different from any other book jacket I've ever seen. It captures the book . . . Oh, I love it." Regan looked up from the cover to Nina. "It's perfect. Just perfect."

"Leo will be thrilled when he hears how much you like it."

"Well, he won't have to wait. I'll call him right now." Regan picked up the poster and gestured for Nina to come along. "Let me get you something to drink while I make the call."

Nina followed Regan into the back entry, though a small hall, and into the kitchen, which opened to a sitting room on the left. A large rectangular island topped with blue granite commanded the center of the room, and white cabinets with glass doors lined the walls. The windows along the back wall offered a sweeping view of the Chesapeake Bay, and on the floor in front of the windows stood a tall bright yellow vase filled with grasses that looked as if they'd been picked that morning from the marsh.

Regan grabbed the phone and dialed even as she chatted with Nina.

"Did you want coffee? Or something cold? I have iced tea, soft drinks—mostly diet, I'm afraid—and I have . . . Leo? It's Regan Landry. Nina just arrived with your miraculous artwork, and I just had to call immediately and thank you for doing such an incredible job . . ."

Regan pointed to the coffeepot, opened the refrigerator door, silently asking Nina her preference. When Nina nodded in the direction of the iced tea, Regan took out the pitcher and opened a cupboard and grabbed two glasses. She poured as she chatted, and handed a glass to Nina. Thanking the art director one last time, Regan disconnected the call and returned the phone to its base.

"I'm going to have this baby framed," Regan told Nina. "I'm hanging this one right out there in the front hallway."

"Well, I'm certainly glad you like it. We're planning big things for this book, you know. The jacket is just the first step toward getting this book noticed."

Regan hunched her shoulders and appeared to shiver slightly.

"It's a little scary for me, you know. *Fallen Angels* is the first book I wrote entirely by myself. I've always worked with my dad in the past." Regan leaned on the granite counter. "I'm afraid I won't do him justice."

"You're going to do just fine. The book will be wonderful. I loved the proposal. And if you have any questions, or problems, or concerns, you know I'm always there for you."

"Thank you. From the bottom of my heart. I don't know what I'd do without you."

"You'd write a great book, and someone else would edit it," Nina told her, adding, "Okay, maybe not quite as well . . ."

Regan laughed. "Definitely not as well."

"You're easy to work with, Regan. There'd be fewer editors with gray hairs if everyone was as easy." Nina sipped her iced tea. "How is the book coming along, by the way?"

"I'm a week away from sending it to you. I need one more pass through, then you may have it." Regan toyed with the petals of the orchid that stood in a vase at the end of the counter.

"I can't wait to read it."

"And I can't wait to eat." Regan changed the subject. "I have tuna ready for the grill, which needs maybe six or seven minutes to come up to temp."

In what seemed like the blink of an eye, Regan had the tuna on the grill while Nina put the finishing touches on the salad. Less than a half hour later, they were seated at one of the tables on the deck, eating and sipping wine, and chatting like the old friends they were.

"I still remember the first time I met you," Regan said. "The first time I came to New York with my dad. I was twenty-five and just getting out of grad school, no idea what I wanted to do with myself, and Dad insisted that I come along with him to meet Carlos. I was totally intimidated by the whole publishing thing and didn't want to go, but I was afraid he'd be hurt if I begged off."

"I remember, too. Carlos was so full of himself; he loved it when his big authors came into the office. And your dad was a big author. His books were among the first at Griffin to make the major best-seller lists. He helped put Griffin on the publishing map." Nina smiled, remembering her first few years as an assistant editor. "We were all so intimidated by your father. He was so tall and handsome and charming. All of the young editors were in awe of him."

"What I remember most about that trip was how Carlos shrugged me off onto you. He wanted to talk to Dad, but he always treated me as if I were the biggest pain in his ass. I don't think Dad ever saw that, though. He had to look hard to see the negative in people he cared about. And he did enjoy working with Carlos."

Nina laughed. "He'd called me into his office before you and Josh arrived that day, and told me to take you shopping. 'Take her to lunch, take her to Saks, take her someplace. Josh and I have work to do.' We had a great time that day, though, in spite of our most senior editor's annoyingly chauvinistic attitude toward you."

"I know he was shocked after Dad died and I told him I'd only work with you." Regan stabbed at a piece of apple in her salad. "Though he should have seen that coming. Friendship aside, you're a terrific editor. Your input into *Fallen Angels* made a good idea even better. I can't wait until you read it."

"Then give me a copy of what you have, to take back with me. I don't care if it needs work."

"I'll have to print a copy for you."

"No hurry. I'll be around for a few days." Nina ate the last of the fish. "The tuna was fabulous. What was in the marinade?"

"Lime and garlic and a few other goodies. I'll give you the recipe." Regan drained her glass. "You said you'd be around for a few days?"

"My stepmother passed away over the weekend. The service was today."

"Oh, I'm so sorry. Were you close?"

"Not at all." Nina frowned without realizing it. "We've had little contact since my father . . ." Nina paused just the slightest bit. "Since my father died years ago."

"How old were you when you lost your dad?"

"I'd just turned twenty."

"And your mother?"

"She died when I was fourteen. Complications from back surgery, if you can believe that. She and my father were divorced when I was five, and I lived with my mom until her death. I'd spent some vacation time with my dad every year, but I never felt I got to know him at all. He married Olivia when I was twelve, so they'd only been married for two years when I came to live with them. It was a very awkward situation."

"They had no children together?"

"No. Olivia had a son, Kyle, from her first marriage. He's five years older than I." Nina placed an elbow on the table and rested her chin in her hand. "He was just enough older to always be a stranger to me. He was already in college when I came to live with my father and his mother. Though I have to say, he's been very nice, very considerate, since I came down for the service."

"Well, you're family, more or less, right? With his mother gone, maybe he sees you as still being his sister. Were he and his mother close?"

"I think they were." Nina wished she could tell Regan everything. If there'd ever been a time in her life when she wanted to confide in a friend it was now. But there was no way she was going to tell the whole sordid story. She skipped the ugly parts and went straight to the immediate problem. "Kyle told me this morning that my dad had never added Olivia's name to the deed to the house, that Dad had left the house to me."

"Why do I have the feeling this has not made you happy?"

"I don't want the house. I don't want anything from that house. As far as I'm concerned, Kyle can sell the place, contents and all, and he can keep the money."

"That's very generous of you." Regan put her glass down, and studied Nina's face.

"Not at all. His mother lived there for the past, what, twenty years or so? It was her house, not mine. It rightfully belongs to Kyle."

"You can arrange that with the lawyer," Regan told her.

"You're right. I can." Nina nodded. "And I will. I'll just stop by tomorrow and go through whatever boxes Kyle wanted me to go through, toss out whatever belonged to my father, and then I'm free to go back home."

"I'm sure there are some things in the house you might want. Your father's books or papers or something, photographs . . ."

"There's nothing." Nina's jaw set and her eyes narrowed. "There is nothing I want from that house. I'll drag my dad's stuff out to the curb so the trashmen can pick it up. Kyle can keep whatever he wants. There's nothing there I care about."

"Well, keep an open mind. You never know what you might find there." Regan tugged at Nina's arm. "Come on. Let's take the boat out for a while, and I'll tell you about the idea I have for the next book . . ."

Four hours later, still dressed in the sweatpants and matching sweatshirt she'd borrowed from Regan, Nina made her way back to Stone River in the rented car. She'd planned on stopping at the Cloisters to grab some dinner before heading over to the house. The key Kyle had given her earlier had all but burned a hole in her pocket.

She had called Kyle's cell phone and left the message that she'd meet him at the house in the morning, but now was regretting having made the call. As she and Regan had buzzed along the bay that afternoon, she'd found herself dreading more and more going back into that house. Which meant she'd have to face it sooner rather than later. And there was no time like the present.

Besides, she told herself as she made a left turn onto Oak Drive, she didn't know how she'd react to being there. She'd rather not have an audience her first time inside.

She slowed down as she approached house number one seventeen, and eased over to the curb. She sat behind the wheel of the car with the engine running and her heart racing, and stared at the house she'd lived in for fewer than five years. The smallish Tudor with its faux thatch roof and tan stucco exterior sat square in the middle of its lot. The driveway was to the right, and ended at the garage, which was styled to match the house right down to its dark brown beams and shutters. A rosebush twined over the front of the garage and spread onto the side of the house. *That would have been Olivia,* Nina thought. She'd been fond of roses.

A flash of memory: after her mother had died and her father had brought her here to live, Nina had been too numb to care about where she put her clothes or whether her room had bookshelves on which to place her books and the other precious things she'd brought with her from home. All she cared about was the fact that her beloved mother was lost to her, and she was forced to live with a man she barely knew, and his wife whom she didn't know at all. Her father had carried her suitcases up the steps to the room she always stayed in when she visited. He'd said very little to her that day that she remembered, other than, "Put your things away now, Nina, and come downstairs. Olivia's made dinner . . ."

The door was open, but in her grief Nina had failed to notice that the room had been freshly painted in her favorite shade of blue and the furniture all painted white, as she'd once said she'd like to do someday. A bowl of freshly cut roses stood on the table next to the bed, and their perfume scented the air. She'd thrown herself on the bed and sobbed until her father, utterly lost about what to do with her, had merely closed the door and gone downstairs. Nina had stayed facedown on the bed for hours. Even now it hurt to remember how alone she'd felt then, how abandoned . . .

She recalled the priest's comments earlier in the day, about how Olivia had been abandoned, and Nina felt a pang. She had certainly been as guilty as her father had been on that score, and for the first time, she found herself feeling sorry for her late step-mother. It hadn't been Olivia's fault that she'd come into Nina's life at the worst possible time. It wasn't her fault that her husband had been . . . what he was.

A perpetually cheating husband, a murdering rapist.

Nina swallowed hard. If life had dealt her a few bad blows, she could barely begin to imagine how Olivia must have felt. She'd married a man she'd loved—Nina had never doubted that Olivia had loved her husband deeply—given her heart to him, and her life turned out to be a nightmare that most women could not even begin to imagine.

How does a woman go on when she discovers the man she married is a serial rapist and murderer of the very young women he's been entrusted with teaching?

The same way that the man's daughter goes on, Nina reminded herself. *Except that I never hesitated to leave, to simply walk away. Olivia apparently felt compelled to stay, though God knows why.*

Nina got out of the car and stood on the walk, and studied the house that now, at dusk, was deep in the shadows of the tall trees that dwarfed it. When she'd steadied her nerves, she walked up the brick path, slipped the key into the lock, and opened the door.

The air inside still wore a trace of Youth Dew, Olivia's favorite fragrance. On the table inside the door was a basket of flowers. The card stuck in the plastic holder was addressed to Kyle. Nina closed the door behind her and went into the living room. The furniture was pretty much the same, though the sofa wore a slipcover she didn't recognize and there was a new chair near the fireplace to replace the one her father had always sat in to read at night. The nights when he was home, that is. Nina seemed to recall there were many nights when he'd arrive long after she'd gone to bed. She knew just how many such nights there had been. She never permitted herself to sleep until she heard his car pull into the driveway, his footfall on the steps.

Nina went into the kitchen and turned on the light. A cup and saucer had been rinsed and placed on the counter, the cup upside down. There was nothing else out of place.

She went from room to room, trying to remember what it had been like to live in this house. She knew she'd eaten meals in that kitchen, but couldn't remember one time she'd sat at that table. There had been holidays, of course there had been, but she had no clear recollection of any of them. She walked to the spot where they used to set up the Christmas tree. She knew it had gone here, in the corner of the living room, but she couldn't bring up a picture of it in her mind. There'd been dinners in the dining room, but she couldn't recall what the china had looked like or what she had eaten. It was as if she'd existed there as a ghost-child, rather than a girl struggling through her teens with all the afflictions young girls struggled with, and many unique to her own situation. Mostly, Nina remembered struggling alone.

She went up the steps to the second floor and passed the room her father had shared with Olivia, and pretended not to remember how she'd heard her stepmother's sobs the night Stephen Madden had been arrested. Olivia had died in that room, Kyle had told her when he'd called her on Sunday evening. It occurred to Nina that Olivia had died in that room long before last weekend.

She went straight to her bedroom and pushed open the door. The furniture hadn't changed, though the bedspread and curtains were different and the walls were now pale yellow. Nina had a vague recollection of Olivia mentioning in a letter or card years ago that she'd redecorated the room, so that when Nina came to visit, perhaps the memories wouldn't seem as bad.

Nina'd thought at the time that Olivia was a fool to stay in that house, and an even bigger fool to think that a coat of paint on the walls and a new look to the bed and the windows could do anything to take away the memories Nina had of living in that house.

But now, standing in the quiet room, seeing how carefully Olivia had tried to preserve a place for Nina here, she found herself wishing she'd made the trip back, just once. Her heart pinched her from within, and she felt sympathy for Olivia flood through her for the first time.

"Sorry, Olivia. I should have been kinder to you. I'm sorry . . ."

She turned to leave the room, and noticed the table next to the bed. A half dozen roses, now dried and fragile, had been placed in a pretty dark blue vase. Had Olivia kept fresh flowers in this room, in the hope that Nina might in fact come back to see her after all these years?

Nina would never know.

Filled with a sorrow she'd never anticipated, she went down the steps and out the front door. Locking it behind her with shaking hands, she fled the house at 117 Oak Drive as if she were being pursued by demons.

In a way, she was.

Four

"Nina?" Kyle's voice sounded as if it came from outside the house.

"Down here," she called from the foot of the basement stairs.

A minute later, he was bounding down the steps.

"You're here early," he said. "I thought I'd have to come over to the Cloisters and drag you, kicking and screaming, to get you here."

"Why waste time?" She shrugged. "Besides, I told you I'd give you a hand."

She turned and pointed to a stack of boxes that lined the back wall.

"I poked into those already. I think those must be your mother's. Some of them have old household items—curtains, bed linens, pots, baking pans, that sort of thing—that must have fallen from favor over the years and were packed up and stored down here. There are a few boxes of clothing that belonged to her as well." She turned and pointed to the boxes she'd placed near the steps. "Those boxes contain some of my father's old papers, some books, his doctoral thesis, some files. They can all go to the trash. Those three boxes on the bottom hold some of his old clothes. They can get tossed out or sent to a thrift store, I don't care which."

"You've been busy." Kyle sat on the bottom step.

"I'm determined." She smiled. "Do you have any suggestions on who I should call to pick up this stuff?"

"I have a list of thrift stores that pick up, but I left it in the car. I can get it for you." He started to rise, and she gestured for him to sit back down. "No hurry. I can get it before I leave today."

"Thanks for separating Mom's stuff from Stephen's. I wasn't really looking forward to going through her things just yet." He paused, then added hastily, "But I don't have a problem with it. I know you'll want to be making arrangements to sell everything as quickly as possible so you can get back to New York."

"Well, I wanted to talk to you about that. Let's go upstairs. I picked up some cold drinks on the way over this morning, and I could use one now."

"Sure." Kyle stood and waited for Nina to pass him, then followed her up the steps. When they reached the top, he switched off the basement light and closed the door.

"I can arrange to have someone come and pick up all the stuff in the basement," he told her. "That won't be a problem. And if you'd like, I can have the furniture appraised and sold for you, and send you a check. I know you have an important job and you're probably itching to get back to it. This has to be depressing for you, but I do appreciate your coming. Mom would have been so happy that you were here."

It was on the tip of her tongue to say, *She would have been happier if I'd come while she was still alive.*

Instead, she told him, "Your mother was a good person, Kyle. She had a hard time of it. I wouldn't have wished that . . ." She searched for a word. " . . . that *situation* on anyone. Why she chose to stay in this house, and in this town, I'll never understand."

"Simple." He shrugged. "She had nowhere else to go. She could live here for free—that was in his will—and she had a few friends. And of course, she had Father Timothy."

"Father Whelan?"

"Yes, sorry. We knew him as Father Tim. He and my mother have been friends forever. Since even before . . ." He appeared embarrassed.

"Before my father ruined all our lives. You can say it, Kyle. It isn't as if it's a secret, especially between you and me." She opened the refrigerator door. "Pepsi or Diet Pepsi?"

"Diet, thanks."

She took out two cans and searched the cupboards

for glasses, then finding two, filled them with ice and poured the drinks. Handing one glass to Kyle, she said, "There's something we need to talk about."

"Shoot."

"I called my dad's attorney this morning. I asked him how I could go about putting the house in your name."

"I don't understand. Why would you do that?"

"Because I think it rightfully belongs to you."

"Nina, your father bought this house before he even met my mother."

"It's *her* house, Kyle. She's the one who lived in it all these years, she's paid the taxes and planted the flowers and trimmed the hedges. It was hers. Now it's yours."

"Nina, I don't think you should make any hasty decisions. I mean, it's very generous of you, but you really need to think this through."

"I have thought it through. I thought about it all night last night. I know it's the right thing to do, Kyle."

"I don't know what to say." He was clearly stunned. "Nina, that's incredibly generous of you, but I can't let you give away your inheritance like that."

"It's already done. Or will be, as soon as Mr. Wexler completes the paperwork and I sign it. Which I will do in the morning. And as far as my inheritance is concerned, let's just say I've already gotten everything from my father that I'm going to get."

"I wish I could think of something to say," Kyle told her. "I mean, about your father."

"There's nothing you or anyone could say. He was what he was. Whatever that might have been. He ruined all our lives. You seem to have risen above it all, and I can see why you'd have wanted a career in law enforcement. I've managed to make a life for myself in spite of him. Your mother was the real victim here. I wish I'd been mature enough to realize that before now. No one should be asked to carry the burdens she was forced to bear. I wish I'd . . ."

"Don't, Nina. Don't second guess yourself."

"It's difficult not to, when I go upstairs into my old room and find that she still kept flowers in there, apparently in the hopes that I'd come to visit. Or when I realize that all the years I'd brushed her off as my father's wife and nothing more than that, she'd really tried to be there for me, and would have been if I'd let her." She blew out a long breath. "I was very immature and self-centered to have treated her the way I did, to not have seen how she had tried to help me through that time."

"You were very young, and you had your own burdens to bear."

"That doesn't excuse the way—"

He held up one hand, and said, "She was all right with it, Nina. I think she understood how difficult it had been for you, with your mother dying and you having to move here immediately after. She knew how hard that was. She knew that you had a lot to deal with. I think you're right, she wanted to help you, but she understood why you didn't let her." His smile was sad. "It happens that way sometimes. She didn't hold it against you."

"Well, it was my loss, not hers."

"I think maybe you both lost a little something."

"In any event, the house and everything in it is yours—will be yours—and you can sell it or move into it or do whatever you like with it."

"I don't feel right about this."

"I'm sorry, but I feel very right about it." She patted his right hand and he covered hers with his left.

"We'll split it."

"Uh-uh." She shook her head.

"I'll send you the money for the furniture, then . . ."

"You're not following me, Kyle. I want nada. Zero. Zilch. It's yours." She squeezed his hands, then extracted her own. "You said you and Marcie were separating. Live here if you like. Or sell it and buy something else. Or sell it and put the money in trust for your kids. Start or add to their college funds. Whatever makes you happy."

"I don't know what to say."

"Then don't say anything. Particularly, don't argue with me anymore. There is absolutely nothing you can say that will change my mind."

"How 'bout if I tell you how much the houses in this neighborhood are selling for, would that do it?"

"Sorry, no. I don't care."

"You must be doing very well if you can afford to brush off that much money. Even half would be several hundred thousand dollars."

"Tempting, but no. Frankly, I wouldn't feel right about taking any money from this house. It never felt like mine. It still doesn't. I have no attachment to it whatsoever. Those were not happy years for me, the years I lived here. I'd just as soon walk away, Kyle. I'm hoping you understand."

"I guess I do. I was just thinking it's a lot of money to just give away."

"I don't feel as if I'm giving anything away. I don't feel entitled to it in the first place. You're Olivia's heir. The house was hers. Let's just look at it that way, and talk about something else."

He was just about to say something when the doorbell rang.

"I've no idea who that could be." Kyle shook his head and went to answer it. "Unless it's the mailman . . ."

Nina remained in the kitchen, and was rinsing her glass in the sink, looking out the window and thinking how Olivia had done such a lovely job in the backyard. She heard footsteps behind her and turned to tell Kyle how much she admired his mother's green thumb, when she realized Kyle was not alone.

"Father Whelan," she said, surprised to see the priest.

"Nina, good to see you again." He extended both hands in greeting and took both of her hands in his. "I was hoping to get a few minutes with you yesterday, but you disappeared on us. Welcome home."

Not my home, she bit back the words. *Never my home.*

"Thank you, Father." She smiled at the tall, good-looking priest, whose white hair only made him appear more distinguished than he had as a young man.

"I don't think I've seen you since we buried your father," he was saying.

"That's probably correct." She nodded. "I haven't been back to Stone River until now."

"Olivia missed you, she was very fond of you." He squeezed her hands before letting them go.

"We were just having that discussion, Father," Kyle told the priest. "Nina knows that Mom understood why she didn't come back."

"Good, good." Father Whelan's eyes narrowed. "Don't beat yourself up over it. I can see in your eyes that you have. Olivia was the last person in the world who'd have wanted to make you feel guilty. She sensed that you had to live your life away from here. Just let it go. You made your peace with her by coming now."

"Thank you, Father."

"How long will you be staying with us? I imagine you'll want to settle things here, with the house."

"Kyle's taking care of all that," Nina replied, not bothering to go into detail about the arrangements she'd already made to pass the house into her step-brother's name.

"Good. That's good of you, Kyle." The priest turned back to Nina. "There is something I need to talk to you about, though, Nina. Would you rather we chatted alone?"

"Hey, I can go upstairs and get started on . . ." Kyle began to back toward the doorway.

"Not at all." Nina shook her head. "I can't think of anything we couldn't discuss in front of Kyle. Please, Father, have a seat here at the table. Could I get you something to drink?"

"Nothing for me, thanks, Nina." Father Whelan pulled out a chair and sat in it. "Nina, as you know, I was Olivia's friend. We'd been friends for many years, since Kyle started kindergarten at the parish school."

"That's about thirty-five years, in case you're try-ing to figure that out, Nina." Kyle smiled and took the seat across from the priest. "I'm five years older than you."

"I remembered." She turned to Father Whelan with curiosity. "What was it you wanted to tell me?"

"As you know, I spent a great deal of time with Olivia the past few years, even more so these past months when we knew her time was short. Her can-cer had been in remission for so long, we'd assumed it was gone forever. Then, sadly, it very suddenly came back with a vengeance. There was no stopping it this time." He patted her hand. "But I'm sure you know all this."

"Kyle told me." She nodded, still waiting for him to get to the point.

"A week or so ago, she told me she'd remembered something she'd been meaning to take care of and just hadn't gotten around to it. It seems that after your father's death, the prison gathered his belongings and mailed them to Olivia. She said there wasn't much in the box, some clothes, his watch, his wedding ring, some photographs. She wanted to make sure the box was given to you."

"I don't want it, thank you, Father. I'm not interested in any of his belongings. You can toss it, if you don't mind."

"You may do that, if it suits you. But I'll honor my promise, Nina. The box is in the trunk of my car. You may do with it what you will, but I suggest you take a look inside." His face flushed with color. "I admit to having glanced at the contents as I taped it up the other day. I was thinking I'd have to mail it to you in New York. There's a letter in there from your father to Olivia, and one to you. Neither appears to have been opened."

"And they won't be opened now," she assured him.

"That's up to you, I suppose. But maybe before you toss them aside you'll give it some serious thought. It's the last you'll ever know of your father, Nina. Perhaps there was something he wanted you to know, possibly about the . . . the things he'd been accused of."

"He wasn't merely accused, Father. He'd been convicted."

"That conviction was, if I recall correctly, on appeal. For what it's worth, Olivia was adamant that Stephen was not guilty. She was convinced he'd not committed any of those crimes. She was positive he had not."

"Where was the evidence, then?" Nina asked flatly. "She didn't testify at his trial, and there was nothing produced by the defense to cast doubt on his guilt. He admitted having had affairs with all of the victims. He admitted having had sex with them on the nights they were killed. Are we supposed to believe that someone else came into these girls' bedrooms, raped and murdered them, after he left? That really stretches the imagination, doesn't it? Does that sound logical to you?"

"All I can tell you is that Olivia believed in his innocence. She didn't believe he killed anyone."

"Maybe she had to believe in him, Father. She was married to him. Surely it would have been easier for her to have believed he was innocent than to admit she'd married a serial killer."

"Perhaps. In any event, whatever your father did— or did not do—he was in fact still your father.

Whatever lies unresolved between you may be aided somehow by his last words to you. I understand your predicament, Nina, and I sympathize. But keep in mind that if you throw away his last attempt to communicate with you, you can never bring it back."

The priest rose.

"If you'll come outside with me, I'll give you the box. When—or if—you decide to open it is entirely up to you. For my part, I'll have done what I'd been asked to do."

Nina continued to lean against the counter, her arms crossed over her chest. Finally, she nodded. "Fine, Father. Give me the box. Fulfill your duty."

"You have my number, Kyle," the priest said. "Don't ever hesitate to use it."

"Thank you, Father Tim. I'll be in touch," Kyle replied, but remained seated.

Nina jammed her hands into the pockets of her jeans and followed the cleric through the quiet house and out through the front door. He walked directly to the trunk of his car and opened it.

"Here you go."

The box he placed in her hands was the size of a medium packing box and weighed but a few pounds. She dug the keys to the rental car out of her pocket as she walked to the driveway. Once there, she opened the trunk and dropped the box in. The soft thud it made when it landed gave no indication of its contents.

"Thank you, Father Whelan," she said as she closed the trunk lid. "Thanks for being so loyal to Olivia. I'm sure she appreciated your friendship."

"As I appreciated hers." The priest leaned in to kiss Nina's cheek lightly. "I'll say to you what I said to Kyle. Anytime you feel you'd like to talk, please, call me. I'll always be available to you."

"Thank you. I'll keep that in mind." She walked him to his car, and stood on the sidewalk while he walked around to the driver's side, opened the door, and got behind the wheel.

"Father," she called to him as he was about to pull away from the curb.

He stopped and lowered the passenger-side window.

"Yes, Nina?"

"If Olivia was so convinced of my father's innocence, why didn't she visit him in prison? And why didn't she open the letter he'd sent her? The one you said was in the box?"

"Olivia believed he was innocent of murder, but he'd openly, and very publicly, admitted to his infidelity. And that, she could not—would not—forgive."

He smiled sadly. "Your father apparently was unfaithful to her within months of their marriage. To Olivia, that was the ultimate betrayal. She stood by him when he was arrested, she stood by him through the preliminary hearings. But I'm afraid once he'd

51

admitted to his affairs, she closed the door on Stephen Madden, and she never looked back. Whatever his last words to her might have been, she never read them as far as I know." He paused before rolling up the window. "Perhaps you will . . ."

Five

Nina paused in the lobby of the stone building that housed her apartment, and turned on the switch that controlled the overhead light on the second-floor landing. The building consisted of three floors, three apartments on each. She couldn't believe that neither of her second-floor neighbors had arrived home yet. It was well after seven-thirty on a cold, rainy night. Who would want to stay out if they didn't have to?

She unlocked her mailbox and removed the assortment of catalogs and the few business envelopes and dropped the mail into the brown leather tote that hung over her shoulder. She climbed the steps to the second floor, grateful—not for the first time—that she'd wisely chosen the smaller apartment on floor number two over the larger one on floor number three. There were some nights when she just didn't think she'd make it.

Tonight was one of those nights. She stopped in front of her door, unlocked the locks, and pushed it open with her foot. Once inside, she reset the locks and dropped the tote on the hardwood floor of the small entry. Kicking off her shoes, she removed her jacket and hung it in the closet just inside the door. She grabbed the tote and took it into the room that served as living room and dining room. She removed the manuscript she'd brought home to work on and dropped it on the coffee table on her way into the bedroom, where she changed from her favorite black wool suit into a pair of soft knit yoga-style pants and a long-sleeved T-shirt. In bare feet, she went into the tiny kitchen and opened the refrigerator to forage for dinner. She'd meant to do some on-line grocery shopping today, but knew she wouldn't be home in time to take delivery by six, the cut-off time imposed by her favorite store. Perhaps it was time to find another favorite market, she was thinking as she decided upon reheated Chinese takeout.

She'd planned on a quick trip to the gym tonight, but that was before she'd gotten stuck on the phone with a needy author just before six. Some writers were more high maintenance than others, she'd been warned early on in her career. Jess Witherspoon was one of those who needed her hand held pretty much on a weekly basis when she was writing. Jess had been working on her new book nonstop for the past four weeks, which meant that at least once a week, usually on Tuesday or Wednesday and always at the end of the work day, Jess called and cried on Nina's shoulder. The book was too hard, it wasn't shaping up the way she'd wanted it to. The characters weren't cooperating, the book was falling apart. The book was doomed, her career was over.

Yada, yada, yada.

Nina smiled to herself, recalling Carlos's often-quoted comment that it was better to be the editor, with an all-seeing eye, than the author, with limited vision.

It had taken longer than usual to get Jess back on track, which resulted in her late arrival home. Which meant the trip she'd wanted to make to the gym wasn't going to happen tonight. It was already late; she was hungry and tired and still had several hours' worth of work to do.

She had just settled down on the sofa with a plate of General Tso's chicken and a bottle of water when she noticed the light blinking on her answering machine. She leaned over and tapped the play button, and sat back against the sofa cushions. She stabbed a water chestnut and listened to the first message. Charles, whom she'd gone out with twice last month, had tickets for the Jets game on Sunday. Was she interested?

Was she? She shrugged. Not really.

Next, a call from her upstairs neighbor apologizing if her new pup's nightly crying was disturbing. They were trying to figure out a way to make it stop.

Nina hadn't realized there was a dog in the building.

Finally, the last message and a familiar voice.

"Hey, Nina, Kyle here. Hey, listen, I'm thinking I might want to stay in the house for a while after all. I mean, with Marcie and me splitting up, and her staying in our house with the kids, it just makes sense for me to stay here, at least until I can get the furniture sold. I think some of the pieces in your dad's study might be antiques. I think you should take another look at the desk and that map chest he had in there. And some of the books look like they might be worth some serious money. I don't feel right keeping the money from things like that. So you should rethink what you want to do with those items. I'm happy to sell them for you, but I won't keep the money from the sale. And that's not negotiable." He paused, then added, as if it had just occurred to him, "Oh, and say, I was just wondering if you'd gotten around to opening the letter Stephen wrote to my mom. I guess I'm just curious to know what he'd had to say to her. Well, sorry I missed you. Give me a call when you get a chance."

The machine clicked to signal the message had ended, and she was glad she'd set it to run until the caller had completed saying whatever he or she had called to say. Few things were more irritating than voice mail that cut you off after an invariably short amount of time.

Well, Kyle was welcome to the letter. She had no intention of reading it. She debated for a minute, then got up and went to the closet and took down the box, which remained unopened. She set it on the coffee table and went to the kitchen for a paring knife with which to cut the tape. She'd done her best to get rid of the damned thing, had gone so far as to deliberately leave it in the trunk of the rental car when she'd returned the vehicle. But some well-meaning, conscientious soul at the rental agency had forwarded it to her at her apartment, and she'd arrived home last Thursday night to find it waiting for her. She'd brought it upstairs and tucked it away, refusing to give it any consideration whatsoever.

She slipped the knife through the tape and opened the box, ignoring the envelope addressed to her in her father's small, precise script, and looking for the one with Olivia's name on it. She found what she was looking for, dropped it on the table, and closed up the box, refusing to look upon the photographs that peeked out from under the pair of men's dark brown leather shoes. Probably the shoes he was wearing when he was arrested, she thought as she returned the box to the shelf.

She sat back on the sofa, pretending not to see the letter on the table that was formally addressed to MRS. STEPHEN J. MADDEN, 117 OAK DRIVE, STONE RIVER, MARYLAND.

Nina picked up the manuscript and went back to work. Forty minutes later, she finally admitted she'd been staring at Olivia's letter for at least the past ten minutes.

What if he'd said something terrible to her in that letter? Nina found herself thinking. Something unforgivably painful, like, I never loved you, I never cared about Kyle.

What if he confessed to having murdered those girls?

What if he told her things that would hurt Kyle to hear?

She was still staring at the letter. Maybe she should take a look . . .

She slit open the envelope with the paring knife and began to read. Before long, her bottom jaw had dropped and her heart had all but stopped beating.

She read all three pages again, certain she had misunderstood. But the words were the same, and the meaning was perfectly clear.

My dear Olivia,

I know I've been a failure to you in so many ways and have caused you nothing but grief and heartache, and I'm more sorry than I can say for what I've put you through. I know an apology alone is unacceptable—there's no atoning for what I've done to you—but I've come to the realization that there is one way I can give you peace of mind.

I know your secret, Olivia, and I will keep it. I will go to my grave professing my innocence, but I will never tell anyone what I know about what you did.

I found what you'd hidden, and I immediately knew exactly what the brown stains on the handle represented. I'd meant to talk to you about it the following day, when I returned from my last afternoon class. Unfortunately, that was the day of my arrest.

It never occurred to me that you'd be following me when I left campus at night, that you'd know where I went, and who I met. Was I so caught up in my own fantasies that I never knew you were watching? I cannot begin to imagine how it must have hurt you. For that, I am more sorry than I can say. I never meant to hurt you, Olivia. And if you believe nothing else, believe that I loved you then, and that I love you now.

My addiction was something apart from what I felt for you. For me, sex was nicotine, it was alcohol, it was cocaine, it was heroin. It was all those things and more. I've long acknowledged, if only to myself, that this is something I can't control. Frankly, I never wanted to control it. I was happy enough to allow my addiction to control me. As long as there were willing partners—and there was never a shortage of girls eager to have me—I was very happy. As happy as a gambler who never lost a hand.

I suppose it was inevitable that you would find

out, and would want to exact your price. But I never—never—thought you capable of such things. When I found the evidence of what you'd done, I admit it made me physically ill.

But all that being said, I know that my actions drove you to do what you did. If I'd been the husband I'd promised to be, none of this would have happened. I know that my sins led to yours, and I am willing to take the punishment for both of us. The fault is all mine.

I can't even begin to ask your forgiveness for all I've put you through. I know I will burn in hell, and that no amount of repentance could be enough to wash this sin from my soul. You, however, can be forgiven.

Talk to Father Tim. It's no secret he's loved you for years, that he'd do anything for you. If you haven't already done so, ask him for absolution, and set your soul at peace.

Your loving Stephen

"Holy shit."

Nina read the letter through a third time, but the words remained the same.

How could her father have thought Olivia guilty when the girls had been raped?

They had been raped, hadn't they? The papers all said that they had.

The Stone River Rapist. Right.

She sat on the sofa, chewing on a fingernail, something she hadn't done since she was twelve and her mother had painted some foul-tasting liquid on her nails to keep her from biting them.

Surely it would have occurred to her father that Olivia could not have raped the four victims. So how could he have concluded that she had been responsible for their deaths?

The more she thought about it, the less sense it made.

And what to do about the letter? She certainly couldn't turn it over to Kyle, not with its blunt accusations against Olivia.

But what if her father had been telling the truth all along, that he hadn't killed those girls? Then someone else—how could it have been Olivia?—had committed four murders, four murders for which her father had been sent to prison.

What was the evidence her father had found that had made him believe Olivia was the killer?

She reread the letter, looking for the part about the evidence. Here, on the first page: the brown stains on the handle.

A knife? Had all the victims been stabbed? She had only a vague recollections of the facts. She'd never wanted to know the details. She'd left Stone River to live with her mother's sister within days of her father's arrest. She didn't follow the news reports and had turned off the television any time there was a mention of it. She'd been so afraid of accidentally finding some reference to Stone River that she'd stopped reading newspapers for several years.

She'd pushed all memories of her father, good and bad, to the farthest reaches of her mind, and left them there.

And now, this.

She'd seen the way her father had been led out of Celestine Hall, his head high and defiant, his eyes cold and icy blue, staring straight ahead. Had he already decided to atone for his infidelity by sacrificing his freedom for Olivia's sake?

After seeing her father's face that day, Nina had never considered that he might be innocent. Now, sixteen years later, the very possibility took her breath away.

She stared at the letter she'd dropped on the table, and wondered what the hell she was going to do about it.

Six

"So, did you get a chance to talk to Regan? What's she thinking about working on next?" Phoebe stood in the doorway of Nina's office.

"She has several ideas she's kicking around. Any one of them would be great. We agreed we'd talk about it again," Nina told her.

"When?" Phoebe leaned a hip against the door-jamb.

"Soon."

"She's coming up for contract. Let's see if we can nail her down. I don't want to lose her."

"I'd be very surprised if that happened."

"Surprised and unemployed." Phoebe smiled and continued her walk down the hall.

Well, that was subtle, Nina thought as she went through the current profit-and-loss statements that she'd found in her IN bin that morning. Phoebe's title may have been director of marketing, but everyone at Griffin knew she was just a few months away from being named publisher. The current president of the company had been hired by Phoebe's grandfather, who'd groomed him for the job, but Phoebe, as majority stockholder, had made it known that she expected to take the reins come the first of the new year.

Nina wasn't worried about Regan, who'd always proven herself to be a straight shooter. If Regan was restless, she'd have said something when Nina was in Maryland. Of course, there was always the possibility that another publisher could come along and dangle a huge contract in her face, but Nina would be surprised if Regan jumped ship. For one thing, she didn't think Regan needed the money, nor did she think that her author's head could be turned by big numbers. She'd already proven that she valued loyalty when she insisted on working only with Nina, rather than with Carlos, who was the big-name editor at Griffin. *No*, Nina told herself, *Regan is solid*.

Still, it wouldn't hurt to keep in touch.

Nina smiled grimly. Who was she kidding? She was dying to talk to Regan, and it had nothing to do with her upcoming contract.

Since discovering the letter from her father to Olivia, Nina had been haunted. She'd barely thought of anything else.

What to do about the letter? How could she find out if in fact her father was right? Could Olivia really have been involved in those murders? What was the evidence her father spoke of, and where was it now?

And even if it was true that Olivia, not her father, was guilty—then what?

And what of Kyle? How could she face him if she was actively trying to prove that his mother—not her father—was a murderer?

And how in the name of God could Olivia have been the Stone River Rapist?

Nina knew she was in way over her head. She didn't even know where to begin to unravel the mess she'd found when she'd read that letter. She'd been tormented for the past week. It tortured her to think that, if her father had been innocent, she'd turned her back on him and had rejected his every attempt to contact her after his arrest. If she somehow found a way to prove or disprove his accusations, there'd be consequences that she—and others—would have to live with. Did she really want to reopen those old wounds?

Then there was the matter of the letter her father had left for her. She still wasn't ready to read that.

Chiding herself for her cowardice, she swiveled around in her chair so that she was facing the one tall, narrow window that graced her office. Outside, clouds were gathering, making good on the weather forecast for more rain. All over the city, the lights in the buildings seemed to glow brighter in the growing dark of late afternoon. Nina moved the chair closer to the window, and watched the clouds roll closer as the storm approached.

If she tried to ignore what she'd found, it would

always be in the back of her mind. It would never go away, and she'd always be wondering. She'd never know the truth.

Without giving herself the opportunity to change her mind, Nina reached for the phone and dialed the number in Maryland.

"Regan, hi. It's Nina. Listen, I was wondering if you had a free day or two this week . . ."

"So, what's this case you stumbled over that you think I might be interested in looking in to?" Regan tossed another small log onto the fire in her cozy sitting room. She'd welcomed Nina warmly, insisted on having her stay there in the house with her instead of at the B and B down the road, and had a wonderful lunch waiting for Nina when she arrived earlier that afternoon. The prior week's warm streak—not quite Indian summer, but close—had come to its inevitable end, bringing with it the clear chill of November. The cord of wood Regan had ordered last week had arrived just that morning, and she'd brought enough into the house to last for a day or so. She'd started the fire right after lunch, and brought their coffee and dessert into the comfortable room off the kitchen. It was her favorite room in the house, with book-lined shelves and deep-cushioned chairs.

She draped a cashmere throw over the arm of her

guest's chair before she snuggled into her favorite seat.

"This is a wonderful room." Nina looked around admiringly. "No wonder it's your favorite place. It would be mine, too, if I lived here."

"I spend more time in here than I do anywhere else in the house. I read here; sometimes I work here on a laptop. I love the view of the bay through the big window there, and I love the little fireplace." Regan smiled. "I'm always comfortable here."

"A warm fire, a cushy place to sit and put your feet up. Good coffee—fabulous coconut cake. I'm not going to want to go back to New York."

"Hey, fine with me. I love the company. And we can justify your stay by talking about work. I have any number of future projects. We can pick one each day and discuss it. By the time we've exhausted my proposals, spring will be sprung."

"I like the way you think." Nina tucked her feet under her and sipped her coffee.

"But right now let's talk about this case you said you heard about. Something about someone being convicted of a crime they've accused someone else of having committed?"

"Here are the bare bones." Nina switched into editorial mode, presenting the scenario as she might propose a book to the staff at Griffin Publishing. "A college professor is arrested and charged with raping and murdering four coeds. He's tried and convicted, gets the death penalty. He appeals his conviction, and while on the way to court, the prison van he's riding in flips over, and he's killed."

"Saves the state a few bucks," Regan murmured.

"I imagine a lot of people were thinking that exact thing at the time. Now, jump forward . . ."

"How many years?"

"Oh, fifteen, sixteen or so." Nina shrugged as if vague on the time frame. "Someone finds a letter the professor had written to his wife accusing *her* of having killed the girls."

"How could that be?" Regan frowned. "I thought you said the victims were raped and murdered. Why would he have accused her?"

"He says something in the letter about having found the evidence she'd hidden, about how he knew what the brown stains on the handle were . . ."

"The girls were all stabbed, then?"

"As far as I know, yes."

"So he writes this letter, says he's going to spill what he knows, or what he thinks he knows?"

"No." Nina shook her head. "Just the opposite. He says he knows that his infidelities—he'd apparently slept with each of these girls, probably many others—caused her to do what she did, so he'll take the blame for her crimes."

"That's noble of him. But why write the letter?"

"I'm guessing to let her know that he knew, and

to let her know that he felt responsible for what she did, and that he loved her enough to take the punishment for her. And he also asked her to talk to this priest they knew. To ask for absolution for her sins so that she could be forgiven."

"Wow. That's some guy." Regan set her cup down on the table that stood between her chair and Nina's. "I've never heard a story like this one. It has everything. Murder, sex, romance, intrigue. The possibility of a wrongful conviction, a jealous wife. A wandering husband . . ."

She stared into the fire for a long minute, then said, "I like it. This one has real possibilities. Where can I find out more?"

"Ah, I'm not sure." Nina was suddenly uncomfortable.

"Well, where did you get your information from? Where'd you hear the story?"

"I read it someplace, some time ago, and it just stayed with me, I guess."

"I guess I could track it on the Internet," Regan murmured.

"How would you go about getting information on the case? I mean, once you had the name of the person who was convicted, you could enter the name and pull up all the news articles, I guess." Nina felt a flush begin to creep up from her collar. She couldn't believe she hadn't thought to do that.

"That's the easy part. Yes, you'd read it, but you

make notes as you go along. You know, who the defense attorney was, who prosecuted the case. Who testified at trial. Who the arresting officers were, the witnesses." Regan reached for her coffee. "You interview everyone you can find—hopefully the key players are still alive and well and can be found—and you get your hands on the old police reports. What evidence did they have that led to a conviction? What evidence did they have that they concluded the victims were all raped? What was the cause of death?"

Nina turned to the window, afraid of what would show on her face.

"I'm assuming the police already know about this letter, right?" Regan was asking.

"I, ah, I don't know. Maybe not."

"Who has the letter?"

"I think a relative."

"Of the professor?"

"Yes." Nina cleared her throat. "At least, that was what I understood."

"And no one else has seen it?"

"I don't think so."

"Then who wrote the article?"

"What?"

"The article you read about this case. If only one person has seen the letter, I'd have to assume the person who wrote the article was the relative who had the letter."

"I suppose." Nina nodded. "That makes sense."

"So why hasn't this person gone to the police with the letter? Wouldn't you think that that would be the first thing they'd do?" Regan turned to her. "If it was someone in your family, wouldn't you want his name cleared as soon as possible?"

"Yes, I do." She caught herself. "I mean, I would. Of course I would."

"What was his name?"

"His name?"

"The professor. I want to pull up everything I can find about him, but I need his name."

"I . . . I don't remember his name."

Nina could feel Regan's eyes studying her. She should have anticipated this, should have realized that Regan would not be content with supposition. She'd want to go straight to the source and find every scrap of information possible about the case. Suddenly, Nina felt uncomfortable, trapped.

"It's really going to be tough to work on this without knowing the names of any of the players, Nina." Regan spoke nonchalantly, but Nina knew there was nothing casual about Regan's curiosity.

She was debating whether to tell her the truth when the phone rang.

Yay, Nina thought. Saved by the bell, literally. She immediately began to think of ways to distract Regan when she completed her call. Maybe she could suggest that they watch a movie. Or go for a walk . . . or shopping . . .

Regan glanced at the caller ID.

"Oh, good. It's Mitch." Her face brightened.

Whoever Mitch was, Nina was thinking, he certainly put a smile on Regan's face. She tried to recall what Regan had said about this new man in her life.

"Hey. Hi," Regan said as she answered the phone. "How are you?"

Regan toyed with her spoon as she listened to the caller.

"I didn't forget. Why not pick me up on Friday, and we'll drive up together? That would be fine. Hey, Mitch? While I have you on the phone . . . I could use those expert computer skills of yours. Not to mention that super-fab FBI equipment . . ."

Nina froze in her seat, recalling the conversation she'd had with Regan a few weeks ago. Her heart sank as it all came back to her. Mitch was a special agent with the FBI.

She gnawed at her fingernails as she listened to Regan repeating the facts she'd shared earlier, and chastised herself for being so stupid. How could she have thought for one moment that Regan wouldn't be able to trace the case? What would she think of her once she found out the truth? Would she ask for another editor? How could someone like Regan, who'd had such a wonderful and open relationship with her own father, possibly understand Nina's situation?

Still chatting, Regan rose and took her coffee cup into the kitchen. She turned in the doorway and mouthed the words, *Would you like a refill?* to Nina, who shook her head to decline.

From the next room, Nina could hear scraps of Regan's conversation. She and Mitch were obviously discussing various ways to prove or disprove the allegations made in the professor's letter. Nina's stomach was in knots. She stood up and went into the hall and grabbed her jacket from the newel post where Regan had laid it earlier. She slid her arms into the sleeves, and went out through the front door. Kicking through the leaves that had fallen from the lone oak tree behind the garage, she walked around the house and followed the walk down to the dock. She stood and watched the fog roll in from the bay, and tried to sort out her feelings.

On the one hand, what would it matter if Regan knew the truth? They were friends, weren't they? Hadn't they been friends long enough that something like this should make no difference in their relationship?

Nina tried to put herself in Regan's place. Would she feel any differently about Regan if Josh Landry had been a killer instead of a talented writer?

Of course she would not. Why couldn't she trust Regan to be as steadfast in her friendship?

She heard footsteps behind her and turned to see Regan coming toward her. Maybe she should just tell her, right now, and get it over with. All she had to do was open her mouth, and say . . .

"Hey, Mitch is going to run some of the info you gave me through his computers and see what he comes up with." Regan was all smiles. "Oh, damn, look there. The moorings on the boat are coming loose. Could you give me a hand with the ropes, Nina? Good thing you came down here. I'd have hated to jump in to go chasing it across the bay."

They struggled with the ropes for nearly twenty minutes. The water was choppy and rough and made it difficult for the two women to secure the boat. When they finally succeeded, Regan patted Nina on the back.

"Thanks so much. I'd have been here all afternoon if I'd been by myself. I think we deserve a little something warming after that. I say brandy by the fire is called for. What do you say?"

"I say that sounds perfect." Nina nodded, and followed Regan back up the wooden walk.

"Did I tell you that Mitch and I have gone in with two friends to start a winery?" Regan was saying.

"No, I don't think you did."

"A friend of mine from college owned a farm she was going to sell, and on it there was an old vineyard. Well, she started seeing a friend of Mitch's—actually, she needed a private investigator to look into some old murders for her—I'll tell you that story over dinner, if you're interested. Anyway, the PI started reading up about growing grapes and making wine, and the next thing we knew, the four of us had thrown in together to start this vineyard. Lavender Hill Wines, we're calling it. Though of course, there's no wine yet . . ."

Regan continued to chat all the way back to the house, much to Nina's relief. There'd be time later, or tomorrow, or perhaps the next day, to tell her about the professor who'd been tried and convicted as the Stone River Rapist.

Seven

The smell of coffee brewing roused Nina shortly before seven the next morning. She rose up on one elbow in the double bed in Regan's guest bedroom and looked out the window. A light rain was falling and a dense mist lay over the marsh. From far out on the bay, she could hear the faint *chug-chug* of an old boat motor and, closer by, the *swish* of restless reeds stirring in the wind. She stretched her arms over her head and threw back the blankets. Her hostess was obviously up and busy in the kitchen. She should join her. Ten minutes later, she did.

"I was wondering if you were a late sleeper," Regan said when Nina came into the kitchen. "Coffee's on, there's a cup on the counter for you. Sweeteners are in the cupboard right behind you—there's an assortment there. Half-and-half is in the little pitcher next to the coffeepot. Help yourself."

"Thanks. It smells wonderful." Nina smiled as she poured herself a cup.

"I wasn't sure if you were a big breakfast person,

a no-breakfast person, or somewhere in between. So I made French toast and sausage, because that's my favorite and I almost never bother to make it for myself. If you'd rather have eggs, I'd be happy to—"

"No, no. French toast is perfect. I never bother to do this for myself, either. What a treat." Nina sipped her delicious coffee and sniffed at the sausage cooking on the stove. "Thank you so much for going to so much trouble."

"It's really no trouble. I just don't bother to take the time to eat this well when I'm by myself. It just seems a waste of time to make one or two slices of toast, one or two pieces of sausage. It's easier to grab a granola bar with my coffee and get to work." Regan looked up from the frying pan where she was cooking two pieces of golden French toast. "You know how it is when you live alone."

"I do." Nina nodded.

"If you'd like to help, you could set the table. The plates are in the cupboard to your left, the flatware in the drawer next to the sink."

"Sure."

Nina placed her cup on the counter and proceeded to set the table. Regan chatted about the weather, the winery, Mitch. It wasn't until they'd sat at the table and started eating that Regan asked, "Did you sleep well?"

"Very well. Thanks." Nina smiled and wondered if Regan knew she was lying through her teeth. All she could think about was how she was going to approach Regan with the truth about her father. She couldn't very well say, *So, Regan, you remember that professor we talked about last night—the one who was convicted of raping and murdering four students—did I mention that he was my father?*

What did one say?

She needn't have worried about how to broach the subject. Regan beat her to it.

"I didn't sleep well at all," Regan was saying as she helped herself to sausage. "I woke up at three this morning and could not fall back to sleep. Don't you just hate when that happens?"

Nina nodded.

"So I came downstairs here, thinking I'd work a little. Turned on my computer, started tracking some research for the book you and I talked about when you were here the last time. I printed out a couple of articles, and was just about to turn off the computer when I started thinking about your story. Your professor."

Nina stopped chewing, and set her fork quietly on the edge of her plate.

"Your father, Nina?" Regan asked gently.

"Yes."

"You could have told me straight away." When Nina started to protest, Regan assured her, "Of course I understand why that would have been hard for you. I'm not blaming you for not coming right out with it. I'm just saying, it would have been all right."

"It's something I never talk about. I've never told anyone about what happened in Stone River. No one."

"You've never discussed it with anyone?" Regan's eyes widened slightly.

"No one. How do you tell people that your father died a prisoner, after being convicted of such terrible things?"

"You were in college there at the time," Regan stated. "The articles I found mentioned you only briefly, right after the time he was arrested, but I noticed there was no further mention of you throughout the proceedings."

"I'd gone to live with my aunt—my mother's sister—immediately after he was arrested. I hadn't been back to Stone River until my stepmother died."

"You didn't keep in touch with her?"

"Not really." Nina shrugged. "Birthdays and Christmases, she sent presents and cards, but I never reciprocated. I just wanted to excise that entire time of my life. I didn't want any reminders. I just wanted to go on with my life."

"And your aunt permitted you to do that?"

"She encouraged it." Nina looked up and saw the look on Regan's face. "I know what you're thinking, and you're right. She didn't like the fact that my father and mother had divorced, didn't like the fact that my father remarried. Even after all those years, she still harbored resentment toward him, and toward Olivia. I think she believed that my father had had an affair with Olivia while he was still married to my mother. I don't believe that was true. I don't think my father even met Olivia until a long time after my parents were divorced, but I'll never know for sure. My aunt believed what she wanted to believe. She was my mother's older sister, and always felt very protective toward her. She was just as happy to have no contact with Olivia whatsoever."

"And your father? Did you have any contact with him after his arrest?"

"Very little. We communicated only about my schooling and that sort of thing through his lawyer." Nina sighed and looked out the window. "At the time, it was what I wanted. I can't even begin to tell you how I felt during all that. I was shocked . . . horrified . . . humiliated . . . I can't put all of my feelings into words. My father was always somewhat distant from me. We were never really close, you understand, but I never, never would have thought for one minute that he'd be capable of . . . all those horrible things he'd been accused of doing. He may have been remote from me, but I'd never seen him act mean or violent, ever. I just couldn't believe it."

"You felt betrayed by him."

"Oh, yes. Totally." Nina shook her head from side to side. "It's one thing to understand that you and a parent aren't particularly close, it's something else entirely to find out that they have committed unspeakable crimes. You just want to run away and hide and never see them again."

"And that's what you did."

"What would you have done?"

"I don't know," Regan answered honestly. "I've always had such a close relationship with my father, I can't imagine how things could have been different. I've never been in the situation you were in. But I hope you don't think I'm judging you, or your actions. I'm not. You did what was right for you at the time. No one has the right to second-guess that, all these years later."

"And if he was innocent?"

"Then you'll make your peace with him any way you can, in this life or in the next. But there's a good chance he'd be more understanding of you than you're giving him credit for."

"I didn't know him well enough to know how he'd react."

"Then I would guess the blame lies with both of you on that score." Regan leaned across the table and squeezed Nina's arm. "Don't beat yourself up, Nina."

"What would you do? I mean, now. If you were me, what would you do?"

"I'd find out if he was telling the truth. I'd get my hands on every report, I'd talk to everyone I could find who was connected with the investigation. I'd look at the evidence upside down and sideways, and then I'd see if there was any chance that someone else had committed the murders." Regan leaned back in her chair.

"Then that's what I'll do. I'll go to the Stone River Police Department and I'll ask for copies of all the reports. That's step one, right?"

"Right. See what the evidence was against your father, let's start with that. Then we'll see if there's any way that your stepmother could have been involved. He must have had a reason for writing that letter, Nina. Let's see if we can find out what it was."

"We?"

"Well, yeah. You don't think I'd turn an amateur loose on a case like this, do you?" Regan smiled. "Now, there's no time like the present. Let's get dressed, and drive over to Stone River. I'd like to take a look at those reports myself . . ."

The Stone River Police Department was housed in an 1892 carriage house that had once belonged to the family that had settled the town and incorporated it. Recently renovated by the local historic society with a combination of public and private funds, the building also housed the small town library and a community room where various groups, from the civic association to the budding arts alliance, could meet. The building was white clapboard and had enough gingerbread to decorate a dozen homes on North Main Street.

"Way to intimidate the criminal element," Regan commented as they walked under a heavily carved arch to get to the front door.

"I'm surprised no one's planted climbing roses over the doorway." Nina grinned. "But frankly, being brought into any police department in handcuffs—fancy arches or not—would intimidate me."

Regan held the door and the two women entered the reception area.

"May I help you, ladies?" a uniformed officer asked from behind a large polished oak desk.

"We wanted to get some reports on an old case." Nina spoke up, having been prodded from behind by Regan.

"How old?" the officer asked.

"Sixteen years," Nina said without blinking, as Regan had instructed her.

Look him straight in the eye, and act as if you expect your request to be fulfilled, she'd told Nina.

"The name of the case?"

"The People of Maryland versus Stephen J. Madden," Nina said.

"You a reporter?" A voice from behind startled both women.

"No," Nina said as she turned around.

There was something vaguely familiar about the man who stood in the doorway. Dressed casually in Dockers and a sport jacket, he was tall and fair-haired, with broad shoulders and cynical pale blue eyes. Cop's eyes, Regan told her later. Eyes that had seen just about everything.

"May I ask why you're interested in that case?" he asked as he came closer.

"May I ask what business it is of yours?" Nina replied.

"Just curious, that's all," he told her.

"Detective Powell, you had a call from the medical examiner on the body that was fished out of the river over the weekend." The uniformed officer handed the man in the sport jacket a note.

"Thanks." He tucked the paper into his breast pocket and turned back to Nina. "Was there anything in particular you were looking for in regard to the Stone River Rapist?"

Nina noticeably flinched.

"We'd like to see all the files." Regan stepped forward. "Actually, we'd like a copy of them."

"You'd have to come back for that." The uniform opened the top desk drawer and took out a slip of paper. He handed it to Nina, saying, "Just fill this out. Then, when we locate the files and have someone who has the time to copy them, we'll give you a call."

"We don't mind doing the copy work ourselves," Regan told him.

"We don't hand over our files to the general public, ma'am. If you want the files copied, it has to be done by a member of the police department. Right now, we're a little busy. But if you'll fill out the form, we'll call you when they're ready, and you can come in with a check and pay for your copy."

"It doesn't look like I have much choice, does it?" Nina muttered and began to fill out the form.

"If there's something in particular you need, I'll be happy to help you if I can," the detective told her.

"You have good photocopy skills?" Nina asked.

"Good as anyone else's," he told her. "But in this case I do have an advantage."

"What's that?" Nina asked.

"I was there," he said.

"You were . . . ?"

"There when they arrested Stephen Madden, yes. There when they found his last two victims. So you can understand why I'd be curious as to why someone is taking a look at the case now, after all these years."

"Stephen Madden was my father." Nina's chin rose just slightly, as if defying him to comment.

"I see." He appeared to study her for a long moment. "I thought there was something familiar about you."

She raised a questioning eyebrow.

"The day your father was arrested, you fainted in the lobby of the building that housed the English department."

"I did." She nodded slowly. She'd all but forgotten. "How did you know that?"

"I'm the cop who caught you on the way down."

Eight

Wes Powell had remained hidden behind his dark glasses for the long moment it took him to place Nina Madden. In retrospect, he realized that, in all likelihood, he'd not have recognized her as the panicked young woman who'd collapsed in his arms on that cold February afternoon in 1989. That girl had had long black hair, deep green eyes that had been filled with terror, and the look of innocence about to be lost. The woman who stood before him now wore an air of maturity, of authority. The hair was shorter, the innocence long gone, but the eyes were the same. Deep green, long black lashes, the panic replaced with a wariness. Looking at her now, he could see the young girl she'd been.

He had remembered her because that day was so strong in his memory. He'd been on the force for exactly ten days when the last victim of the Stone River Rapist had been found facedown in her bed in her tiny off-campus apartment. Hers had been the first dead body he'd gotten up close and personal with, and he'd never forgotten. Just as he'd never forgotten being in Celestine Hall when the detectives had led Dr. Stephen Madden through the lobby, hands cuffed behind his back.

Wes had thought at the time that he'd never seen anyone so defiant. In the years since, he'd not seen anyone who'd worn the mantle of guilt as completely as Professor Madden had that day.

And now, here was Madden's daughter, the pretty young girl he'd reached out to catch as she crumbled to the floor.

An uneasy thought occurred to him.

"Any particular reason you're wanting to look at those reports now?" *Please God, don't let her be taken with the notion that her old man might have been innocent.*

Stephen Madden's daughter exchanged a glance with the woman who accompanied her, then looked at Wes and said, "I'm thinking about writing a book about my father."

"A book," he said flatly. Of course. Didn't everyone want to write a book these days?

"Detective . . . Powell, was it?" The Madden woman's friend was petite and had a mass of light auburn curls that framed her pretty face. She smiled and extended her hand. "I'm Regan Landry. I write true crime, and am currently looking into the Stone River Rapist story. Ms. Madden has kindly offered to assist me."

"Landry." Wes nodded. Of course he knew the name. "Josh's daughter."

"You knew my father?"

"We'd met on several occasions. He was quite the character."

"That he was."

"So, about those reports," Madden's daughter reminded him.

"Sure." Wes sighed. He was late for a meeting with his chief; he'd been in Baltimore for the past thirty-six hours trying to connect the dots on a case that had been driving him crazy for the past three weeks, but he'd have to play nice. Regan Landry was a VIP, and he'd have to treat her like one. "I'll be happy to have the files brought out from storage and copied, but I'm afraid I can't promise it will be today. A lot of the old files were moved about five years ago, and it may take some time to locate them."

"That's fine. Just call and let me know when it's ready. My name is Nina Madden, by the way. Let me give you my cell phone number. I just realized I only put my office and home numbers on the form I filled out." She searched in her purse for a small leather case that held business cards. On the back, she wrote her number.

"I'll make sure it's taken care of." Wes glanced at the front of the card. *Nina E. Madden, Senior Editor. Griffin Publishing, New York, New York.*

"Thank you, Detective. I appreciate your help." There was a trace of coolness in Nina's smile.

"My pleasure." Wes held the door for the two women.

"Wes, the chief . . ." Janice Mayfield, the sole woman detective on the force, stepped into the hallway.

"Yeah, yeah, I know. I'm coming." Wes looked over his shoulder at the desk sergeant. "Would you mind putting in the request for all the files on the Madden case? You can have them delivered to my office."

"You gonna be copying them yourself, then?"

Wes flashed a dark look.

"Yeah, that's what I thought," the sergeant muttered as Wes closed the door behind him.

"What do you think?" Nina asked after she and Regan had gotten into Regan's Land Rover. "Do you think we'll ever see those files?"

"No question," Regan assured her. "He's been around long enough to know how to play the game."

"What's the game?"

"We get what we asked for, or I go over his head," she said. "I don't usually like to say it this way, but the Landry name does carry a lot of weight in law enforcement. Dad had a tremendous readership among cops, coast to coast. He was very much pro-law, and they all knew it. He'd do book signings at small stores in small towns all across the country, and the place would be mobbed with cops. Same thing in the cities. They shared a very tight relationship. So I am not the least bit concerned about whether we'll get the files. It's simply a matter of when."

"I'm looking forward to going through them." Nina paused to reflect for a moment, then added, "At least, I think I am."

"It's not going to be pretty, I should warn you. You're going to see and read a lot of things you might wish you'd skipped." Regan slanted a sideways glance at Nina. "You know, I could always look through the files first, if you'd like. I've gone through countless police files. It takes a lot to rattle me."

"Thanks, Regan, I appreciate the offer. But I think I need to do this myself." Nina fell silent.

"You'll read some things about your dad that might upset you."

"I've been upset about my dad for almost half my life," Nina said softly, staring straight ahead.

"This will be different. There will be reports in there detailing his relationships with all of these women. There will be statements that will be very upsetting to you."

"I understand."

"Well, just keep in mind that you can always count on me. If you want to talk things over, if you have any questions about things that don't seem right . . ." Regan's voice trailed away.

"I'm sure I'll have questions. I'm sure we'll have lots to talk about. And actually, if we're going to try to piece this thing together with an eye toward proving or disproving my father's allegations, you're going to have to go through it all yourself. I'm sure you'll pick out things that aren't obvious to me. I've had no experience reading police reports, whereas you've been reading them for years."

"Hey, when other kids were reading Golden Books, I was reading autopsy reports and witness statements at my father's knee."

"I could almost believe that." Nina smiled.

"Well, just keep in mind that you're allowed to skip things. Don't feel you have to read the entire file."

"I know. Thanks."

A few minutes later, Nina said, "You're right about one thing. I'm not looking forward to reading in-depth accounts of my father's relationships with these girls."

"That's going to be tough," Regan said softly.

"For me, personally, that whole older man–young girl thing has always been creepy. Throw in the fact that the old man is my father, and it raises the *ick* factor to new heights."

"I can't even begin to imagine. I often wondered if my father had any relationships with any of the women he knew, after my mother died. If he did, he never gave any indication."

"You think he kept them from you?"

"My dad never was much for secrets." Regan shook her head. "He always liked things right out there on the table."

"Still, you're wondering about it."

"I am. There was a woman named Dorothea who used to call the house from time to time. Dad would take the call in his office and close the door. I always wondered what was going on there."

"You think they got together when he was doing book tours?"

"I don't know when he would have. I was usually with him." Regan smiled. "It just always made me curious. It's sort of intriguing, thinking about your parents having secret lives."

"*Intriguing* isn't exactly the word I'd choose right now."

"Oh, for God's sake, I can't believe I said that." Regan's face went scarlet. "I'm so sorry. Of all the thoughtless things to say . . ."

"It's okay." Nina smiled in spite of herself. Regan was the last person on earth who'd deliberately try to make anyone feel embarrassed or self-conscious.

"I think I'll just shut up for a while now."

"No need. Really," Nina assured her. "We've beaten that horse to within an inch of its life. We'll deal with whatever's in the files once we have them. Let's talk about something else."

"Let's talk about the ice cream sundaes right up the road here at Harry's," Regan said. "There's a little art gallery in the back room. Maybe you can find something to brighten up that little office of yours back in New York. At the very least, the hot fudge is homemade, and to die for."

"You're on. And while we're eating, you can tell me more about this shopping outlet mecca I keep seeing advertised on the billboards around here."

"Rehoboth, Delaware." Regan smiled knowingly. "Just the right distance for a road trip. How does tomorrow sound?"

"Tomorrow sounds wonderful," Nina said, relieved to shift the spotlight from herself and her father's case onto something less dark and serious, something fun.

The way Nina saw it, the next few weeks promised precious few light moments. She might as well smile while she still could.

Nine

A sharp gust of wind greeted Nina as she rounded the corner on her way to the subway on the following Wednesday morning. Her head down, she hoisted the leather tote over her shoulder and felt the manuscript inside shift. How, she wondered, would she tell the agent representing the work that she was going to have to pass on the book?

She was a block from the subway when her cell phone rang.

"Ms. Madden?" a male voice asked.

"Yes?"

"Detective Powell, Stone River PD."

"Oh, yes, Detective Powell. How are my files coming along?"

"They're sitting right here on the floor of my office. Copied, boxed, and ready for pickup."

"Terrific. Would Friday night be all right for me to come in? Will someone be around?"

"We're the only place in town that never closes," he told her. "Someone will be here."

"And you'll take a check for the copy work?"

"Yes, with the proper ID."

"Driver's license okay?"

"Sure."

"Well, thank you, Detective Powell. I appreciate the follow-up."

"You're welcome."

She closed her phone to disconnect the call as she descended the steps to the subway. As eager as she was to view the contents of the files relative to her father's case, at the same time there was a knot of apprehension in her chest. This was, she acknowledged, one huge can of worms she was about to open. She wasn't sure how she was going to feel once she was confronted with the facts she'd been avoiding, or what the consequences might be.

She got onto the subway and stood near the door, clutching the tote to her chest, grateful to have something to hang on to besides the metal bar. Ten minutes later, still clutching the tote, she got off the subway and walked up the steps, planning her agenda. She had a meeting right at nine, another at nine forty-five. She'd have to fit in a call to Regan to let her know she'd be back this weekend to pick up the files. They'd already discussed the possibility, and Regan had made it clear that Nina would be welcome there any time, whether Regan was at home or not. She'd sent Nina back to New York with a spare house key, just in case she'd be away when the files were ready.

Which, as it turned out, had been a bit of pre-science on Regan's part.

"I've had a change of plans for the weekend," Regan said when Nina finally had time to make the phone call later that morning. "A month or so ago, I placed an ad in some Illinois newspapers, looking for information on a man named Eddie Kroll. Someone called me claiming to have known him, but it turned out to be someone who'd only known him in grade school and thought someone—namely, me—was paying for information. She really had nothing that helped me. Last night, I got a call from a woman claiming to be related to him, though she was vague about the relationship. I'm flying out in the morning to meet with her in a little town called Sayreville."

"Who's Eddie Kroll?" Nina asked.

"That's what I'm hoping to find out. All I know about him is that, when he was thirteen, he and two of his buddies were convicted of killing one of their classmates. He was tried as a juvenile, since he was the youngest of the three and therefore everyone assumed he was the most impressionable. He got out of juvie when he turned twenty-one and seems to have disappeared off the face of the earth."

"Sounds like another book in the making. Assuming, of course, you can find out what happened to him."

"Well, whoever he was, my dad was interested enough in him to keep his grade school report cards.

I found them in the basement of Dad's house, along with bits and pieces of information on other assorted crimes and criminals." Regan chuckled. "My father was such a mess when it came to keeping things straight. He'd have a half-dozen files going on the same case because he could never remember where he put the others. It's made going through his records a nightmare, but it's been interesting all the same. He left enough notes for me to write for the next thirty years."

"You just made your editor a very happy woman."

"Yes, but that doesn't solve your problem. I expect you to stay here in my house, but I won't be able to pick you up at the airport or the train station."

"Don't give it a second thought. I'm grateful for the bed. I'll rent a car and drive out, like I did when I came down for Olivia's funeral."

"Speaking of which, what do you hear from your stepbrother? Do you think he has any idea of what was in your father's letter?"

"I'm sure he doesn't. The sealing tape on that box was pretty old. I think maybe Olivia just opened the box, took one look inside, and taped it back up again."

"Without reading the letter?"

Nina hesitated for a long moment. "Father Whelan told me that Olivia claimed she hadn't opened it, but I'm not one hundred percent positive of that. The back of the envelope appeared to have been resealed, as if someone had steamed it open, then reglued it. Of course, I could be totally wrong about that."

"Why would she have read it, then sealed it back up again?"

"I don't know. You'd think if she'd read it, she'd have destroyed it. Why would she have wanted anyone to know that my father believed her to be the killer?"

"Was she the type of person who would have wanted the truth to come out after her death?"

"I honestly can't answer that. I didn't know her well enough. Kyle might be a better judge of that, but I just can't bring myself to tell him what my father suspected."

"Does he know about the letter?"

"Father Whelan mentioned it in front of him."

"Don't you think it's strange that his mother didn't leave the letter for Kyle?" Regan noted.

"Maybe she was thinking, my father wrote it, it contained his thoughts, therefore it should go to me. I have no other explanation. Unless she thought the letter contained something else."

"Like what?"

"Like . . ." Nina thought for a minute, then said, "Like the fact that he'd left the house to me rather than to her."

"Maybe. It just seems to me there's more to it than that." Regan, too, was thinking. "And it bothers me that if she knew what was in the letter, she didn't destroy it outright."

"So maybe she was telling Father Whelan the truth. Maybe she didn't open it."

"Something isn't adding up," Regan said. "If she did open it, why would she want you to know that your father suspected her? And if she didn't open it, why not? Why not leave the letter for Kyle?"

"I have no answers. The more immediate problem is what to do about Kyle. He's called twice, wanting to know if I'd read the letter, and what did it say."

"What did you tell him?"

"I couldn't bring myself to tell him the truth. I just couldn't do it."

"So what did you say?" Regan asked.

"I lied through my teeth. I told him I'd left the box in the trunk of the rental car." Nina paused. "Which wasn't a total lie. I had left the box in the trunk of the car. However, some well-meaning soul at the rental agency forwarded it to me."

"I trust you left that part out when you were talking to Kyle."

"I didn't exactly talk to Kyle. I left the message on his answering machine."

"So you wimped out all the way around."

"I'm afraid so."

"Well, you're going to have to come up with a better way of dealing with him than simply ignoring him, or leaving him voice mail."

"I know. Maybe after I look through the files, I'll have a better feel for whether or not my father's allegations could be true. Assuming I can tell the difference."

"When things are really off, they stand out. And if need be, we can always have Mitch take a look. He's pretty good with the cold cases. And he's very good on the computer. If there's something out there, he'll find it, if we can't."

"Good to know we have backup."

There was a rap on Nina's door. Hollis poked her head in the door and whispered, "Sales meeting in the conference room has been moved back. It's starting now."

"Regan, I have to run. I can't thank you enough for everything. For the use of your house, for your moral support. I honestly don't know what I'd do without you."

"Well, then. I seem to recall having said those exact words to you not so long ago. It appears we're now even."

Nina's flight was late, her reserved car turned out not to be, and by the time she got to the Stone River Police Department, it was nine thirty-five. She'd missed Detective Powell by nineteen minutes.

"I'm sorry, miss," the officer in charge told her,

"but I don't generally go into the detectives' offices and take things."

"I'm sure it will be fine. He requested several boxes of files for me, and he had them photocopied, and I told him I'd be in tonight to pick them up. Didn't he mention someone would be in to pick up some boxes?"

"He said someone. How do I know you're that someone?"

"Can you give him a call, tell him that I'm here? I'm sure he'll say it's all right for you to go in there and get my files."

Nina paced a bit while the call was made. She strained to listen to what was being said, but couldn't hear.

"He said okay, he said he was sorry he left but he figured you weren't coming, since you hadn't called or anything to say you'd be late." The officer got up from his desk and walked down the hall. "I'll be back in just a minute."

Nina paced a little more, wondering why Powell hadn't called her before he left. He had her number. She looked at the display screen on her phone. *1 missed call*. She checked the number.

"What's the number here?" Nina asked when the officer returned carrying a box.

"It's 402-555-5700."

"It figures." She snapped the phone closed. Detective Powell had tried to call her at eight-fifteen.

Right about the time she was arguing with the car rental agent. She must not have heard the phone ringing.

She should have called when she realized how late she was going to be.

"There's another box." The officer disappeared around the corner again, and returned a minute later carrying one more file box.

He sat the box on top of the desk and handed her a receipt.

"You can make the check payable to the Stone River Police Department."

Nina took her checkbook from her handbag and wrote out the check and showed him her driver's license without waiting to be asked. The bill was for way more than she'd expected—but she hadn't realized how much paper was involved. There was no question what she'd be doing for the rest of the weekend.

She lifted the first box from the desk and took it out to the rented Taurus, and placed it in the trunk. She turned and found the officer coming down the walk behind her.

"I thought I'd give you a hand with this," he told her.

"Thanks so much." She stood back while he set the second box next to the first.

"Don't mention it." He slammed the trunk closed for her. "Sorry about the mix-up."

"It's all right. I should have called." She got behind the wheel, turned on the ignition, and drove off.

The roads outside of Branigan, the small town where Regan lived, were windy and poorly lit. She slowed down as she approached several driveways before realizing they were the wrong ones. She found Regan's almost by accident. At night, every drive and every house seemed to look the same.

She parked next to the deck, and opened the house, turning on all the floodlights at the back. When she'd finished removing her belongings, she locked the car and went back into the house, but she left the bright lights on. The house was very quiet, very isolated, and she felt just a bit edgy.

Regan had kindly left soup in the refrigerator, along with yogurt, fruit, cheese, diet soda, and white wine. Nina made herself a light supper, poured herself a glass of wine, and settled down with the boxes in the sitting room, after checking to make certain all the doors and windows were locked.

She'd just finished eating when her phone rang. The sudden intruding noise caused her to startle.

"Hello?"

"Ms. Madden. Detective Powell."

"I'm so sorry I missed you, Detective. I was delayed on my trip down from New York."

"You could have called."

"Yes, and I should have. I apologize if you waited

beyond whatever time you would normally have left."

"There is no normal."

"Yes, I have a job like that."

"I doubt it," he muttered, and she could hear the weariness in his voice. "I'm calling to let you know that you're missing a couple of boxes."

"I am?" She frowned. "There are two here."

"There should be four. One for each victim."

"I'll drive back to Stone River tomorrow and pick them up. Thank you for telling me."

"You're staying in the area?"

"I'm in Branigan. At a friend's."

"I'd be happy to drop them off. I'll be passing through there in the morning."

"Really, you don't have to do that. I'll make the trip."

"I should have waited. I knew you'd be there, after you made such a point to request the files." He softened slightly. "I'll be passing through Branigan early in the morning. You an early riser?"

"Actually, I am, but I really don't think . . ."

"Give me the address."

"Fifteen Shore Drive."

"Easy enough. I'll see you in the morning."

He hung up without waiting for her to say goodbye.

"Okay, then," Nina said. "I guess you will . . ."

* * *

Nina read until the fire had burned out, but she'd barely noticed. It was after two in the morning when she stopped to stretch her legs, and she was shocked to see how much time had passed. Normally a fast reader, she'd taken her time, making notes of the facts she felt were important. She wondered if Regan would agree.

She folded over the notebook and, leaving it on the chair, closed the fireplace flue and turned off the lights. Her eyes were begging for a break, and her back and neck were stiff from having remained in the same position for so long. Her body was telling her to wrap it up for the night, and she did. She went up the steps to the loft room she'd stayed in the last time she was there, and kicked off her shoes. She lay across the bed for just a moment, and was asleep before she knew it.

Early the next morning, the sun woke her as it shone directly in her face. She was surprised to find that she'd slept on top of the comforter, still dressed in her clothes from the night before. Not quite certain just how early was early to Detective Powell, she got up and showered and changed, and was downstairs by seven-thirty.

She made it with eleven minutes to spare.

The kitchen clock read seven forty-one when the Jeep pulled up to the deck and parked next to the Taurus. She watched through the window as the detective took the boxes from the backseat of his car, one atop the other. He stood in the driveway as if uncertain which way to go. Nina unlocked the back door and stepped onto the deck.

"Good morning," she called.

"Oh, hey. Good morning. I was just trying to figure out where the front door is." He walked up the stairs and across the deck.

"To tell you the truth, I'm not sure I know. I've only come and gone through this door." She smiled and held out her hands for the boxes. "Here, I'll take them."

"They're really heavy. Let me just put them down on something." He went past her, into the kitchen, and set the boxes on the counter. "Wow. This is really something. I didn't know granite came in that shade of blue."

"I hadn't seen it before, either. I don't know where Regan found it."

He glanced around the room admiringly, his eyes going back twice to the coffeepot, which was beeping to announce it had finished brewing.

"I was just making coffee. Would you like a cup?"

"I'd kill for one." He visibly cringed as soon as the words were out of his mouth. "Sorry. Bad choice."

Ignoring his faux pas, she took mugs from one of the cupboards and poured the coffee, handing his to him with a caution. "It's really hot."

"Thanks."

She got out a container of cream.

"How do you take it?"

"Just cream is fine. Thanks."

Nina passed the cream to him and poured sweetener from a pink paper packet into her own cup.

"So, you're staying with Ms. Landry for a few days?"

"Actually, she's away this weekend, but she offered to let me stay here."

"Good friend."

"She is."

"And you're her editor as well."

"How did you know that?"

"I read it in the front of her book, that last one. *In His Shoes*. She dedicated it to her editor, Nina Madden. That would be you."

"You had the book?"

"Actually, I picked it up at the bookstore the other day after you left the station."

"Why?"

"Why?" He considered the question. "I wanted to see if she was any good. I'd read a few of her father's books, and I knew she lived down around the bay someplace. I was curious. I wanted to see if she was legit."

"Satisfied?"

"Very."

He took a sip of coffee and leaned back against the counter.

"This new book you're working on with her. What's the deal with that?"

"What do you mean?"

"What brought that about?"

"Regan thought it would be a good story."

"That's all?"

"What else should there be?"

"Just checking." He took another sip. "I'm just relieved to hear that's all there is to it. I was hoping it wasn't going to be one of those situations where someone, years after the fact, got the notion that an innocent man had been railroaded, that the cops had screwed up, that the wrong man was convicted. That sort of thing."

He stared at her levelly, then continued.

"Because I was there that day, you know? I was part of that investigation. I was at the crime scene when they found the body of the last victim."

"Maureen Thomas. I just read about her."

"Her friends called her Mickey. She was twenty-two years old, one semester away from graduating with honors in English."

"I know. I read the file."

"She was a beautiful, intelligent . . ."

"I said, I read the file." Her voice rose slightly. "Why do you feel it necessary to reiterate what I've already read?"

"Because I want you to understand who the victims were. What was taken from them."

"If you're trying to make me feel like shit, you're doing a damned fine job of it." Nina's eyes began to sting.

"I just want you to understand—as difficult as it might be to accept—that your father was guilty. There were no mistakes made." His voice softened. "I just don't want you to go into this"—he waved one hand at the boxes on the counter—"thinking you're going to find something we missed that will prove he was innocent. I'm sure this was a terrible ordeal for you back then. I would just hate to see you go through it again for no good reason."

Anger welled inside her. "I don't think it's your place to oversee the choices I make."

He put his mug down on the counter.

"Hey, I know how these things go. I've seen dozens of 'em. Relatives get it into their heads that their loved one was railroaded, that some cop had it in for them. Look, I can understand why it's hard to accept. I swear, I do. It must have been terrible for you back then. And I'm sure it's been a big question in your life all these years. Did he, or didn't he?"

"You're wrong. I never questioned whether or not my father was guilty."

That clearly surprised him. It took a moment for him to recover.

"Then why," he asked, "has this conversation turned defensive on your part?"

"Let me ask you this, Detective. Suppose there *was*

some evidence that turned up that at least cast doubt on my father's guilt. What would you do?"

"There's no such evidence. I'm telling you, I worked this case. I worked it inside and out. I dotted every *i* and I crossed every *t*. There's nothing to turn up. We had it all."

"Let's put that aside for now." She crossed her arms over her chest. "Just play along with me. Tell me what you'd do, if some piece of evidence was found that indicated someone else was responsible for the deaths of those girls. Would you reopen the case?"

He stared at her for a very long time.

"Well, Detective?"

"You bring me something that shows me that someone other than Stephen Madden was the Stone River Rapist, and yes, I will reopen the case."

"Thank you. That's all I needed to hear you say."

"So, am I supposed to guess now what you have? You're not going to tell me what you've found?"

"Oh, I haven't really found anything. Yet. If and when I do, trust me, Detective Powell, you will be the first to know."

"I'll hold you to that." He turned and rinsed out his cup, then placed it upside down on the counter, as he might do if he were home. He glanced at the clock on the wall. "And with that, I'll be on my way. I have a soccer game in less than an hour."

"You play soccer?"

"Me? Ha. Not with these knees." He smiled for the first time since he'd stepped into the kitchen. "My son plays."

"How old is your son?"

"Nine. And if I don't get there on time, his mother will end up taking him to his game and I'll never hear the end of it. It's my Saturday."

"Then you best get going. Thanks for dropping off the files." Nina walked him to the door. "And for your insights into the case."

"I'm still not sure I understand what exactly you're looking for, or what your motive might be, and of course, it's none of my business. But dredging this up without a sound reason is going to cause pain to a lot of people. The victims' families. Their friends. The college."

"I understand that."

"I wonder if you do, Ms. Madden." He turned and walked to his car. "I have to wonder if you really do."

Ten

The task Nina had set for herself turned out to be more difficult than she'd imagined. The closest she'd ever come to reading police reports was in Regan's books, where all the little shorthand words and phrases that law enforcement personnel used had already been deciphered. Trying to interpret the real thing was something else entirely. The pages she had difficulty reading went into separate piles for each of the four victims. After a time, she realized the "ask Regan" piles contained most of the reports.

The hardest part, she'd decided, was reading about the victims. By the time she'd finished reading all the witness reports in each of the files, she felt as if she'd known each of the murdered girls personally. Lana Shuman collected comic books from the 1950s, as Nina had done for a time. Sara Maynard took horseback riding lessons as a young girl, much as Nina had when her mother was alive. Barbie Hughes read everything she could find about ancient civilizations, still one of Nina's favorite subjects. But most shocking to Nina was the fact that the last victim, Maureen—Mickey—Thomas, had been one of several roommates freshman year with Clare Murphy, a sister of one of the girls in Nina's world history class.

She closed the file she'd been reading. She simply could not reconcile the man portrayed in those files—the sleazy professor who used his position, his charm, and his good looks to prey upon innocent young students—with the man who, admittedly, hadn't been much of a fixture in her day-to-day life, but who had always treated her well.

She tried to conjure up specific memories of things she'd done with her dad as a child, and had to admit there were precious few to choose from. Once, when she was about nine or ten, he'd taken her to the Bombay Hook National Wildlife Refuge on the Delaware Bay, and they'd spent hours walking the trails. He'd pointed out rare birds—Caspian terns and stilt sandpipers and glossy ibis; she still recalled their names though not what they looked like—and they'd stopped on the path to watch a mother fox lead her brood of pups across the road. They hadn't talked much that day, but it was the first time she'd ever felt any bond with him, and she'd never forgotten it.

And, of course, there'd been that trip to London, but she never allowed herself to look back on that.

She tried to call up other such times, but all she could think of was the night before he was arrested. He'd arrived home around eleven—not unusual for him—and she'd heard him moving around in his study below her bedroom. She'd gone downstairs—she'd been a little anxious about finding out the next day if she'd be asked to join the sorority she'd so longed for—and stood outside the study door for a moment, debating whether or not to knock. She could see the light under the closed door, but had hesitated before knocking. From behind the door, she could hear the sound of drawers opening and closing—desk drawers or file cabinets, she couldn't tell which. Finally, she'd knocked, and walked in. Her father was standing behind the desk looking edgy and distracted, and uncommonly rumpled. He'd listened to her fears of rejection by the sorority of her choice, and had made some vague comment like, "It will all work out for the best, I'm sure."

A few minutes after she'd gone back upstairs, she'd heard a door close below. She looked out the window and saw her father going into the garage. At first, she thought he was going out again, which would have been strange, since his habit was, once home, to stay home. She'd leaned on the sill, watching and waiting for at least ten minutes, but her father didn't come back inside, and the car didn't leave the garage. Finally, she gave up, and got into bed. Later, as she was drifting off to sleep, she thought she'd heard his footfalls on the step and the door at the end of the hall close softly.

She'd never had the opportunity to ask him what he'd been doing that night.

Strange, she thought now, that one of most vivid memories of her father was her last one.

Not quite the last, she reminded herself. She'd been there the next day, in Celestine Hall, when he was arrested.

She thought again of the unread letter in the box on the closet shelf, and wondered how much longer she could put off reading it.

Nina slipped the handwritten statements back into the folder—one from Sara Maynard's sister telling of Sara's reluctance to discuss her social life in the months before she was murdered, another from Sara's former roommate—and dropped the file on the floor. It had been a depressing day filled with depressing tasks, and she needed a break. She drove into Branigan and made a stop at the drugstore in the center of town. After twenty minutes of browsing the magazines, she purchased one, and returned directly to the house. She read the magazine straight through, then tossed it onto the floor next to the files. She went through Regan's selection of DVDs hoping to find a light comedy, and settled on *Don't Tell Mom the Babysitter's Dead*. Not exactly what she'd expect to find in Regan Landry's film library, but it was just what Nina needed. She microwaved some popcorn she found in the pantry, poured herself a diet soda, and settled down for a little mindless entertainment.

"So what do you guys want on your pizza?" Wes turned to his son, Alec, who was busy playing rock-paper-scissors with his best friend, Reed, while they waited in line at the cafeteria-style restaurant.

"Pepperoni." Alec laughed as his rock smashed Reed's scissors and Reed yelped.

"That okay with you, Reed?"

"Sure." Reed grabbed a red plastic tray from the stack behind him and thrust it at Alec, who was still laughing as he lunged for a tray of his own.

Wes stepped between the two just as the boys began to duel with the lunch trays.

"Enough," Wes admonished the boys. "I would have thought you'd have worked off all your energy running up and down the soccer field."

"We did." Alec giggled. "But Mrs. Garrity was snack mom today and she brought cupcakes with little candy bars on top for after the game, and we've got sugar highs."

"Yeah, we've got sugar highs," Reed said as the two boys collapsed on each other in laughter.

"Okay, settle down, both of you." Wes was going to have to ask the coach to have a chat with Mrs. Garrity about suitable after-game snacks. "Sugar high or no, you need to remember you're in a public place, and acting like goons is not acceptable."

"He's the goon." Alec poked at Reed.

"You're the goon." Reed poked back.

Another round of silly laughter followed.

Wes paid for the pizza and drinks and led the boys to the back booth.

"Water?" Alec wrinkled his nose. "We want Coke."

"Sorry, bud. Something has to wash all that cupcake sugar out of your system."

"We're gonna pee sugar-water." Alec dissolved in a fit of hysteria.

"Eat." Wes rapped his knuckles softly on the table. "Enough silliness for one meal, okay? Just settle down."

The boys tried, but every once in a while, one of them would snicker.

Wes tried to distract them.

"That was a good game you guys played today," he said.

"We sucked." Alec picked the pepperoni from his slice, tilted his head back, and dropped the meat into his open mouth.

"Yeah, that's why we lost." Reed nodded. " 'Cause we suck."

"Well, you know, it's just a game, fellas. You play hard, sometimes you win, sometimes you lose. But it's just a game."

"That's not what my dad said last time, when we won," Reed told Wes. "He said you're supposed to play to win."

"Well, you hope to win, that's why you always play

your best." Wes nodded. "But there's something to be learned from winning and from losing."

"What did we learn today?" Alec asked him.

"That even when we suck, we still get pizza." Reed elbowed him in the ribs.

It seemed to Wes that the rest of the afternoon went downhill from there.

His ex-wife, Claudia, topped it off for him when he dropped Alec off.

"For God's sake, Wes, can't you ever be on time for anything?" She met him at the door where she'd obviously been waiting.

"Sorry. The game ran late, then we stopped for pizza . . ."

"You could have forgone the pizza."

"I promised Alec and Reed we'd stop."

He shoved his hands in his pockets. Something about the way Claudia expressed herself always made him feel as if he were a child being scolded for a very disappointing deed. He hadn't appreciated it when they were married, and he didn't appreciate it now. With Alec standing next to him, he wasn't about to take her to task for it. It never did any good, anyway. Claudia was Claudia. Gorgeous, brash, and bossy. Always had been, always would be. There had been a time when Wes hadn't minded quite as much.

"I said I was sorry. I'll try to keep better track of the time next weekend."

"Alec and I are going to see my mother next weekend."

"Right. The following weekend, then."

Claudia sighed. "No, you won't. You'll have all good intentions to. But you won't. And you'll be late again. And you'll make me late for whatever it is I'll be waiting to do."

"If you're so late, why are you standing here arguing with me?"

"Point well taken." Claudia grinned and closed the door in his face.

Alec tapped on the window to yell good-bye. Wes waved and got into his car. It was coming up on six P.M., already dark, and the storm clouds were gathering. He drove back toward Stone River, and somehow found himself on Shore Drive.

He slowed to a near stop as he drove past Regan Landry's driveway. He couldn't see the rambling contemporary house from the road, but he thought he might have been able to make out a bit of light back through the scrub pines.

He still couldn't believe that Stephen Madden's daughter was digging into that old case. That man had been guilty as sin. There'd never been a question in Wes's mind.

He couldn't help but wonder how Nina was going to feel when she wasn't able to find any evidence that would convince him to reopen the case.

Or how he'd feel if she did.

Eleven

When Regan returned to Maryland on Tuesday night and found that an early-morning storm had washed out Shore Drive, she did what she always did when the road was impassable. She went to the marina outside of town, left her car, and borrowed a small outboard motorboat from the owner. Twenty minutes after leaving the marina, she was pulling up to the dock behind her house and tying the craft to the pilings. When the road was reopened, she'd return the boat to its owner and drive her car home. It was a small price to pay for the joy of living right on the Chesapeake.

Swinging her overnight bag over her shoulder, she trudged up the walk to the house. The heavy rains had redistributed quite a bit of the mulch from the beds around the deck, and she'd have to remember to rake it back into place. But later, she told herself. Not tonight.

Tonight she was going to take a long hot bath and mull over all she'd discovered about the mysterious Eddie Kroll during her trip to Illinois.

And all she hadn't learned.

Elusive bastard, she reflected as she unlocked her back door and stepped inside. If not for the sticky note Nina had left on the refrigerator door, Regan would never have known that she'd had a weekend houseguest. All the dishes had been washed and put away and the floor had been cleaned as well. She stepped into the study, which was as neat as a pin, except for the pile of boxes Nina had left standing against the bookcase, along with copies of the notes she'd made, as Regan had asked her to do. She'd get to those in another day or two. Right now, Regan had notes of her own to review.

First of all, there was the matter of Dolly Brown. In her mid-to-late sixties, Dolly had dyed pale strawberry blond hair and lovely deep blue eyes, and was ten or fifteen pounds short of plump. She'd called after seeing an ad Regan had placed in a local newspaper, and told Regan she'd known Eddie Kroll as a child and that her family had lived next door to the Krolls. Regan had flown to Sayreville to meet with Dolly, who'd proven to be a bit of a puzzle herself.

For one thing, who Dolly Brown was in relation to Eddie Kroll seemed to change on a daily basis. First, she claimed to have been a neighbor. But when Regan pressed Dolly to tell her what happened to Eddie after he left juvenile hall, she claimed not to know.

"Well, where do you think he went?" Regan had asked. "What was the talk in the neighborhood?"

"The talk was that he died."

"In juvie?"

Dolly had paused. "After he got out."

"How did he die?"

"I never heard that part."

"Where is he buried?"

"I don't know." Dolly had shaken her head.

"Why can't I find a death notice, or a death certificate?"

Dolly had shrugged.

"The parish doesn't even have any records on Eddie's death. How likely is that?" Regan had persisted.

"I think maybe he didn't die around here." Dolly had looked down and started picking at the chipped nail polish on her left thumbnail. "I think maybe he didn't come back here after he got out."

"Well, where do you think he went?"

"I don't remember. I don't know that I ever knew. I was younger than he was. I just didn't pay a whole lot of attention."

"Can you show me where he used to live?"

"What?" Dolly had appeared surprised by the question.

"The house Eddie used to live in. You must remember where that is, if you used to live next door."

"Of course I remember." Dolly had grown indignant.

"Show me how to get there, then." Regan opened the car door, and Dolly got in the passenger side with what seemed to Regan to be a great deal of reluctance.

Dolly gave the directions, and Regan followed them. A few minutes later they were parked in front of a small, neat, white clapboard twin house. On the side where Dolly said the Krolls had once lived, an old man sat on the porch and rocked in a wooden chair that was painted the same bright blue as the shutters.

"Let's go talk to him." Regan pointed to the man. "Maybe he knows where Eddie is."

"He's lucky if he knows where *he* is." Dolly made no effort to move from the front seat. "Carl has Alzheimer's, and on any given day, doesn't remember his own name."

"But on any given day, he just might." Regan got out of the car and started walking toward the house. Dolly still gave no indication she was going to follow until Regan banged on the side of the car door.

Dolly grumbled, but got out.

"I'd prefer not to agitate him," Dolly said.

"He doesn't look agitated. He's smiling."

"He does a lot of that these days. He just doesn't know any better."

"Well, he seems to know you. He's waving for us to come up to the porch."

Regan waved back and started up the cement walk to the porch.

"You coming?" she called to Dolly without looking back.

"You coming to see me, pretty lady?" the man asked as Regan approached.

"I certainly am." Regan smiled. "I can't resist a chance to chat with such a handsome guy."

"You sit right down here, honey." He pointed to the chair next to him.

Regan sat, and was about to speak when the door opened and a woman leaned out.

"May I help you?" She looked upon Regan with suspicion.

"This here is Regan Landry." Dolly hurried up the walk. "She put an ad in the local paper, looking for someone who knew Eddie Kroll, and I answered it."

"Oh. Really." The woman stepped onto the porch and closed the door behind her.

"Yes. You are . . ."

"Stella. Carl's wife, Stella." She regarded Regan curiously.

"It's nice to meet you, Mrs. . . . ?"

"Everyone just calls her Stella," Dolly told her.

"Dolly, you remember that time me and Eddie caught all those little fish down in the stream there at Holman Park and brought them home and put them in the frying pan?" Carl looked over at Stella and began to laugh. "Mom came in and found all those dead, blackened little bait fish all over the place, liked to kill the both of us."

"I remember, Carl," Dolly said softly.

"So, you knew Eddie pretty well, did you?" Regan asked.

"Sure, I knew Eddie. We were . . ." A look of confusion crossed his face and he looked to his wife for help. "What were we again?"

"Brothers, sweetheart," Stella told him gently. "You and Eddie were brothers."

"That's right," Carl said as if reminding himself of something important. "We were brothers, me and Eddie."

He looked up at Stella and asked, "Is he still alive?"

"No, sweetie, he died." She leaned over and patted his hands. "Both of your brothers died."

"Harry died, too?" The look of confusion returned.

"Harry, too." She smoothed his steel gray hair back from his face. "You're the last brother, Carl. The last of the Kroll boys."

"The last one." He head moved slowly, side to side, as if amazed by the news. "The last one . . ."

"Mrs. Kroll, do you know what happened to him? To Eddie?"

Stella paused, then turned to Regan. "No, I'm sorry, I don't know. It happened before I met Carl. No one ever seemed to want to talk about it, so I never pushed it. Sorry."

She touched Regan gently on the arm and said, "It was a pleasure to meet you. It really was. I wish you luck in your search, and in your life. And with your books." Stella turned back to Carl. "Right now, I'm going to take my sweetie into the house and give him some lunch. Dolly, I'll be talking to you."

With Dolly's help, Stella got Carl out of the chair, and together the elderly couple walked into the house and closed the door behind them.

"Guess you'll be wanting to be heading back to the airport." Dolly brushed her hands together in a sort of "that's that" motion. "Mind dropping me off at my house?"

"I don't mind." Regan rose from her seat. "But my flight isn't until Tuesday morning. I have all the time in the world."

When they got into the car, Regan turned to Dolly and asked, "Why didn't you tell me that Eddie's brother still lived in this house?"

"Because I didn't know what kind of a day he'd be having. Some days he remembers things like it was yesterday. Other days, just the mention of Eddie's name sets him off and he gets really agitated, and then Stella has a real hard time with him. I didn't want you coming over here and getting something started that Stella was going to have to deal with."

"You seem to know a lot about the situation," Regan said as she started the car.

"Me and Stella been friends for a long time." Dolly stared straight ahead.

"Dolly, I'm not here to upset anyone, or to disrupt anyone's life."

"Right. You just want to know about Eddie because your father had his report cards." There was a hint of sarcasm in Dolly's voice.

"Well, now, how do you suppose that could have happened?" Regan drove slowly, prolonging the ride as long as she could. "How would my dad, a writer who'd spent so much of his life in England, come to have the report cards of a young man who'd disappeared years earlier in Illinois?"

"I have no idea."

"Don't you think it's odd? I mean, Eddie's family is still living in the same house he'd been living in when he was arrested. Wouldn't you think they'd have kept his things?"

Dolly shrugged.

"I suppose I can always go back and ask Stella if she knew if any of Eddie's things were tossed out."

"Stella has enough on her hands, with Carl not knowing from one day to the next who he is or where he is. You call her about Eddie's things, and the next thing, you're going to want to start talking about what happened that got Eddie sent away."

"You must have still been living next door to him at the time. Why don't you tell me what happened?"

"You can learn everything you want to know from

the newspapers. I'll bet you're real good at finding things out on the Internet."

"Actually, I am. Thank you." Regan tried not to smile. "And I have read the articles. Every one I could find. But I know enough to know that there's always so much more to a story than what you see in print."

Dolly sat rigid in the passenger seat, staring out the window.

"Let's start with the basics, then," Regan said. "Did Eddie do it? Was he guilty of killing his friend?"

"Yes. He did it. He wasn't alone, and he was led into it by the other two, but he never denied that he'd hit the boy."

"The others were James Cash and Leonard Wilson."

"Yes, those two. Big fifteen-year-olds, used Eddie to lure Joey into that vacant lot."

"How'd he do that?"

"Eddie knew Joey from school, the other two boys didn't know him as well. They told Eddie to tell Joey that he'd stolen some cigarettes from the drugstore, and that he'd sell him some cheap."

"What was the motive? Why did they want to kill this boy?"

"Eddie said he didn't know they were going to kill him. He thought they were only going to rob him."

"How much did they get?"

"Twenty-two dollars and nineteen cents," Dolly said quietly. She was still staring out the window. "They gave all the money to Eddie."

"I don't understand. Why would they do that if the idea was to rob this kid? Granted, it wasn't much of a haul, but why do it and not split up the money?"

"They didn't do it for the money. That's just what they told Eddie, so that he'd go along with it. Jimmy and Len were planning all along to hurt Joey."

"Why?"

"Because he'd done some things with Jimmy's sister and spread it all over school."

"The newspapers said that all three of the boys—Cash, Wilson, and Kroll—took part in beating Joey to death with rocks and bricks."

"Eddie admitted having smacked Joey in the head with a board he found lying on the ground."

"For twenty-two dollars?" Regan frowned.

"The other two told him Joey would have a couple hundred on him." Dolly turned to look at Regan. "Joey's father owned the dry cleaners in town. Joey used to brag that on Friday nights, he helped his father close up, and then his father would go to the tavern on his way home. Instead of taking all the week's receipts with him, he'd send it home with Joey. Turned out not to be true, but there wasn't a kid in town who hadn't heard Joey brag about how some nights he'd have hundreds of dollars in his pockets."

"So Joey was a talker. Talked about the girls he scored with, talked about how much money he carried around with him."

"He had a big mouth, all right." Dolly nodded. "My mother always said a big mouth would get you in trouble every time. Joey's big mouth got him killed."

"Was Eddie friendly with these other two boys?"

"Not friendly, so much as . . . I'm not sure, but I think he was sort of in awe of them. They were two years older, they were sort of the big guys in the neighborhood, you know what I mean? The cool guys. All the freshmen looked up to them."

"So when they needed someone to get to Joey, they just picked one of the younger boys to lure him to the vacant lot."

"Right. The way I understood it at the time, they could have picked anyone. It just seems that Eddie came along at the wrong time."

"The newspapers said that both of the other boys claimed that Eddie had been behind the whole thing. That he'd planned it; he'd recruited them because they were bigger and stronger.

"They said he'd asked them to help rob Joey, that he'd split the money with them. That when things didn't go well, he was the one who started hitting Joey with the brick."

"That was disproven at the trial, though, wasn't it?" Regan frowned, trying to remember the details.

"Yes. Thank God, the attorney who represented Eddie understood something about how blood flies through the air when something is hit. He showed in court how, if Eddie'd been the one hitting Joey, his clothes would have had a pattern of blood on them. His didn't. Jimmy Cash's did."

"They were both tried as adults. Cash and Wilson."

Dolly nodded. "They were both released after serving their sentences. Lennie Wilson died a few years ago. Lung cancer. Jimmy Cash is still around somewhere. I don't know where."

Dolly looked over at Regan. "I really don't know where he is. I didn't bother to keep up with him."

"So Eddie was railroaded by the two who planned the whole thing. You're telling me he was just a good kid who got caught up in something that got out of hand?"

"Eddie was a good kid." Dolly turned her face back to the window, and that was that.

Regan had felt there'd been a whole lot more to the story, but something in the set of Dolly's jaw made it clear that there'd be no more questions entertained about Eddie Kroll. Even Regan's offer to take the widowed Dolly to dinner at one of the area's nicest restaurants hadn't been enough to bring Dolly around. Regan had spent two more days in Sayreville, but she wasn't able to get Dolly to return her calls.

Now, back home, Regan tried to look back on her conversations with Dolly with a bit of detachment. There'd been something off about the woman, Regan had picked that up the minute she met her, but there was something more, some question that had lingered on in her mind for days. And there'd been something that Stella had said . . .

Well, it would come to her. Right now, that cold November wind was picking up again, and her whirlpool bath was calling her name. There'd be time enough later to review her notes so she could go over them with Mitch when he drove out on Friday night. Though maybe she wouldn't wait that long. Maybe she'd call him later and give him a few names to run down for her. She'd met a lot of people out there in Sayreville, some related to Eddie Kroll, some who claimed to be childhood friends. Their stories had all been the same. Eddie'd been used by the older guys, set up just as surely as Joey had been. Eddie came out of juvenile hall and vanished. They'd all heard he'd died, but no one seemed to know where, when, or how.

As she turned off the downstairs lights and started up the steps, it occurred to her that she'd returned from her fact-finding trip with just as many questions as answers.

Twelve

Nina stretched to reach the ringing phone she'd pushed to the farthest corner of her desk without looking at it. "Nina Madden." As soon as she heard the voice on the other end, she wished she'd checked the caller ID.

"Nina, it's Kyle. Damn, but you are hard to get ahold of."

"Oh, Kyle, hi. I'm sorry, I've been really busy, and I . . ." She rested her elbows on the manuscript she'd been reading and put her head in her hands. He was the last person in the world she felt like dealing with.

"Hey, not a problem. I've been busy myself. So tell me how you're doing? Besides busy. Everything all right up there in the Big Apple?"

"Everything's fine, thanks. How are you doing? You and Marcie talking things out?"

"Not really. I don't know how that's going to go, frankly. We'll see. Listen, while I have you on the phone, I called the car rental place and they told me that if you'd left a box in the trunk of the car, they'd have sent it on to you." He paused. "Did you get the box back yet, Nina? It should have arrived by now."

Busted. Damn.

"Actually, I did get it back, Kyle. I've been meaning to call you about that."

"So, did you read the letter that Stephen wrote to my mother? Ordinarily, I wouldn't be so curious, but all things considered—him dying so soon after he wrote it, her dying recently—it's just been on my mind."

"I can understand that."

"So, do I get to see it?"

She hesitated just a little too long.

"Nina?" His voice was a little more forceful.

"Actually, Kyle, I don't think you want to read it."

"Why not?"

"Because I think the contents will upset you."

"Nina, I think I can handle whatever it was your father had to say to my mother."

She bit her bottom lip. She couldn't bring herself to say, *Dad thought your mom was the killer.*

"Nina?"

"Let me do this. I'm going to be in Maryland over the weekend at a friend's house. She doesn't live too far from Stone River. How about I meet you at the Oak Drive house and show you the letter. I think it's better that you read it yourself."

"Terrific. What day works best for you?"

"How about Saturday afternoon?"

"That will be just fine. Thanks, Nina. I'm looking forward to reading it. And to seeing you again, of course."

"I'll talk to you then."

Kyle said good-bye and hung up. Nina dropped the receiver into the cradle and put her head in her hands. She berated herself for not being able to carry through with the lie she'd planned on telling. And why couldn't she have just said, yes, the box came but the letter isn't in it? What would have been the problem with that? Now she'd have to face Kyle, hand over the damned letter, and let him read it.

She couldn't even begin to wonder how Kyle was going to react. Well, she'd find out soon enough. Today was Thursday. She'd be leaving for Regan's after work tomorrow, taking the train into Newark, Delaware, where Regan would pick her up. Regan and Mitch had plans to visit the vineyard they'd invested in, and would be leaving on Saturday morning. They'd have all Friday evening to powwow, as Regan called it. By then she'd have made some notes on the case, and was hoping to be able to talk it over with Mitch before Nina arrived on Friday.

Nina was hoping they'd be able to come to some studied conclusion. Either there was a chance that her father had been telling the truth, or he'd been playing some cruel hoax on Olivia.

She couldn't help but dismiss that thought. She'd

never have suspected her father of being capable of that kind of cruelty.

Then again, no one would have suspected him of being a murderer, either.

She pushed it all from her mind. There were decisions to be made on the manuscript she'd been working on when the phone rang, and she had to make them before the end of the day. She'd deal with Kyle—and her father's letter—over the weekend.

"You must be Nina," said the tall, good-looking guy who stood on the deck behind Regan's house.

"I am. Mitch?" She walked toward him while Regan parked the car back near the garage.

"Right." With his right hand, he shook hers. With his left, he grabbed her overnight bag. He turned to Regan and asked, "Where's my pizza?"

"I'll have to go back out to get it. I forgot the number so I couldn't call from the car."

"That is the lamest excuse I've ever heard," he told her. "But no matter. I have come prepared. I have three really nice steaks marinating in the fridge."

"You do?" Regan stopped in her tracks.

"I do." He nodded.

"You're my hero." She kissed him on the side of his mouth.

"Damn right I am." He followed the two women

into the house. Once inside, he held up Nina's bag and asked, "Which room?"

"I put her in the room at the end of the hall," Regan told him. "We're supposed to have a fabulous moon tonight, and you'll be able to see it from that little balcony if you want," she told Nina.

"I'll take it right up. Be back in a flash."

"Thanks, Mitch," Nina said. "Regan, did you finish going over those notes I left for you?"

"No shop talk till after dinner," Mitch called as he headed upstairs with Nina's bag. "Gives me indigestion."

"He's cute," Nina whispered.

"In a slightly geeky sort of way." Regan grinned.

"I don't see the geek factor."

"You've never watched him on the computer."

"Besides," Mitch was saying as he came back down the steps, "I've been up to my ears in bad guys this week. Let's put it on ice for just a little while."

"That's fine with me," Nina said, then turned to Regan. "Besides, I'm dying to know what you found out about Eddie Kroll while you were in Illinois last weekend."

"I don't think I learned a damn thing about him, although I did get some insight into the murder he was sent away for." Regan frowned. "Oh, and I found the house he grew up in. His brother and sister-in-law are living there."

"You met his brother?" Nina's eyebrows rose.

Regan nodded and took a plate of cold shrimp from the refrigerator and placed it on the counter. She hunted up napkins and small plates.

"Dig in," she told Mitch and Nina. "And yes, I met his brother, Carl. The last of the Kroll brothers, they said."

"Well, what did he tell you about Eddie?"

"Just that he caught a bunch of bait fish when he was a kid and tried to cook them for dinner by dumping them in a frying pan."

"That's it? You didn't ask him what happened to him?"

"Wouldn't have done any good." Regan bit into a shrimp. "He has Alzheimer's."

"Oh, no."

"Oh, yes. The wife, Stella? Claims she met Carl after Eddie died. Or disappeared. Or whatever the hell it was that happened to him."

"And this woman you went out there to meet?"

Mitch piled a mound of shrimp onto a plate and excused himself to start the grill.

"Well, she did give me a lot of information about the actual crime that Eddie was convicted of. It seems Eddie was duped by two older boys into taking part in killing one of the kids from the neighborhood. Eddie thought they were going to rob the kid. Eddie's part was just supposed to be to lure the kid to a vacant lot. The others knew the victim wasn't going to leave that lot alive." Regan perched herself on one of the counter stools. "Which doesn't make Eddie an upstanding citizen, but doesn't make him a hardened killer, either."

"And you got all this from Dolly?"

"Yes."

"So she was helpful," Nina pointed out.

"Yes, but reluctantly. And there's something funny about her."

"Funny in what way?"

"Evasive. She clearly knew a lot more than she was telling me, but no matter how hard I tried, I couldn't get her to break and spill all of what she knows."

"Why would she call you and have you come all the way out there, if she wasn't going to tell you everything?" Nina helped herself to a few shrimp.

"I have no idea. But I know there's plenty she was holding back from me. And there was something else, too, that I thought was weird."

"What's that?"

"Every once in a while, I'd find her staring at me. Not in a rude way, just . . . staring. I can't explain it."

"Maybe she's a fan and was impressed to have met you."

"We never discussed the fact that I'm a writer, and my father's name was never brought up." Regan seemed to consider that for a moment. "That in itself is odd. Everyone always asks about my father. Dolly never mentioned his name."

"Maybe she didn't make the connection."

"Maybe."

"So where does that leave you, as far as Eddie Kroll is concerned?"

"It leaves me trying to figure out my next move." Regan reached for another shrimp.

"It leaves you in my capable hands." Mitch came in through the back door. "Give me a few hours with the names of those buggers and my computer, and I'll find something for you."

"I'm counting on it. I think at this point, if I had some direction, I could figure it out."

"I'll do my best." He squeezed her shoulder. "You want to check those baked potatoes I put in the oven before you got home while I throw the steaks on the grill? Nina, you could get the salad out of the refrigerator and toss a little dressing on it."

He opened the refrigerator door and grabbed the dish that held the marinating steaks and was out the door in a flash.

"Does he always take over the kitchen like this?" Nina asked. "Not that that's a bad thing."

"Only when it's his weekend to cook." Regan grinned and opened the oven door. She poked at the potatoes with a long-handled fork. "They look perfect."

Nina tossed the salad while Regan set the table in the breakfast room for three. Within ten minutes, they were seated and eating the steaks Mitch had expertly prepared.

"So tell me more about this vineyard you two bought into," Nina said.

"Not much to tell yet," Mitch replied. "We'll know better in the spring if any of the grape vines are going to make it. They've been overgrown for so many years, we're still not certain if all of the vines weren't choked out by the weeds and trees that had sprouted up."

"And we thought the trellises could all be salvaged, but it turns out that most of them have to be replaced or, at the very least, repaired," Regan added.

"It sounds like an interesting project, though," Nina said.

"We're all sort of captivated by the idea," Regan told her. "I really hope it works out. For one thing, because it is, as you say, interesting and could probably be fun, if we can make a go of it. And for another, it's fun to be in business with your friends, people you care about. We all have high hopes for this venture."

"I hope it's a huge success," Nina said.

"Thanks." Regan smiled. "We do, too."

"So, now that the dinner hour is winding down, let's talk about Nina's dilemma." Mitch placed his knife and fork across his empty plate. "Regan has already filled me in on the background. We've talked about what we feel we need to do."

"Shoot," Nina told him.

"Here's our idea." Mitch leaned back in his chair, his arm draped casually over Regan's shoulders. "We think we want to try approaching this as if we were trying to prove that Dr. Madden was in fact innocent. The prosecutors proved to a jury's satisfaction that he was guilty. We're going to look at their evidence and see if that holds up, or if the same information can be turned around to prove his innocence."

"Where's their proof, in other words, Nina." Regan touched her arm lightly. "What did they use, and what, if anything, did they miss?"

"To hear Detective Powell tell it, they didn't miss a damned thing," Nina told them. "He was pretty adamant that my dad was guilty and trying to prove otherwise was a colossal waste of time."

"Well, it's our time, right?" Mitch noted. "Besides, I'm intrigued by the idea that your father continued to maintain his innocence, yet privately believed he was taking the blame for someone else. Usually, if someone is trying to get out of a conviction, and he knows or has reason to suspect that someone else committed the crime, he wastes no time giving up the name, believe me. Especially in a murder conviction. But confiding in the person he supposedly believed was guilty, and not giving her name to the police? That's a new one."

"You think he could have been just playing with her?" Regan asked.

"He claimed to have loved her. Would he have been so cruel to someone he loved?"

"And then there's this matter of the rapes," Mitch said. "How could Dr. Madden have thought his wife was guilty, if in fact the girls had been raped?"

"We'll need to take a good look at the evidence there, see what they had." Regan nodded. "Right now the main question in our minds is, were the girls really raped?"

"Well, what about DNA? If they had DNA from my father linking him to the girls . . ." Nina shrugged.

"There was no DNA testing available back in 1989," Mitch reminded her. "And even if there had been, there's a strong possibility that, since your father admitted having had affairs with each of the victims, his DNA would most likely have been present."

"Did the cops assume that the girls had been raped because there were signs of a struggle?" Regan thought out loud. "Or because Dr. Madden admitted having had sex with them on the nights they were killed?"

"Why didn't they connect him sooner?" Mitch wondered. "Why wasn't he linked to the first girl right away?"

"All of the girls lived alone, and while all four had alluded to friends or siblings about a hot romance, none of them told anyone who he was." Nina appeared embarrassed. "He must have told them all that they couldn't tell anyone. I'm sure he convinced them they had to keep the relationship quiet, or he'd lose his job."

"Then how was he linked to the last vic?" Mitch asked.

"Fingerprints on a glass found in the kitchen," Nina replied. "And a book he'd left in her bedroom. They matched up the prints, and when they started talking to him, he admitted they'd been having an affair. Later, a neighbor of the second victim identified him as being the man she'd seen leaving the apartment building on several occasions."

"So they had the case all sewed up." Mitch rubbed his chin.

"I'm sure they thought they did. Older man, popular, good-looking professor. Pretty, young, starstruck coeds. Stephen Madden isn't the only man in that position to sleep with his students. I'll bet it's more common than you think," Regan said.

"I admit, it looks like an easy catch. Maybe too easy," Mitch told Nina. "I've been tempted to take the easy way out myself, many times. I'm not judging the cops. But it's always been my experience that if something looks too obvious, it generally is."

"So you think we should at least look into it?" Nina asked.

"Oh, yeah. If nothing else, it'll give Mitch and me something to do. Think of it as a sort of parlor game.

Some people like chess, some people like puzzles. We like to look into old murders."

"Well, just for the sake of argument, let's suppose my father did not kill those girls. And let's say they were raped. I think we'd all agree that would take Olivia out of the picture." Nina looked from Mitch to Regan. "Who else is there?"

"An excellent question. Who else would have had motive to kill those girls and pin the blame on the professor?" Regan got up and went into the study, and returned a moment later with a notepad and pen. She wrote POSSIBLE SUSPECTS on the top sheet of paper. "Any thoughts on that, Nina?"

Nina shook her head. "I can't even begin to imagine who would have done something like that."

Regan added several question marks to the page.

"What would motivate someone to kill and put the blame on someone else?" Nina asked. "For that matter, what would have motivated my father to have killed those girls?"

"The prosecution's theory was that the affairs were coming to an end and he was afraid they'd tell someone," Regan pointed out.

"There are statements in those files from other girls who'd slept with my father over the years. Quite a few of them. I'd think if he'd been afraid of someone talking about their affair, he'd have started killing them off long before he did."

"Good point." Regan nodded, and jotted down MOTIVATION???? under her previous notations.

"The murder weapon was never found, was it?" Regan asked.

Nina shook her head. "Not by the police, anyway. My father claims to have found it."

"Right, the letter he wrote to Olivia." Regan nodded.

"I would have liked to have seen that," Mitch said.

"You can." Nina rose. "It's in my handbag. I brought it with me because Kyle insists on seeing it."

"Your stepbrother? Olivia's son?" Regan asked.

"Right. I was really trying to avoid having him see the letter. I didn't want to share with him the fact that my father thought his mother killed those girls. But he was adamant, he wants to read it." Nina turned to Regan. "I ran out of excuses not to show it to him. I did tell him I didn't think it was a good idea, but he wants the letter."

"Don't let him keep it," Mitch told her.

"Why not?"

"Because we might need it later," he explained.

"Oh, right, he's going to turn it back over to me so that I can use it to prove his mother was guilty? That's not going to happen."

"May I see it?"

"Sure, Mitch." Nina took her bag from the counter and opened it.

"Is your copy machine working?" Mitch asked Regan.

"Yes."

Nina held out the envelope, and Mitch took it, opened it, and read the letter through one time before handing it to Regan.

"Would you mind making a copy of this for Kyle?" he asked.

"It'll just take me a sec." Regan went down the hall in the direction of her office.

"He's going to want to know why he's getting a copy and why I'm keeping the original."

"You can tell him that the original letter is in the hands of the FBI." Mitch grinned. "And you won't be lying."

Regan returned in a minute and handed the copy to Nina. Mitch reached out for the original, and read it over one more time.

"He says he found the weapon—clearly a knife—but he doesn't say what he did with it." Mitch looked up at Nina. "You have any thoughts on that?"

She shook her head.

"No, but since he's accusing Olivia, wouldn't he have found it around the house someplace?"

"That's what I'd think," Mitch agreed. "And if he found it there, he probably left it there, wherever it had been hidden."

"He says he'd planned on talking with Olivia the next day, when he got home after his last class." Regan picked up the copy that lay on the table and scanned it. "So if the police didn't find it the day they arrested him and searched the house, then maybe your father returned it to the hiding place."

"So we go back to the house and try to get in and search for a logical place," Mitch told them. "Assuming the house is still standing and we can find out who owns it now."

"No mystery there," Nina replied. "Dad's will provided for the house to come to me upon Olivia's death, but I signed it over to Kyle. It's his house now."

Mitch cut to the chase. "So, in other words, if we want to search for the murder weapon there, we're going to have to get his permission to look for it."

"The murder weapon we need in order to prove his mother killed four girls and framed my father."

"What are the chances he's going to let us do that?" Regan asked.

"What do you think?" Nina rested her elbow on the table, her chin in her open palm.

"Yeah." Regan grimaced. "That's what I was afraid you'd say . . ."

Thirteen

Nina's hands were sweating on the steering wheel as she parked in front of the house on Oak Drive. She was worried about how Kyle was going to react to reading her father's letter, and she was concerned about the fact that sooner or later, the premises were going to have to be searched for a murder weapon that may or may not have been hidden there. How was she going to pull that off with Kyle now holding the keys? She wouldn't be at all surprised if he got really angry and tossed her off the property.

She tried to put herself in his place, and wasn't sure how gracious she'd be. It was all she could do to remind herself that she was only the messenger. Of course, throughout history, it had been the messenger who'd been shot.

"Hi." Kyle came out the front door. "Watch that pile of stuff there."

He pointed to the boxes that lined the curb.

"I called for a trash pickup for this week, and the borough was supposed to send a truck over on

Friday, but it never got here. I'm hoping it doesn't rain over the weekend and make a mess, because I'm not going to drag all this back inside." He waited on the sidewalk for Nina to round the front of the car, where he gave her a quick hug. "Most of that is from the basement. You won't believe all the stuff in the attic. You should take a look at it, by the way. I think there are some things that belonged to your father."

Before she could respond, he hastened to add, "I know you said you didn't want anything from your father, but there are some old photographs. Might be his parents, his grandparents. You might want to take a look."

"I think I'll do that. Thanks." She nodded. She'd never known her father's family very well. After her parents divorced and she lived with her mother, she rarely saw relatives on her father's side.

"Come on in." He held the door aside for her.

"Hey, you've been busy." She walked into the living room, where the walls had been freshly painted pale beige. "This looks great."

"I'm trying to go room to room. Whether I stay for a while or sell, the house has to be freshened up a bit. I spoke with a Realtor the other day, and she said I'd need to do stuff like that, brighten up the rooms with paint. Painting is easy and it's fast, so I thought I'd start with that right away."

"It really has made a difference."

"Well, she also told me to throw some slipcovers

on the sofa and chairs. Do something different on the windows, since those drapes have been there for as long as I can remember."

"Guess it's time, then."

"Yeah. It's time." He gestured for her to come into the kitchen. "I was just having coffee. I'll pour a cup for you and then we can get down to business."

"Business?" She sat at the kitchen table and draped her purse over the back of the chair.

"The letter." Kyle handed her the cup he'd just filled for her.

"Oh. The letter." She smiled as if it had merely slipped her mind, when in fact she'd thought of little else since he'd asked her for it. She slipped her handbag off the chair and took out the folded piece of paper. "Actually, I made a copy for you. Whether or not you're going to want to keep it after you read what my father had to say, well, that's going to be up to you."

"Well, let's see." He sat opposite her at the table and put out his hand.

Nina gave Kyle the letter, then sat back and sipped her coffee. He began to read, and she rose and walked to the back window. She looked out as if she were seeing it all for the first time.

She stood with her back to him and heard the rustling of the papers as he went from one page to the next. When she finally turned back to the table, he was rereading the first page. She sat back down, and watched his face as he read, searching for some indication of what he might be feeling. He'd not said a word, nor had his expression changed. What, she wondered, could be going through his mind?

Finally Kyle looked up and said, "Of course, this is all nonsense."

"I don't know what it is, Kyle."

"You can't believe for a minute that my mother was the Stone River Rapist?" His eyes narrowed and his mouth slid into a smirk. "A fifty-two-year-old woman did not rape and murder those four girls."

"I can't explain why he thought what he thought." Nina shrugged. "I can't imagine how she could have been guilty, and yet I can't imagine him just making up such a thing."

"And this part here"—Kyle's voice rose slightly— "this part where he refers to what must have been the murder weapon. If he'd found it, and he thought she'd used it, why didn't he tell his lawyer? Why didn't he tell the DA?"

"I think he's pretty clear on that point. He felt his actions were responsible for causing her to do what she did. What he *believed* she'd done," Nina explained. "He says he knew he'd caused her terrible pain, and that—"

"Well, he got that much right." Kyle tossed the letter onto the table between them. "She was devastated by all his affairs. Sometimes I'd come home from school and find her crying. Just sitting someplace, crying. Weeping as if her heart was breaking. Which of course, it was."

"She told you that? She told you that my father was cheating on her?"

"Not at first. But later, she did. She said they'd only been married for a few months when he had his first affair." He looked at Nina darkly. "Can you imagine how that must have made her feel?"

"Why did she stay with him, all those years? Why didn't she leave him?"

"The way your mother did?" He held his mug by the base and not by the handle as he drank from it. "That's why your mother left, you know. Because he cheated on her, too."

"No. I didn't know that." She felt her spine straighten just a bit as she spoke. "But I'm not surprised. If he was unfaithful to Olivia so soon after their marriage, it stands to reason it was a pattern that had already been set."

"Well, he says it right in his letter. The man was a sex addict. Just couldn't get enough of those young girls," Kyle said bitterly.

"Apparently not," Nina replied softly.

"Oh, God, Nina, I'm so sorry." Kyle reached across the table for her hands. "Honest to God, I wasn't thinking. This has just come as a shock to me, that's all."

"I understand. It came as a shock to me, too." She

squeezed his hand, then slipped hers out of his grasp. "I wasn't sure how you'd react to it."

"I just don't believe it." He picked up his mug with both hands and raised it to his lips. "I don't give it any credence whatsoever."

She fell silent, both hands in front of her on the table. She began to pick at her nail polish.

"Nina?" Kyle set the mug on the table. "You don't think there's anything to this, do you?"

"I believe that my father found what he believed to be the murder weapon, and for reasons that I don't understand, he believed it pointed to Olivia as the killer."

"He doesn't say what he found or what he did with it." Kyle skimmed the letter again. "Except that he hid it someplace."

"Someplace here," Nina told him. "Maybe in his study, in the garage, in the attic."

"I seem to remember that the police searched this place pretty thoroughly and on more than one occasion," Kyle reminded her. "If it was here, how did they miss it?"

"I don't know. I don't know if it will ever be found."

"I suppose you were planning on taking a look."

"I wasn't even going to ask. I can't imagine how I'd feel if I were in your shoes." She avoided meeting his eyes.

"Hey, if you want to go through this place, turn it

inside out and upside down, you go right ahead. If you think you can find what all those cops couldn't, I say, go for it."

"Are you serious?" She looked up.

"Of course I'm serious. And I'm that certain there's nothing to be found. I don't know why your father had this crazy idea—maybe being in prison did something to his mind, who knows?"

"Well, I'd like to take a look around." She nodded. "I can't thank you enough for being so understanding about all this. I wasn't sure how you'd react."

"Thought I'd toss you out on your ear?"

"The thought did cross my mind."

"Never. We're the survivors. I can't be angry with you for something your father did." He drained the last bit of coffee from his mug. "By the way, what did you do with the original of the letter?"

"Oh, a friend of mine is looking it over," she replied without thinking, then immediately regretted it.

"A friend?" He tilted his head at a slight angle. "No offense, Nina, but this isn't the sort of thing you'd share with a friend."

"My friend is a writer. She's also one of my authors, one of the authors I edit."

"Regan Landry."

"Right. How did you know?"

"I've read some of the books she worked on with her father."

"I'd heard that a lot of people in law enforcement read them."

"Her father was damned good. Damned shame about that whacko shooting him to death like that."

"Yes, it was. Josh Landry was a great guy."

"So, are you two planning a book about your father?"

"Not really. I would like to know the truth, though." She looked at Kyle across the table, and took a deep breath. "I didn't know my father very well. The things I've learned about him, through reading the police files . . ."

"You've seen the police files?" His eyebrows rose. "On the cases he was convicted on?"

"Yes."

"Why?"

"Because I wanted to know." She shrugged. "I wanted to know what happened. After all these years of pretending that none of it mattered to me—that he didn't matter to me—I want to know the truth."

"I think the jury found the truth."

"Perhaps they did. And maybe you're right. Maybe the stress of the trial distorted his thinking or made him delusional or paranoid, who knows?" She leaned forward in her seat. "I want to know, Kyle. I want to know the truth."

"And you think that by reading the files, by talking to Regan Landry, you're going to find the truth?"

"Hey, I'm open to suggestions. You have a better idea, or a different starting point, let's hear it."

"I don't think trying to prove my mother was the killer is a good place to start to look for the truth."

"Well, let's take her out of it, then. And for the sake of argument, let's take him out of it, too. Let's start with a blank slate. If it wasn't him, and it wasn't her, who was it? Who else would have had a motive?"

"I'm sure the police asked themselves the same thing."

"Not on your life. Why would they have done that? They thought for sure they had the right man. Why would they have wasted time looking for another suspect? My father admitted to having had affairs with each of those girls. I'm sure they felt that alone was sufficient to have made him guilty."

"Don't you?"

"Why would he have killed his girlfriends when the affairs were going so well?"

"Maybe they weren't. Maybe he was trying to dump them and was afraid they'd start talking about the relationship."

"I think that's what the police decided on as motive, but I think that's the easy way out. I've read through all the police files. The detectives did a good job talking to the friends and close relatives of the victims. They all said they knew the girls were involved with someone, they didn't know who, but the girls—each of them—had let it be known that they were very happy in the relationship. That doesn't sound like a girl who's about to be dumped."

"Maybe she didn't know she was going to be dumped."

"Following your logic, then she'd have no reason to start talking."

He sat silent for a long minute.

"The point is, there might have been someone else who had motive to want my father discredited, to have him out of the picture. The letter he wrote indicates to me that he believed Olivia did it to get back at him, to punish him. I know it's really, really hard, but if you could try to be as objective as you're asking me to be, is it such a stretch that a woman who was betrayed the way your mother was—a woman who'd had to put up with so much over the years— is it so hard to believe that she'd want to get back at him for all he'd put her through?"

Kyle rubbed his temples.

"No. I suppose it's not a stretch for a woman to want to retaliate in any way she could, if she'd had enough of it." He nodded. "Theoretically, of course. I still don't believe my mother did it."

"I don't think I do, either."

"So where does that leave us? You take Mom and Stephen out of the picture, who's left?"

"That's what we'll need to figure out." Nina leaned back in her seat. "Can you think of anyone else who'd have had a motive to set my father up?"

"No. Remember, I'd already graduated from college by the time this happened. I'd moved on."

Nina opened the letter Kyle had left on the table and idly reread passages. She came to the bottom, and read the last paragraph over several times.

"I know this is going to sound outlandish, but do you really think Father Whelan was in love with your mother?"

"Not so outlandish." He smiled sheepishly. "I don't think it's a big secret. He's always had a thing for her. Nothing ever happened between them, I'm pretty sure of that, but I do believe he loved her."

"Did he know about my father's affairs?"

"She might have told him." He thought about it for a second, then said, "She probably did tell him."

"Well, if he'd loved her all that much, and my father was hurting her so much, is it out of the question that he'd want to hurt my father? To get my father out of the picture, or fix things so that he couldn't hurt Olivia anymore?"

"I think that's a real stretch. I think that would be easy, you know? The priest in love with the beautiful woman whose husband didn't deserve her . . ."

He shook his head.

"Just smacks of a trite mystery plot. Not very original."

"Sometimes trite is true," she told him. "There's a reason why things become clichés."

"It just doesn't ring true to me." He tapped his fingers on the tabletop. "Now, if it were Dr. Overbeck we were talking about, I'd say there could be some smoke from that fire."

"Overbeck?" Nina frowned. "He was at your mother's funeral. I remember him. He was in the English department. I heard my dad say once that Dr. Overbeck would love to have Dad's position in the department."

"Your father's position wasn't the only thing Overbeck coveted."

"What do you mean?"

"I mean Father Whelan wasn't the only one who'd had a thing for my mother."

"Overbeck had his eye on her, too?"

"And her on him." He sighed and rested an elbow on the table.

"You mean, Olivia and Dr. Overbeck . . . ?"

"Right." Kyle nodded. "Dr. Overbeck and my mother had an affair."

"How long . . . ?"

"Oh, the affair lasted for several years. Started some time before your father was arrested; I never asked Mom exactly when it began. Lasted about five years after that."

"When did you find out about this?"

"Just a few months ago. I guess when she realized just how sick she was, she felt the need to spill it."

"Then the police wouldn't have known about it when they were investigating the murders."

"Probably not. Though I don't know if it was any great secret. Overbeck's such a pompous ass, it would have been tough for him to have kept his mouth closed."

"In other words, if they'd have looked hard enough, they'd probably have been able to find out."

"My mom seemed to think that everyone knew."

"But the police already had such a strong suspect in my father, they figured there was no reason to look further." She spoke softly, as if she were thinking aloud.

"Even if they'd known about the affair, though, would it have changed the way the case turned out?"

"Well, I guess that's a question that has to be asked." She rose and swung her bag over her shoulder. "And I'm going to do exactly that . . ."

Fourteen

Nina was dialing Wes Powell's cell phone number even as she was walking to her car. She'd be searching the house, as Kyle had agreed to permit her to do, but first things first. The cocky detective had promised to reopen the case if she brought him anything that proved someone other than her father was the guilty party. Well, she had no actual proof, but she had what she thought to be a damned good theory, and she was going to do her damnedest to sell it to Powell.

She was disappointed to have to leave voice mail for the detective.

Not a problem, she told herself. *Gives me more time to prepare my case. By the time he calls back, I'll have all my facts in* . . .

The phone rang in her handbag. By the time she found it, the message screen read *1 missed call.*

Damn. She hit the call-back button. Wes answered on the second ring.

"Detective Powell?"

"Yes?"

"Nina Madden."

"Yes, Ms. Madden. What can I do for you?"

"Well, you said to call if I had evidence that someone other than my father could have been the killer."

"I think what I said was more like, if you had evidence that proved that someone else was the killer." He paused, then asked, a little more sarcastically than Nina would have liked, "Don't tell me you've solved a fifteen-year-old case in—what's it been, a week?"

"Sixteen years." She corrected him calmly.

"What?"

"Sixteen years. The case is sixteen years old."

"So who really did the deed, Ms. Madden?"

"Actually, I'm not sure who the killer is, but I do have something you should see."

"And what might that be?"

"I don't think I care for your dismissive tone, Detective. You don't need to patronize me."

His sigh said it all.

"Sorry, Ms. Madden, but I don't have time for games."

"Neither do I. And I assure you, this isn't a game to me."

"You have something you think will prove that your father was not the Stone River Rapist." His voice held a challenge and more than a bit of impatience.

She chose to ignore it.

"Maybe not prove, in and of itself." She picked her words carefully. "But something important enough that it deserves your consideration."

"Something that hasn't surfaced until now."

"Yes."

"Something credible."

"The FBI thinks so." *Okay, that was a stretch, but Mitch had been interested.*

"The FBI," he repeated flatly.

"Yes. Agent Mitch Peyton looked it over last night and thought you should see it." Another stretch, but it was the best she could come up with. Detective Powell was getting on her nerves.

"Nice of him."

"So? Are you interested?"

"Sure. Bring it in first thing Monday morning and I'll be happy to take a look at this mystery evidence of yours."

"Actually, first thing Monday morning, I'll be back in New York."

"Well, that is unfortunate."

"I was hoping to meet with you sooner."

"Where are you now?" His voice sounded increasingly pained.

"On the road between Stone River and Branigan."

"Have you crossed Temple Road yet?"

"The big intersection with the movie theaters?"

"That's the one."

"I think it's about ten minutes farther up the road, if memory serves."

"I could meet you there in about thirty minutes."

Nina paused, and he added, "Sorry. That's the best I can do."

"That would be fine, thank you. I appreciate your taking the time to see me on such short notice."

"There's a park right there on the corner. I'll meet you in the lot. What are you driving?"

"A white Land Rover."

"Nice."

"It's Regan's." She somehow felt obligated to tell him.

"See you there."

Wes pulled into the lot at Temple Park five minutes early. The Land Rover was one of four other vehicles in the first row. He parked his Outback next to the Land Rover and got out. Her car was empty, so he took the path to the only real attraction the park held.

She was standing at the edge of the small pond with her back to the path. He walked up behind her and without turning around, she held up a bag of potato chips.

"Help yourself," she told him.

"That was risky," he said, taking the bag. "You offer to share your snacks with anyone who comes along?"

She pointed down to the water.

"I could see your reflection." She turned and smiled.

Wes took a few chips from the bag and passed it back to her.

"So, what do you have to show me?"

She stuck her hand in her purse and handed him an envelope.

"That's the original," she told him. "Try not to get potato chip oil on it."

"I'll do my best." He opened the envelope, took out the pages, and began to read. It was all he could do to keep his face rigid. *Was this a joke?*

Finally, he finished reading, and asked just that.

"Is this supposed to be a joke?"

She reached for the letter.

"Is that the best you can do?" She grabbed at the letter. "I thought you'd be interested. You obviously have a closed mind. I should have known better. Give it back, and I'll take it back to the FBI and let the professionals handle this."

He continued to hold the letter out of her reach.

"I asked you a serious question," he said with a calm he didn't feel.

"Of course it's not a joke."

"Well, forgive my skepticism, but this case has been closed for a long time. You and Ms. Landry pop up one day looking for the files, and the next thing I know, you're back with this?" He looked at the letter again. "What the hell is this, anyway?"

"It's a letter that my father wrote to his wife, Olivia Madden, shortly before he died."

"And it just appeared out of nowhere. Just like that." He snapped his fingers.

"Close enough." She held her arms crossed over her chest, as if trying to hold her anger in.

"Where did you get this?"

"It was in a box of things that the prison warden mailed to Olivia after my father died. She stuck it in a closet and before she died a few weeks ago, she gave it to a friend of hers. Father Whelan. Timothy Whelan."

"I know Father Whelan. He teaches a course at St. Ansel's."

"Right. I was visiting with my stepbrother when Father Whelan brought the box over to me."

"How did he know you'd be there?"

"I imagine Kyle—my stepbrother—must have told him." Her arms remained crossed.

"So Father Whelan shows up with the box, and you open it, and find this letter."

"Not right away. Actually, I tried to lose it, but the rental car people found it in the trunk of the car I'd turned in and mailed it to me."

His soft laughter surprised her.

"Why didn't you just throw it away yourself if you didn't want it?"

She shrugged. "I don't know. I guess I thought if I simply left it someplace, I wouldn't have to deal with whatever was inside."

"What did you think was inside?"

"Father Whelan told me there was a letter from Dad to Olivia. He was of the opinion that she hadn't read it, but I'm not so sure. The envelope looked as if it had been opened, then resealed, but I could be wrong about that." She relaxed, and her arms uncrossed. She slid her hands into her jacket pockets.

"What else was in the box?"

"I'm not sure. I didn't look at everything carefully. There was a pair of his shoes, the ones he wore when he was arrested, I think. A few articles of clothing. A letter to me." She paused. "I'm not certain what else."

"May I ask what the other letter contained?"

"The letter to me?" She shrugged. "I have no idea. I haven't read it."

He studied her carefully for a long moment, then asked, "Aren't you curious about what he had to say to you?"

"We're discussing the letter from him to Olivia." She looked at him through pale green eyes that looked as if they could bore a hole right through him.

"I only asked because if he had this to say to his wife"—Wes held up the letter—"maybe he'd said something similar to his daughter."

She seemed to consider this. "I'll take a look when I get home. Maybe. If there's anything in it that is relevant to the case, I'll let you know."

"I'm going to hold you to that."

She reached for the letter, and this time he permitted her to take it. "I'll make you a copy of this, if you're really interested."

"That would be fine. When are you going back to New York?"

"Tomorrow afternoon."

"I can take the letter and copy it at the police station, if that's more convenient."

"Regan has a copier. I can make one for you there."

"You're staying at Landry's?"

She nodded.

"I'll swing by tomorrow and pick up the letter, if that's all right."

"That would be fine. Anytime before three would be good. I'm planning to leave around then to catch my train."

"Let me ask you something, Ms. Madden." His tone softened considerably. He didn't want to antagonize her, since she obviously believed her father's letter to contain the truth. He was going to have to help her follow what he considered case logic. "If we were to believe that Olivia Madden was the killer, how do we explain the fact that the girls were raped?"

"Regan and I talked about that. We didn't see a lot of evidence in the file to support the rape allegations."

"You have got to be kidding." He stared at her. God save him from the amateurs. He started counting backward from ten.

He'd only gotten as far as seven when she said, "We were wondering if we could see what you had that proved the girls had been raped."

"You have copies of the lab reports, Ms. Madden, and they indicate—"

"They indicate that the victims had engaged in sexual intercourse within hours of being murdered, yes. And if we are to believe that my father had been having an affair with each of these girls at the time of their deaths, it's likely they'd had sex." Her hands came out of her pockets and she crossed her arms again. "Show me where they were raped."

"The reports all indicated some vaginal injury. So unless your father and his girlfriends were all into rough sex, tears and bruises usually indicate that the woman was forced."

He hadn't meant to be so blunt, but much to his surprise, she didn't so much as flinch.

"Did you talk to any of the others?"

"Any of what others?"

"Any of his other girlfriends?"

"If you looked at the files I copied for you, you know that we did. The statements were all there." His thinning patience had all but worn through. It was evident in his voice.

"Yes, their statements were there. But I didn't see

one that indicated that they were asked about what kind of acts they engaged in, or if they ever got rough or were into anything kinky."

She faced him without blinking. He had to concede she had balls. Most women could not discuss their father's sexual proclivities without blushing or stammering. Nina Madden did neither.

"So what you're saying is that your stepmother could have been the killer, because the girls weren't raped, but rather merely engaged in rough sex with your father."

"No. What I'm saying is, if my father did not engage in rough sex with his girlfriends, he probably didn't cause the internal damage you're describing. Which means someone else did. If he routinely had sex with these girls, why would he have raped them?" She frowned. "It just doesn't make sense to me. He really wasn't a violent person, Detective Powell. I know that relatives always say things like that, but it's true. And if he thought Olivia was the killer, it was because he wasn't convinced that the girls were raped."

"Look, I appreciate how you must feel. But your reasoning is a little faulty. Just because he'd had an ongoing relationship with the victims at the time of their deaths doesn't mean that he never acted out of character." *If in fact it was out of character,* but he was going to let that go for now. "The point is, there's really no proof that Olivia was involved in this."

"Did you look for other suspects, Detective Powell?" Her jaw set squarely.

"No, we did not." He sighed deeply. This was going nowhere fast. He knew he shouldn't have made that call back.

"Were you aware that my stepmother was having an affair with a man in my father's department? A man who openly coveted my father's position?"

Before he could respond, she continued.

"Or that Father Whelan was in love with her? With Olivia?"

"No, I wasn't aware of either of those things. But it wouldn't have made a difference." His patience was just about gone. "We had evidence . . ."

"You knew that he'd had an affair with each of the girls, and you decided that was enough to make him guilty."

"Well, frankly, that's pretty damned telling, you know? He was the only one who'd had a relationship with each of the victims at the time they were murdered. We knew he was in the apartment of the last victim on the night she was killed, and—"

"The witness said she saw a tall man leaving the apartment," she interrupted. "Both Dr. Overbeck and Father Whelan are tall men."

"That may be, but it was Stephen Madden's prints we found in the apartment, and the book with his name in it."

"He admitted he'd been there." Her voice dropped

slightly, and from the look on her face, he suspected that her arguments were starting to sound lame even to her.

"Look, I'm sorry, I really am. If you had something more concrete, I'd be happy to take another look at this. I swear I would." Her look of defeat quashed his anger. "I'm just not sure what you want me to do."

"Isn't there anything that can be tested? Clothing from the victims, the bedsheets, something?"

"You mean DNA testing?" He raised his eyebrows. "Ms. Madden, try not to take this the wrong way, but there's no way my chief would use up our precious lab time for something like that. The county lab isn't equipped to handle the active cases. They're backed up as it is."

"I understand that." She nodded slowly. "It makes sense to spend your resources on the cases that are ongoing. It could make the difference between catching a killer or a rapist who's out there now, and not catching him at all."

"I'm glad you understand." He relaxed and fought the urge to look at his watch. He was hungry, tired, and wanted to go home.

"I do. Thanks. I'm sorry I took up so much of your time." She smiled and offered her hand.

He took her hand and held it for just a moment. He found he didn't want to let go, but of course he did. He also found himself wishing they'd met under different circumstances.

Who am I kidding? he asked himself as they walked side by side down the path on their way back to the parking lot. *I barely have time for Alec. I barely have time for a life.*

"Nice park," she was saying.

"What? Oh, yeah. It's nice. They ice skate back there on the pond when it freezes."

"Do you skate?"

"A little. Mostly I drag my son around, and after about twenty minutes, he's cold, he wants hot chocolate, he has to go to the bathroom." Wes couldn't help but grin. That described his last time out on the ice with Alec to a T.

"How was his game?"

"What?"

"His soccer game last week. How'd he do?"

"They lost." Wes shrugged. "He's nine, and at that age they're still learning to play."

"I played soccer when I was in high school," she told him as they reached her car. "A little in college, too."

"Where'd you go to college?" He wasn't sure why he asked. The question just seemed to come out of his mouth.

"Immaculata. It's in Pennsylvania." She opened the driver's door. "You?"

"St. Joe's." He smiled. "I used to date a girl from Immaculata."

"What was her name?" She leaned against the car. "Maybe I knew her."

"Karen Michaels."

"Tall, blond, leggy . . ."

"That's the one."

"She was a year ahead of me. She was nice."

"I only went out with her a few times."

Nina nodded and got into her car. He closed the door for her.

"Sorry I wasted your time," she said as she started the engine.

"You didn't waste my time." He stepped back from the car and waved as she passed by.

He stood and watched the Land Rover merge into traffic at the light, and wondered why he had the feeling that, despite her having appeared to concede defeat, Nina Madden had not given up the fight.

Fifteen

"So you feel Detective Powell just brushed you off?" Regan asked Nina. She and Mitch had returned home from their weekend at the vineyard, and she now sat in the chair closest to the fireplace, her legs pulled up under her as Mitch stacked wood in the fireplace to dispel the afternoon chill.

"Oh, he definitely dismissed me. So I let him think I was okay with it, that I understood his position, and was leaving quietly."

"And he bought that?" Mitch asked.

"I believe he did." Nina nodded.

"Man has a lot to learn about women," Mitch muttered.

"He did say he'd stop over for a copy of the letter, but I'm not holding my breath," Nina added.

"Okay, so the locals aren't willing to reopen the case. You asked, he answered. On to door number two," Regan said. "We'll just go on from there."

"If I could just interject something here," Mitch said from his place in front of the fireplace. "It may not be so much that this guy is uninterested, or unwilling. You have to put yourself in his place, ladies. The guy's probably overworked, underpaid, and has more cases on his desk than anyone could possibly clear. Time is a real factor in a lot of folks' lives." He turned to Regan. "Except for your deadlines, which are generally well spaced out, from what you've told me, your time is pretty much your own. You set your schedule, you decide what you want to do on any given day. Most people do not have that luxury. Cops, in particular, have no luxuries at all, when it comes to their jobs."

"I understand that," Nina said. "And I'm not angry with him. I'm just going to move past him and find a way around him."

"How shall we begin to—" Regan stopped and tilted her head to one side, listening. "Did you hear a car?"

"I heard something outside," Nina told her.

Regan stood and looked out the window.

"Speak of the devil," she said. "Guess he decided to play along with you after all."

"Powell is here?" Nina frowned. She really hadn't expected him to show.

"Yup." Regan slipped on her shoes. "I shall invite him to join the party."

"He doesn't strike me as being much of the party type," Nina told her. "He doesn't seem to have much of a sense of humor, either."

"Hey, he's a cop. He doesn't need a sense of humor," Mitch said. "Cops don't have time to be funny."

Regan tossed a pillow from the sofa in the direction of Mitch's head as she headed for the back door.

Nina stayed on the sofa, straining to hear the conversation in the next room, but could only hear soft, muffled words. A minute later, she heard two sets of footsteps.

"Detective Powell, this is Mitch Peyton." Regan introduced the two men as she came through the doorway. Her face was pale, and she appeared shaken. "Of course, you know Nina Madden."

Wes nodded to Nina and extended his hand to Mitch. "Your name is familiar," he said.

"Mitch is with the FBI," Nina told him.

"Oh. Right." He nodded. "The agent you mentioned yesterday."

"Detective Powell, I think you need to tell Mitch and Nina what you just told me." Regan gestured for him to take a seat.

He sat on the sofa, at the opposite end from Nina.

"I guess there's no good way to do this," he told them. "There was a murder at St. Ansel's last night. The body of a young woman was found in the Towers, one of the on-campus apartment buildings. She'd been raped, and stabbed multiple times."

"Oh, my God . . ." Nina covered her mouth with her hand. "Do you know who . . ."

"No suspects. No witnesses. We interviewed the girl's roommates and several of her friends. She wasn't dating anyone, she just transferred here from another college."

"Maybe someone from her old school, an ex-boyfriend . . . ?" Regan suggested.

"According to her friends, there was no ex-boyfriend." Wes turned to Nina. "I don't know what this means in the context of the discussion we had yesterday, but I was there, on the scene, in the apartment of the last of the Stone River Rapist's victims sixteen years ago. I can tell you that the scene I just came from was eerily similar."

"In what ways?" Mitch closed the fire screen and sat in the chair opposite Regan.

"Both girls were partially clothed, and left in the middle of the bed. Legs crossed at the ankles. Arms crossed over their chests. Head facing the wall. All the lights in the room were on—the overhead as well as a lamp on the table next to the bed and the desk lamp. These are details that were never released to the press, by the way."

"I did notice that in the reports I read," Regan said. "The bodies of all the victims had been similarly posed. I wondered at the significance, especially of the girls' heads facing the wall. And the lights being left on."

"A good profiler could nail that in a Broadway minute." Mitch looked over at Wes. "I happen to know someone who—"

"Uh-uh. This case isn't going to the Bureau." Wes's eyes narrowed and his jaw hardened. "Don't think for a minute that we can't handle this, or that we're going to invite you in to take over."

"Whoa. Slow down," Mitch told him. "No one's interested in taking your case. Especially if there's a chance it's connected to your old one. You caught it the first time around, you caught it now. End of story."

Wes did not appear reassured.

"Besides," Mitch continued, "I have more than enough files on my desk. That being said, if there's anything I can help you with—unofficially, of course—I'm happy to do that. If I can ease some evidence through our lab—hey, no problem. But I'm not interested in taking the case."

"Sorry if I overreacted," Wes told him.

"Hey, the Bureau has that reputation, I can't deny it. In most cases, it's well deserved. And if your chief requests that we come in, I'll have no control over that. But let's not get ahead of ourselves. Let's get back to the reason for your visit." Mitch leaned back in his chair. "Unless it was just to let Nina know that maybe her father wasn't so far off the wall after all."

"Half off, at best," Nina said. "Remember, he accused Olivia."

"Yesterday, we talked about three possible suspects." Wes turned to Nina. "I remember you mentioned Father Whelan, but I don't recall the name of the other man."

"Dr. Overbeck. Nathan or Nathaniel, I forget which," Nina told him.

"He's the man Kyle told you had had an affair with his mother?" Regan asked Nina.

Nina nodded.

"You said three suspects, Detective Powell. You and I only talked about Dr. Overbeck and Father Whelan," Nina reminded him.

"I'm thinking we can't discount your stepbrother," Wes said. "I'm thinking his motive could be as strong as the priest's or the professor's. Maybe stronger."

"Detective Powell, with your permission, I'd like to discuss this case—and the old ones—with one of our profilers. Just to get some insight into the type of personality we're looking for." Mitch realized his mistake as soon as the words left his mouth. "The personality you're looking for."

"What's your interest in this?" Wes asked him bluntly.

"It's sitting right there." Mitch nodded in Regan's direction. "She's looking at this thing from a totally different perspective than you or I might. She's looking at it through the eyes of her friend."

Nina said, "I came to Regan after I read my father's letter to Olivia because I had nowhere else to go with it. I knew she had experience investigating old cases, and I knew if anyone would be willing to help me sort through this, she would."

"Didn't it occur to you to take it to the police?"

"I tried that. Yesterday. You blew me off," she reminded him.

"Ouch." Wes rubbed the back of his neck. "I guess I asked for that."

"May I ask what your plan is, Detective?" Mitch asked.

"I plan to talk to the two men Ms. Madden named as having relationships with her stepmother. Frankly, I don't know that I'm convinced there's anything to it, but it's a starting point I wouldn't otherwise have."

"A minute ago I mentioned talking to one of our profilers, and you got your back up," Mitch said. "I don't know what you think profilers do, but I can tell you what our best one does."

"Go on," Wes said, resigned to listen as if he already knew what Mitch was going to say.

"She learns as much about the victims as she can, then she'll study the evidence. There's no voodoo to it, there's no wild guesses or strange formulas. The woman I'd like to discuss this case with is a psychologist, and she's the best in the business. She'll do it unofficially for me—and for Regan—because she's a friend, and she can't turn away a friend. There will be no FBI file, there will be no report. She will tell you what she thinks, and not commit any of it to writing, so that her fingerprints won't appear anywhere on the case. Understand?"

"I understand." Wes shrugged. "But I have to be

honest, I've never seen a profiler yet who wasn't so full of themselves that they didn't think they had all the answers."

Mitch smiled and said, "You haven't met Annie."

"Go ahead. Bring her on." Wes shrugged again. "What do I have to do?"

"Get Regan a copy of the reports—and the photos, if you can—and we'll take it from there. Annie can look over the old files here or I'll take them to her at her apartment, whichever she prefers. She'll do this on her own time."

"Are you sure about that?" Nina asked. "You're awfully free with this woman's time. Maybe she's too busy right now."

"Annie is never too busy to help a friend." Mitch grinned. "Besides, she owes me big time on something I helped her with a few months ago. Getting her to look this stuff over shouldn't be a problem."

Wes nodded. "All right. I'll get a copy of everything on this case as soon as it's available. May not be till the end of the week, but you'll have it when I have it."

"You can call me and I'll drive up to Stone River and pick it up at the police station," Regan told him. "I'll get it to Annie. It will be interesting to see what she thinks. She's a really smart lady."

"Well, we'll see how smart she is." Wes stood. To Nina, he said, "I apologize for the way I treated you yesterday. I still have serious doubts about this whole thing, but I'd be a fool to dismiss your theory in light of this new murder."

He ran a hand through his hair, and all of a sudden he looked very tired.

"I have to tell you, I was totally stunned when I walked into that room this morning and saw that girl lying there like that. Took me right back." Wes shook his head. "What are the odds, I kept asking myself."

He looked at Nina and said, "It's even stranger when you consider that you and I just had that conversation yesterday, don't you think?"

A shiver went up Nina's spine.

"It's creepy," she said. "The timing is just positively creepy."

"It makes me wonder, Ms. Madden, what set this guy off? I mean, if it is the same guy from sixteen years ago, what's set him off now?"

"That's a question for our profiler," Mitch told him.

"If she can nail that, she'll make a believer out of me," Wes said.

"I got twenty bucks says you'll solve this case based on something she tells you." Mitch leaned back against the fireplace mantel, looking amused.

"I've got fifty says I'll solve it on my own."

"You're on, Detective Powell."

The two men shook on their bet.

"Oh, the letter." Nina stood. "You wanted a copy of that. I'm assuming you still do?"

"Actually, I would like a copy." Wes nodded.

"Here, Nina, I'll take care of it." Regan held out her hand for the letter Nina was retrieving from her handbag. She took it and disappeared down the hall.

While they waited for Regan's return, Nina asked, "Detective Powell, were you involved in the search of our house, before or after my father's arrest?"

"Actually, I was. Why?"

"In the letter, my father says he'd found what she'd hidden, that he understood what the brown was on the handle. We know the victims were stabbed, so we're assuming he's referring to a knife. I was just wondering how thoroughly the house was searched."

"Inside out, upside down," Wes said. "Attic, basement, the entire yard, the cars, the garage. I can't think of an inch of that place that we could have missed. We also searched Celestine Hall—his office, his files, his classrooms."

"Then what happened to the knife?" she asked.

"Good question. The letter didn't say where he'd found it, or what he did with it."

"Since he assumed that Olivia had hidden it, and she rarely went over to the college, I think we could assume that he found it someplace in or around the house. Maybe he left it where he'd found it," Regan said as she came back into the room. "Then later, the person who'd hidden it—the person who used it—could have come back and retrieved it, before the police searched the house."

"Which of the three had access to the house?" Mitch asked.

"All of them," Nina said. "Father Whelan was a frequent visitor. I wouldn't be surprised if Dr. Overbeck was, as well, given his relationship with Olivia."

"You're forgetting the son," Wes reminded her.

"No, I'm not forgetting." Nina shook her head. "There's no way I could believe Kyle could have done something like that. I saw the pictures in the files. He just couldn't . . ."

"That's exactly what everyone said about Ted Bundy," Wes told her. "My advice to you, until we know for certain what's going on here, is to stay away from your stepbrother. I'd really hate to see you end up like that girl we found in the Towers this morning."

His facial expression softened.

"I'd really hate for the next victim to be you . . ."

Sixteen

Nina sat on her living room sofa with the worn cardboard box on her lap, the lid partially open, and asked herself for the hundredth time why it was so difficult to open the letter her father had left for her. What was she afraid of?

That she'd learn something about him she didn't want to know?

Too late. She'd lived for sixteen years with the belief that he was a serial killer and an adulterer. What could be worse than that?

That maybe after all these years of telling herself that none of it mattered, that he'd taken her in after her mother died because he had to, that maybe she'd discover that it did matter after all?

Getting close.

That maybe after having convinced herself that she had no real feelings for him, she'd discover that she had cared for him, and him for her?

Or that he hadn't cared at all? And that she cared more than she'd wanted to admit?

Bingo.

This is silly, she told herself. *Stop making excuses and just open the damned envelope.*

She reached into the box. She found the envelope under one of the shoes, and she opened it as soon as she removed it from the box. *No more excuses. Just do it. Get it over with.*

My dear Nina,

Well, what a sorry state of affairs this is.

I can only begin to imagine what a nightmare this has been for you. I saw you in the lobby the day I was arrested, and I have never felt such humiliation in my life. I can't imagine anything worse than being led away in handcuffs, accused of the most vile crimes, with your only child watching. The others standing around—my colleagues—barely mattered. But my child. My daughter.

There are no words to tell you how I ached for you. How humiliated you, too, must have felt.

I was relieved when I'd heard you'd left Stone River, and prayed that you would not come back for the trial. My greatest fear, going into the courtroom, was not that I'd be convicted as much as that you would be there to witness my shame, and, therefore, feel ashamed yourself.

My greatest remorse was for what you went through because of me. Even if I'd been guilty of all the things they accused me of, I doubt I could have brought you greater pain. It seems that my entire life has been spent bringing pain to those I loved the most. Your mother. You. Olivia. I suppose in the afterlife that will be judged to have been my greatest sin. That I caused such pain to those who loved me.

Regardless of what you may have heard, please believe that I am innocent of killing those girls. Guilty of having toyed with them, guilty of breaking my promises to Olivia, guilty of not being able to control my passions. Perhaps my sins led others to commit those terrible crimes, but you must believe that I did not kill them. I swear on your mother's life that I did not murder those four girls.

Someday, if you can find it in your heart, please remember me in your prayers.

I am, and will always be,
Your loving father

Nina blew out a long-held breath and wiped the tears from her face as she read the letter through again. She still wasn't sure how she felt about her father, but she felt consoled, somehow, by his words.

He claimed to have loved her. She'd never permitted herself to think that he had. All these years she'd believed she'd been no more than a peripheral part of his life, some loose little tangent, and now here he claimed to have loved her. You don't love loose threads.

Even now, in her mid-thirties, it was heady stuff.

She read the letter through two more times, then folded it carefully and returned it to its envelope. Stephen Madden may not have been a very good father—and God knew he'd been a lousy husband to both of his wives—but by his own admission, he'd loved his child. What did she owe him in return for this late gift?

She stayed on the sofa for almost an hour, thinking back over her childhood, the times when he was gone, the times when he came back. The summers after the divorce, when she'd stay with him for a few weeks in the summer—weekends during the school year—they'd been so awkward with each other. He didn't seem to understand children at all.

And then, the summer she turned twelve, he'd taken her with him to London. It had been the best two weeks of her life, but later she'd blocked out the trip as if it had never occurred. It had been too good to be true, and as with so many such things, had been too painful to remember after he'd fallen from grace in her eyes.

For those two weeks, her father had taken her everywhere—she needed to see London, he'd told her, it was the most beautiful city in the world. *When you're in college,* he'd promised, *you can take a semester here, or a year, if you like.* She'd believed him.

They'd walked in Hyde Park and listened as a woman dressed in men's clothing stood on Speakers' Corner and talked about her plan for universal salvation, and he'd taken her photograph standing beside the statue of Peter Pan in Kensington Gardens. They'd strolled Portobello Road, and he'd bought her a tiny ring in one of the antiques stalls. They visited the Tower of London and Madame Tussaud's, and St. Marylebone Church, where Elizabeth Barrett married Robert Browning. He'd taken her to the Sherlock Holmes Museum and the Victoria and Albert and the British Museum, whose treasures had inspired a keen interest in archaeology that she'd never lost. They'd had high tea at Harrad's and shopped for books on Charing Cross Road. That summer had been the first time in her life that she'd felt as if she had a father, and he was wonderful.

He'd stayed in London to teach a semester, and he'd sent her back home wondering how her mother could have left such a glorious man, how could she have kept Nina from knowing her incredible father for all those years, allowing her only brief bits of time with him. She'd anxiously awaited his return at the end of the summer, certain there'd be more adventures for them in the fall.

And then, shortly after he'd returned to the States

and to St. Ansel's, he'd called to tell her he was getting married. She'd never forgotten the feeling that had spread through her. She'd felt as if he was abandoning her all over again, and she'd known instinctively that she'd never feel close to him again. She never got her semester in London, and she'd never returned to the city.

And she'd never quite forgiven Olivia, or him.

It had been years since she'd permitted herself to look back on that summer, but once she did, the memories washed through her in a flood.

Damn, but it hurt.

She got up and went into her bedroom in search of a tissue with which to dry her face. She brought a handful back to the living room, blew her nose in one and took it into the kitchen to toss into the trash. She took a cold bottle of spring water from the refrigerator and drank half of it standing up near the window that overlooked the fire escape. By the time she'd returned to the sofa, her emotions were under control and her focus clear.

First thing in the morning she'd call Detective Powell and assure him that there was nothing in the letter from her father that would be of interest to the police, other than his denial of having been involved in the murders.

She looked into the box and saw the brown leather shoes her father had been wearing at the time he was imprisoned. His shoes, his white shirt, his tan cashmere sweater to which a faint trace of cologne still clung. A fat brown envelope lay in the bottom under a Bible with a worn brown leather cover. Several personal items—the tortoiseshell comb he'd always carried in the pocket of his sport jacket, a small phone book with a black cover, a handful of change—were scattered through the box.

She opened the brown envelope and was surprised to find photographs of her and her mother among the pictures of Olivia and her father on their wedding day. The envelope had been sealed, and it occurred to her that perhaps he'd had memories that he'd found too raw to face, too, memories he'd had to hide away in dark denial. She picked up the envelope to slide the photos back in, and felt something in the bottom. She reached in and pulled out the small gold ring he'd bought her in London. How had it gotten into the envelope?

She'd sent it back to him, after his marriage to Olivia had caused her so much confusion and hurt. It was the only thing she could think of—as a twelve-year-old with an overactive sense of the dramatic—to express her rejection of his affection after he'd sprung this new wife on her out of the blue.

Nina slid the ring onto her pinky and admired the tiny amethysts set in the center of the little golden rose. It fit, so she kept it on.

So, that's done, she told herself as she closed the

box and returned it to the closet shelf. She'd faced what she'd feared, and she was fine. Better than fine. There'd be more to think about, more to digest, but she'd had her fill of emotion for one night, and needed to put it aside.

When she went to sleep that night, for the first time in her adult life, it was with the thought that perhaps her father had loved her after all.

Seventeen

Wes stood on the sidewalk in front of the Tudor-style stucco home for several minutes before approaching the front door. He wanted to get a feel for the place, to understand the layout of the property. To the right was the driveway, at the end of which was a two-car garage that mimicked the architectural style of the house. The house and garage were connected by a brick path, and the front and back yards were separated by a white lattice fence with a gate. Rosebushes climbed high and stretched from the house to the roof of the garage. At either side of the property was a stand of very large evergreens. A low hedge ran across the front of the house, and large holly bushes obscured the windows on both sides of the front door. The house and garage were set back a bit from the street, so that the overall impression was of a tidy house that fit snugly in its seclusion.

He wasn't really sure that this wasn't a waste of his

time. On the drive over from the police station, he'd asked himself what he wanted to accomplish by coming here, to the house Stephen Madden had shared with his wife and his daughter. The best answer Wes had been able to come up with was that he wanted to get a feel for the three men who had been close to Olivia. Somehow, her relationships with them—and with Stephen—felt pivotal to the case, and his gut told him it would be wise of him to get to know her, too.

He walked to the door and was raising his hand to ring the doorbell when it opened. A man who appeared to be in his late thirties or so stood in the doorway. He wore a light green crewneck sweater and olive Dockers and a cautious expression.

"Mr. Stillman?" Wes inquired.

"Yes. Detective Powell?" The man's voice was smooth and steady.

"Right."

"Come on in." Kyle Stillman stepped aside to permit Wes to enter the house. "I was just about to come out to get you. You looked as if you weren't sure this was the right house."

"I wasn't certain at first. I had a hard time finding the house number."

They stood in the foyer, which, like the living room, appeared to have been freshly painted. Wes commented on that.

"Oh, yes, I've been busy," Kyle told him. "Just sprucing up the place, since I'm thinking about selling it. I guess you spoke with my stepsister. I imagine she told you about the deal with the house."

"I don't know that she mentioned it."

"Come on in the kitchen." Kyle gestured toward the arched passage behind him. "We can sit and talk in there. I just finished the last of the coffee, but I'd be happy to make a fresh pot, if you'd like some."

"No, thanks. I've had my two-cup-per-day limit already." Wes went directly to the table and took the chair facing out from the corner. There was something about Kyle Stillman that made him uneasy, something that made him want to not sit with his back to the room. "So what was the deal with the house and your stepsister?"

"Nina's father owned this place before he married my mother, but after they were married, he never put Mom's name on the deed. Turns out he made provisions for Mom to live here in the event he died before she did, but upon her death, the house was supposed to pass directly to Nina." Kyle sat down across from Wes.

"So you're telling me that Nina owns the house."

"Nina did own the house. She signed it over to me. You believe that? She *gave* me the house. Said she'd never been happy here, it only held bad memories, that it should have belonged to my mother, and if it had, the house would now belong to me. So she signed it over. You ever hear of anyone doing something like that?"

"No, actually, I haven't. That was very generous of her."

"It just shows you the type of person she is."

Before Wes could respond, Kyle said, "So, you said on the phone you wanted to talk about the letter Stephen wrote to my mother shortly before he died. I'm assuming you read it. What did you think of it?"

"Strange idea he had."

"Strange? It's ludicrous." Kyle laughed. Wes thought it had a hollow ring. "How someone as smart as Nina could take that seriously . . . I just can't fathom it. It's a crazy idea."

"Well, no doubt Dr. Madden's affairs had to have hurt your mother terribly."

"You have no idea what she went through on his account. He just . . . " Kyle looked away. "She was just destroyed by him."

"Wouldn't she have wanted to destroy him in return?"

"Mother?" He shook his head. "She wasn't the murderous type. She was really a very good, very sweet woman. Everybody loved her."

"But she had to have been angry with her husband."

"I'm sure she was for a while, those first few years

they were married especially." He shrugged. "But after a while, I think she accepted that that was the way he was and he was never going to change."

"Well, just to set your mind at ease, I agree that it's not likely that your mother was the killer. But I am interested in his claims to have found the weapon." Wes kept his eyes on Kyle's face. "If Dr. Madden had found the murder weapon here, in or around this house, I would imagine that he'd have immediately suspected she'd been the one who'd hidden it. No one else had access to the house, except for her. Who else could have hidden it?"

"You're not taking this seriously, are you?" Kyle asked.

"Just dotting the *i*'s and crossing the *t*'s. We do have these new allegations . . . and the mention of finding the murder weapon. Which as you probably know, we never did find."

"I seem to recall that." Kyle nodded.

"Well, here's the important part, Kyle. Yesterday morning, a young woman named Allison Mulroney was found dead in her apartment on campus. She'd been stabbed to death."

"I saw that on the news. Kind of like déjà vu all over again."

"Here's something you didn't hear on the news, Kyle. The wounds on this girl are identical to the wounds on those girls who were killed sixteen years ago. Same width, some length, same depth. One would venture to guess, same knife in the same hand."

"How could that be?" Kyle frowned. "Stephen Madden's been dead for almost fifteen years now."

"That's what I'm going to find out. You think of any likely suspects, anyone you recall having spent a lot of time around the house back then, you be sure to give me a call . . ."

"Well, you know, Father Whelan spent quite a bit of time here. I don't think a day passed when he did not stop by to see my mother. And then, of course, there was Dr. Overbeck."

"Dr. Overbeck?" Wes asked with a straight face, as if he hadn't already heard the story. "Who is Dr. Overbeck?"

"He was—still is—a professor of English at the college. My understanding was that he was a bit of a rival of Stephen's."

"A rival for what?"

"For the top position in the department. Stephen definitely had the inside track there. Or at least he did until he was arrested." Kyle stared at Wes for a moment, then said, "And there was also my mother."

"What about your mother?"

"She and Dr. Overbeck had an affair."

"Really?" Wes raised his eyebrows and tried to look surprised. "When was that?"

"I believe Mom said it started about a year or two

before Stephen was arrested. She ended it after Stephen died."

"Was he married?"

"He wasn't at the time. I think he may have married since, but I'm not sure about that."

"So you're saying that Dr. Overbeck would have had access to the house because he was here occasionally with your mother?"

"It was more than occasionally. *Quite frequently* is more accurate."

"Would he have been here often enough to find a good hiding place if he'd had something to hide?"

"Sure."

"What do you suppose his motive could have been for killing Dr. Madden's girlfriends?"

Kyle shrugged. "Hey, it's just a guess on my part, but maybe he thought, with Stephen out of the way, he could just skate right into his life. You know, the job, my mother . . ."

"Why not just kill Dr. Madden, then? Surely if he was smart enough to kill four girls and get away with it for—what was it, eighteen months or so?—he'd have been smart enough to have killed one man and gotten away with it."

"Who knows what he was thinking?"

"You think it could have been him?"

"If it wasn't Stephen, then, sure. It could have been him."

"How about Father Whelan?"

"I don't see him as having a motive. Oh, yeah, he was in love with my mom, I guess Nina told you that. But it's too easy, you know? I just don't see it."

"Who else might have had a motive, Kyle? Can you think of anyone else?"

"No, really, I can't. But if I think of someone, I'd be happy to give you a call."

"You do that." Wes stood to leave. "Say, do you mind if I ask what you do for a living?"

"I'm a security guard. I'm on disability right now, damaged the tendons in my shooting hand, can't use my gun anymore." Kyle shrugged. "Can't send a one-handed man out on the street with a gun, and my company does almost all armed work, so they put me out on disability."

"You having any therapy for that?"

"Oh, I was, for several months. They said I'd reached, what did they call it?"

"Maximum medical improvement?"

"Yeah, something like that. So unless they can find something for me to do that doesn't require me to use my right hand too much, I'm pretty much at home these days."

"Sorry to hear it."

"Yeah. I miss the job." Kyle stood and walked partway to the door. "Anything else I can do for you?"

"No, I think we're okay for now." Wes rose and followed him.

The two men walked outside together.

"What's the name of the company you work for?" Wes asked.

"White Shepherd. Why?"

"I was just thinking, I know a few guys who own guard services. If I hear anything you might be interested in, I can give you a call."

"That'd be great. Thanks. And if anything else comes up, or you have any other questions about my mom or whatever, give me a call."

"I'll be sure to do that." Wes shook Kyle's hand and got into his car.

Wes glanced in his rearview mirror as he drove toward the stop sign at the end of the street. He could see Kyle still standing on the sidewalk, where Wes had left him, watching the car drive away.

Odd duck were the two words that came to Wes's mind as he made his left onto Locust Drive.

He was early for his appointment with Dr. Overbeck, so Wes took the opportunity to take a walk around St. Ansel's campus. Even two weeks earlier, there'd have been leaves on the trees, but with the cold snap they'd had, there was little color left clinging to the branches of the maples that lined the campus walks. Groups of students passed by, all seeming to chat at the same time. He saw few girls walking alone, and wondered if the news about Allison Mulroney had put the fear of God into them. He hoped it did. He hoped, too, that they'd be doubling up at night. The chief had held a press conference earlier that morning, and had suggested that any girls living alone should get together or stay with friends until the killer was caught, but Wes figured most of these girls had probably missed the broadcast. When he returned to the station, he'd suggest that flyers be printed up and passed around the campus, just to make sure everyone got the message: There's safety in numbers.

He wandered back toward Celestine Hall, and thought about the approach he'd take with the professor. He was still thinking about it when he knocked on Overbeck's office door.

"Hey, come on in," Dr. Overbeck greeted him from behind his desk. In seconds he was at the door, his hand extended, shaking Wes's hand enthusiastically. "You're Detective Powell, right?"

"Right. It's good of you to make time to meet with me."

"Hey, whatever we can do here on campus to help you out." He gestured for Wes to take a seat in one of the dark green leather chairs that stood on the opposite side of the desk. He was tall and wiry, with blond hair that had grayed and small dark eyes. He was dressed casually in jeans and a sweater vest over a shirt with a button-down collar. He stood behind his chair for a moment before sitting. "Terrible tragedy, that poor Mulroney girl, isn't it?"

Dr. Overbeck made a *tsk-tsk* sound and shook his head.

"She was just a lovely girl. Good student. Friendly. A little on the quiet side, but not overly shy. Terrible tragedy," he repeated. "I suppose you want to know if I've noticed anyone following her from class, or if anyone seemed to hang around her, but honestly, I never noticed. I mean, if there was someone bothering her, or following her, she never mentioned it. But then again, why would she? I mean, I only have her for that one class. And as for her social life, I'm afraid I can't help you there. I did hear that she dated one of the boys on the basketball team, but I don't know who."

The professor stopped and looked at Wes, as if waiting for the detective to say something. When he did not, Overbeck said, "Well, that's what you wanted to know, right? What I knew about Allison Mulroney?"

"While I appreciate the information, actually it was another murder I wanted to discuss with you."

"Another murder?" Overbeck frowned. "Good God, there's been another one?"

"I'm referring to the murders sixteen years ago. The ones Dr. Madden was convicted of." Wes kept his eyes on Overbeck's face, and watched the surprise register.

"Why would you be interested in those? As you say, there was a conviction in that case." Overbeck's face took on a wary expression. "What has that case got to do with this one?"

"There are similarities between the murders." Wes leaned back in the chair and spoke slowly, drawing it out. Watching Overbeck's eyes.

"What kind of . . . what are you talking about?" Overbeck drew his hand through his hair. "I'm sorry, Detective, but I'm simply not following you at all. Stephen Madden died years ago. So any similarities between those murders and this one . . ."

"Need to be explored," Wes interrupted him. "We need to take a look at the big picture here, Dr. Overbeck. Sixteen years ago, we had four young women killed in exactly the same manner. The bodies left in the same position, the clothing handled in the same manner. Obviously someone methodical, right? Now here we have a young woman who's been killed in the same manner, left in the same position. Clothes folded the same as the others. Makes you think."

"Makes you think about what? That there's a copycat killer on the loose at St. Ansel's?"

"Makes you think maybe Stephen Madden was telling the truth when he said he hadn't murdered those girls."

"You have to be kidding. Stephen was guilty, all right. He'd had affairs with each of those girls, and then what happened? He wants to end the relationship, they threaten to tell the dean, he kills them. It's as simple as that. I can't believe no one put it together sooner than they did."

"No one put what together?"

"Well, that it was Stephen's girls who were getting killed."

"But I was under the impression that, at the time, no one knew he'd been having these affairs." Wes caught Overbeck's gaze and held it, refusing to let the man look away. "That until Madden was arrested for the last of the murders, no one had known he'd had any involvement with the others."

Wes let that sink in before asking, "Are you telling me now that you knew Dr. Madden had been involved with the others?"

Overbeck continued to stare.

"Because if you knew, I'd have to wonder why, after the first girl was found murdered, you didn't come forward and say something. There was, what, something like five or six months between the first murder and the second? And if you'd known about his affairs, surely you would have wanted the police to know, right?" Wes leaned forward and rested his forearms on the desk. "I mean, given your relationship with Mrs. Madden, I'd think you wouldn't have minded if Dr. Madden had been taken out of the picture sooner."

Dr. Overbeck broke eye contact at the mention of Olivia Madden.

"You were having an affair with Dr. Madden's wife, correct?"

Overbeck sighed heavily. "Yes, I had an affair with Olivia."

"You know, what I find interesting is that you managed to keep that a secret during the entire investigation and trial." Wes shook his head. "I was one of the investigating officers back then, and the only time I heard your name mentioned was as a colleague of Madden's."

Wes stopped and looked around Overbeck's office. He stood and walked outside, and looked up and down the hall, then came back in.

"Now that I think about it"—Wes sat back down—"this was his office, wasn't it? Madden's?"

Dr. Overbeck cleared his throat before answering. "Yes. Yes, it was Stephen's office."

"I also seem to recall that back then, Dr. Madden was next in line for the head of the English department when . . . help me out here, who was the head of the department back then?"

"Father Candelori."

"Right. Father Candelori." Wes nodded. "Madden was his choice to take over the department when he retired. Which was supposed to be the following year, right?"

Overbeck nodded.

"Who was finally named head of the department back then, Dr. Overbeck?"

"Actually, I was."

"Really," Wes said flatly.

"Really." Overbeck stood. "I don't know where you're going with this, Detective, but I think you've taken enough of my time for one day. I'm devastated that another young girl has lost her life here at St. Ansel's, but I don't know what the point is to your bringing up Stephen or Olivia or any of that. It was all a long time ago. Stephen was convicted, he went to prison, he died. Olivia, as I'm sure you're aware, has died recently. I can't see where there's anything more to be said."

"Well, here's the thing. Without boring you with the details, Madden's daughter just got her hands on a letter that Stephen had written to Olivia shortly before he died. In the letter, he tells her about having found what he believed to have been the weapon that killed those four girls, way back when." Wes paused to watch Overbeck's eyes begin to widen. "Apparently the weapon was hidden in Madden's house; at least, that's what the letter seemed to indicate. He seemed to think the weapon implicated Olivia somehow, though that's crazy, right? I mean, since the girls were all raped, Olivia couldn't very well have been the killer."

"I don't know anything about any of that." Overbeck had gone pale.

"But you knew Olivia well, didn't you? Your affair lasted . . . how long? Two years?" Wes stood. "Two very critical years in Olivia's life, wouldn't you say? Her husband gets arrested and charged with murder, she finds out about all of his affairs . . ."

Wes rubbed his chin, as if something had just occurred to him.

"Unless, of course, she knew about them. I don't suppose she ever told you that she knew he was having these affairs with his students?"

Overbeck considered the question carefully before answering. "Olivia knew Stephen was having an affair. I do not believe she knew with whom."

"Well, that helps." Wes started toward the door, then stopped and asked, "What was she like, Olivia? I met her years ago but, of course, didn't get to know her. My impression of her is one of a very beautiful, very strong woman."

Overbeck nodded slowly. "Yes, she was beautiful. And strong."

"Were you in love with her?"

"Absolutely," Overbeck said without hesitation.

Wes took out his wallet and retrieved one of his business cards. Handing it to the professor, he said, "All of my numbers are on here. Will you give me a call if you think of anything that might be helpful?"

"I will. Yes, I'll do that." Overbeck appeared to be relieved to see Wes go. He walked with the detective to the door, and the minute Wes was in the hallway, Overbeck closed it.

Smiling with satisfaction, Wes walked to the stairs

and down to the first floor. Once in the lobby, he checked his watch. He had plenty of time before he had to meet with Father Whelan. He'd grab lunch, then head back to the building on the other side of the campus where Father Whelan's class was being held.

There was only one of Olivia's men left to talk to. He wondered what the priest could tell him that he didn't already know.

Eighteen

Wes had just made it to the other side of the campus when the students from the two-fifteen classes were beginning to spill out of St. Ambrose Hall and down the wide double stairs in the front of the building. He was halfway up the steps through the crowd when his cell phone rang.

"Powell," he answered and stepped to the side of the staircase.

"Detective, it's Mitch Peyton. I thought I'd give you a call and let you know that we have a date for the profiler to meet with you. She'll be available all day Thursday."

"This coming Thursday?"

"Yes, day after tomorrow. Where would you like to meet? She said she'll go to the police station, or she'd go to Regan's, your choice."

"Do you think Ms. Landry would mind if we met there?"

"Are you kidding?" Mitch snorted. "She wouldn't miss this for anything."

"And I suppose Ms. Madden will be there as well?"

"Oh, yeah, she'll be there. Regan says Nina took some personal time—apparently she has a lot of days accumulated, and with everything that's going on, she thinks she'd rather stay around for a while than continue to travel back and forth between here and New York."

"Well, maybe by Thursday I'll have something to bring to the party."

"What do you mean?"

"I spent my day divided between Kyle Stillman and Dr. Overbeck."

"And . . . ?"

"And frankly, I don't know which of them I dislike more."

"This has promise. How about the priest?"

"He's next up." Wes turned his wrist to look at his watch. "As a matter of fact, he's up right now."

"Great. I'll be interested to see how your impressions fit in with Annie's psychological profile. Wouldn't it be nice to find a neat fit?"

"You ever see a neat fit, Agent Peyton?"

"Nah. But we all have our dreams, Detective."

Father Timothy Whelan leaned on the dark oak podium in the front of the large room on the second floor of the last building on campus. He appeared to be listening patiently as first one student, then another, stopped to say a few words. The priest had a response, or a smile and a pat on the shoulder, for each kid. Wes waited until only the priest remained. When he entered, Father Whelan was packing some papers into a leather briefcase.

"Father Whelan," Wes said, and then introduced himself, "Detective Powell. We met very briefly, years ago. I was part of the Madden investigation."

"That explains why your name rings a distant bell." Father Whelan set the briefcase on the desk and turned to Wes with very blue eyes that stared out from a ruddy face. "How are you coming along with your investigation of this horrible murder?"

"Still looking for leads, Father." Wes sat on one of the seats in the first row. "I have to admit, right now we have none."

"Well, surely there's some evidence, fingerprints, shoe prints, whatever."

"The crime scene techs found lots of prints in the apartment, Father. But unless one of them goes through the computer and bounces back with a match on record, we may never know whose prints we're looking at. And as for footprints—" Wes smiled. "Father, have you been watching *CSI*?"

"Oh, guilty, there." The priest smiled, too. "I'm afraid I'm addicted to crime shows. I never miss one, if I can avoid it."

He glanced down at several papers on the podium, then stacked them and added them to the briefcase.

"Of course, with my class here, and my classes at St. Ansel's Prep, I don't have as much time as I might like some nights to just relax and watch TV." The priest closed the briefcase with a snap. "Now, tell me what you think I can help you with."

"We've been talking to some of the instructors who had Allison Mulroney as a student. We're looking for any information you could give us about her personal life, her friends, that sort of thing."

"I would think you'd get more of that sort of information from the students who lived in her apartment building."

"Oh, we're talking to them as well." Wes nodded. "But we're looking at this from every angle. Sometimes you might notice something in class that the victim's friends or roommates might have missed."

The priest nodded. "Of course, of course. I can tell you she was a good student. Quite a fine writer, by the way. She did a paper last month on Christopher Marlowe that was just terrific." He leaned on the podium as if in thought. "She usually came in to class alone, but almost always walked out with Andrea Bollen. They always sat together there in the front." Father Whelan pointed toward the left side of the room. "I seem to recall she liked to look out the window. I didn't blame her for that. There's a pond down there with a pair of swans. I watch them myself when I can sneak a peek."

Wes took his notebook out of his pocket and scanned the first few pages.

"We did talk to Andrea Bollen. She lived with two other girls in the apartment across the hall from Allison. She was the one who told me about your class, by the way. She said she and Allison had different classes right before this one, but would meet here and after class would go to the coffee shop for a snack, then stop at the library for an hour or two, then go home. She said the routine rarely varied."

"So anyone watching her for any period of time would know where to find her," Father Whelan said.

"All those crime shows appear to be paying off. You're starting to think like a cop, Father."

"Unfortunately, this isn't our first brush with a killer here at St. Ansel's, Detective Powell."

"The Stone River Rapist." Wes nodded. "I remember it well."

"Do you now?" The priest stared at him. "Did you live here in Stone River then?"

"I did, but I was also on the force at the time. It was my first big case. And you know, you never forget that first homicide."

"Well, that was an easy one, though. I mean, in terms of solving it. It was obvious who the killer was."

"Not to us," Wes told him. "At least, not until we found that book Dr. Madden had left in the apartment of the last victim."

"Lucky thing, that. Who knows how much longer the killings would have gone on had you not caught him then."

"Luck?" Wes leaned forward in his seat and rested his arms on his thighs. "I never thought about it being luck. At the time I thought it had been uncommonly stupid for a killer who had been so clever up until that point."

"Well, it was an oversight on Stephen's part, I'm sure. But it doesn't matter, since it led to his arrest and conviction. And no more of our girls had to die."

"I understand that you were close to Dr. Madden's wife." Wes decided to toss that out there.

"Why, yes, I was." Father Whelan's hands gripped the podium, and he stared at Wes. "Olivia and I had been friends for years."

"Yeah, so her son told me." Wes stood and walked to the window and looked out. "Oh, yeah, the swans are out there on the pond. Don't they fly away in the winter?"

"No. You saw Kyle recently?"

"Just this morning, as a matter of fact." Wes turned

back to the room and leaned on the wide windowsill. "It seems that after Olivia's death, Nina—Stephen Madden's daughter—came into possession of a letter that her father had written to Olivia."

"Yes, she did. I delivered it to her, as Olivia had asked me to do before she died."

"Had you read the letter before you passed it along, Father?"

"Of course not." The priest crossed his arms over his chest.

"You weren't tempted? As close as you and Olivia were, you weren't interested in what her husband had to say to her from prison?"

"Not at all."

"But you were aware of the problems in their relationship. Of Stephen's wandering eye."

"Olivia told me that Stephen had been unfaithful to her."

"Why do you suppose she didn't leave him?"

"I never asked her that. I guess she must have loved him." The cleric averted his eyes.

"Were you her confessor, Father?"

The question seemed to catch the priest off guard. "On occasion, yes. When she was ill the first time, several years back, then later, toward the end, yes, I heard her confession."

"Were you aware that she'd had an affair with Dr. Overbeck?"

"I can't discuss her personal life with you,

Detective. It would be a breach of confidentiality, of her trust."

"Only if she confided in you during her confessions. Did she do that, Father? Did she talk to you about her affair in her confessions?"

"You know I cannot discuss anything that was revealed in the course of a confession. As a priest, I am bound to silence by the church, by my vows. I'm sorry, Detective Powell, but if you're looking for 'dirt' on Olivia Madden, you're going to have to find it elsewhere." Father Whelan picked up his briefcase. "I fail to see what this has to do with Allison Mulroney."

"There are several striking similarities between this case and the Madden case," Wes told him, "so we're taking a second look at that."

"You can't be serious." Father Whelan stared at Wes as if he'd suddenly sprouted a second head.

"Serious as a heart attack. That's not for publication, by the way. We're still looking into it, but there are too many similarities to ignore."

Father Whelan stood riveted to the spot.

"Why would . . ." he wondered aloud, then stopped. To Wes, he said, "I have a meeting in ten minutes on the opposite side of campus. I'm sorry."

"I'll walk with you. I left my car over by Celestine Hall." Wes walked to the door and waited for the priest to follow him.

Wes tried to engage him in further conversation,

but Father Whelan appeared distracted as they made their way back across campus. When they reached Celestine Hall, Wes tried one more time.

"Father, what can you tell me about Olivia Madden?"

"What do you mean?"

"What kind of person was she?"

The priest seemed to consider the question carefully.

"Olivia was very beautiful. Very emotional. She had depths of emotions . . . " He shook his head, then said, as if nothing further was necessary, "She wasn't like anyone I ever knew."

"Kyle seems to think you were in love with her."

"Detective," Father Whelan smiled weakly, "I never met a man who knew her who wasn't."

Nineteen

When Mitch suggested bringing in a profiler to review the case, Nina hadn't been quite certain what to expect, but it definitely wasn't the woman she watched get out of Mitch's car and walk across the deck on Thursday morning. The cool-looking blonde being welcomed with hugs from Regan was totally feminine, casually dressed in cashmere and tweed. From the second-floor window, Nina could see the rope of pearls twined around the woman's neck and the sparkling diamond on the ring finger of her left hand.

"Nina, come down and say hi to Annie," Regan called from the first floor.

Nina hastily ran her fingers through her hair and hurried down the steps.

"Annie, this is my friend—and editor—Nina Madden. Nina, Dr. Anne Marie McCall."

"It's Annie," the profiler told Nina with an easy smile. "So you're the one who put this ball in motion."

"I did, I'm afraid." Nina nodded.

"Well, it's certainly been an interesting read." She patted the briefcase that hung from her shoulder before turning to Mitch. "Where's our cop?"

"Just pulled in the driveway," Mitch told her.

"Good. We need him," Annie said. "Regan, may I get a cup of tea before we start?"

"Certainly. Nina? Anything?" Regan asked on her way to the stove.

"Nothing, thanks."

Mitch went to the back door and opened it.

"You're just in time," he told Wes as the detective strode up to the door. "We're all assembling— Regan, where are we holding this little powwow?"

"How about right here in the kitchen?" She turned to the door and greeted Wes. "Come in, Detective Powell. Meet Dr. McCall."

"Good to meet you." Wes went directly to the table, his hand out for Annie's. "I heard you might be able to give us a little insight into this case."

"I'll do my best." Annie took his hand, then pointed to the chair next to Nina's. "Why not sit opposite from me, so that we can face each other. I have the feeling this conversation will be mostly between you and me."

"Hello, Ms. Madden," Wes said as he pulled out the chair next to hers and sat.

"Detective." Nina smiled.

"Must we be this formal?" Annie frowned. "It

makes me uncomfortable. Does anyone have a problem with first names?"

Everyone shook their heads no.

"Good, because it drives me crazy." She held up her hand for the mug of tea Regan was passing to her.

"Okay, folks, last call." Regan stood with her hands on her hips in the middle of the kitchen floor. "Coffee, tea, soda, a bottle of water? After I sit down, you're on your own."

She glanced around and, convinced there were no takers, sat next to Mitch, who was on Annie's right.

"First off, I think we need to ask Wes if there have been any developments on this latest murder." Annie addressed the detective.

"Unfortunately, no. There was some trace evidence recovered from the crime scene, but of course it's going to be some time before we get anything back from the lab. If you're asking me if we've identified any suspects, no, we have not. We've found no one in her life who doesn't have an airtight alibi. And believe me, we've been beating the bushes. There's no one who looks even remotely promising. And of course, no witnesses."

"She lived in an on-campus apartment building, though, right?" Annie frowned. "How is it that no one saw or heard anything?"

"Homecoming weekend. There'd been a big party at one of the frat houses on Saturday night.

According to one of her friends, Allison wasn't feeling well and left—alone—around eleven-thirty. Almost everyone else stayed till one or two. There was no one around to hear, or to see."

Wes paused, then added, "But I did meet with the three men we talked about last weekend."

"Father Whelan, Kyle Stillman, and Dr. Overbeck?" Mitch asked.

"Yes." He turned to Annie and explained. "We were thinking perhaps one of the men closest to Olivia could have been involved in the Stone River Rapist case, perhaps as a means of getting Stephen out of the way."

"That's a sound theory. But I think there may be a little more to it than merely wanting Stephen out of the picture." Annie tapped the side of her mug lightly. "I think whoever killed those girls wanted to punish Dr. Madden."

"Punish him for what?" Nina asked.

"For his infidelity. I don't think Dr. Madden was too far off in his theory that Olivia killed those girls. I don't believe she did, but I do think whoever did it thought he was avenging her somehow for the pain Stephen must have caused her. I believe that when you find your killer, you will find someone who was deeply involved emotionally with Olivia."

"That could have been any one of the three," Regan pointed out.

"Whoever killed these girls did so with passion

and righteous anger," Annie said. "If you're merely trying to get someone out of the picture, you don't need to invest yourself in the actual killing. The man we are looking for was doing more than going through the motions. The wounds are too deep, the crime scenes too bloody. He was making a statement. He was very much involved in what he was doing."

"But couldn't he have been making a statement against the girls rather than my father?" Nina asked. "If we're to follow the theory you've set out, maybe the killer was punishing *them* for having slept with a married man."

"Possibly, but I believe it was through killing them that the killer was targeting Dr. Madden." Annie's softness was gone. She was all business now. "I also see this as a message to him. *I know your secrets. See what I can do? You prize these women, but I can take them from you.* The act of taking what Stephen had gave the killer a sense of power."

"Power over the rival," Mitch murmured.

"Exactly so." Annie nodded.

"So which one of the three gets your vote, Wes?" Mitch sat in the seat next to Regan, his arm draped over the back of her chair. "Any of them give you a strange vibe?"

"Frankly, I found them all strange, as far as I'm concerned," Wes said. "I'd be hard pressed to say one was more odd than the other."

"Give me the rundown," Annie said.

"Well, we'll start with Kyle, since I saw him first." Wes wished he'd taken more notes at the interview. He didn't want to leave out any of the details. "I'm thinking he was pretty close to his mother. Nina, do you have any insights into their relationship?"

Nina thought for a moment before responding.

"I was only fourteen when I came to live in that house, and Kyle was nineteen and a sophomore in college already. So we didn't connect, if you know what I mean."

"He was away at school, then?" Regan asked.

"No." Nina shook her head. "He went to St. Ansel's. Because my dad taught there, both Kyle and I were able to attend for free. He lived at home, but I didn't really see him a lot. He had a part-time job in the evenings and, as I recall, a pretty heavy course load."

"What was his major? Do you remember?" Regan asked.

"Criminal justice, I think," Nina told her.

Everyone at the table fell silent.

"How did a man with a degree in criminal justice end up working as a security guard?" Wes asked, breaking the silence.

"I thought he'd gone to the police academy after he graduated," Nina said. "It seems to me he was working for the Maryland State Police when I left Stone River."

"How long did he work for MSP?" Annie asked Nina.

"I have no idea. I pretty much lost contact with him and Olivia for a long time."

"Well, that moves to the top of my to-do list." Mitch rubbed his chin thoughtfully. "Kyle's background is in law. Who'da guessed it?"

"Funny he left that out when I met with him the other day. I've yet to meet the former cop who didn't want to make damn sure I knew he'd been a cop, too." Wes considered the omission. "Then again, maybe not."

"You know how to get what we'll need on his background?" Annie asked Mitch.

"Just a few taps on the keyboard, Miz Annie." He wiggled his fingers.

"Good. I'll be interested in seeing what you find." Annie gestured for Wes to continue.

"Well, I'm thinking that if he knew about Stephen's affairs, he probably would have been pretty pissed off at his stepfather for cheating on his mother. That fits into Annie's theory of anger at Madden as a motive."

"I don't believe it for a minute." Nina shook her head. "I just don't believe for one second that Kyle killed anyone."

"Look, he was Olivia's only child," Wes told her. "Weren't they pretty close?"

"Yes, but . . . "

"And they'd probably been close for a long time," Wes ventured to guess.

"Well, yes, Olivia had been a single mother for a long time. I think her first husband died when Kyle was three or four, so sure, they'd have been close, but that doesn't mean he was a murderer," Nina protested.

"He was a student there on campus, he could have accidentally discovered that Stephen was having an affair. Maybe he followed him one time out of curiosity, found out where the girl lived. Realized what was going on and, like a good son, decided to take matters into his own hands. Avenge his mother, whatever."

"Good theory." Annie nodded. "Depending on his relationship with Dr. Madden, there could have been more involved there. If he'd seen Madden as a rival for his mother's affections, he'd have been happy to have found a way to hurt him. I'd have to know more about his personality, of course, but he could have found great satisfaction in having raped his stepfather's lovers."

"That sounds almost Oedipal," Regan noted.

"It is," Annie agreed.

"I have to go on record right here and now and say that I think you're wasting your time on Kyle." Nina looked around the table at the others in the group. "I just don't see it."

"Duly noted." Annie turned back to Wes. "Anything else on Kyle Stillman?"

"That's it for now. Let's move on to Dr. Overbeck. Nathaniel Carver Overbeck." Wes leaned back in his chair and stretched his legs under the table. It seemed that every time he moved, his thigh rubbed against Nina's and she'd shift slightly in the chair. *Too bad,* he thought. He'd enjoyed the contact.

"Here's an interesting character. He started out almost overeager to help. As long as he was discussing Allison Mulroney, anyway. Had only nice things to say about her, by the way. She was a lovely girl, good student, never noticed anyone harassing her, that sort of thing. But once I brought up the old murders, he definitely grew uncomfortable."

"Shifting around in his seat, nervous gestures with his hands . . ." Mitch said.

"All of the above. Now, when Stephen's name came up, he became positively self-righteous. He had the story down pat. Stephen had affairs, Stephen wanted to end the affairs, the girls threatened him, he kills them off and moves on to the next one. He even made the comment, 'I can't believe no one put it together sooner.'"

"Interesting." Annie nodded.

"Yeah, until I suggested that if he'd put it together, why hadn't he gone to the police with his theory."

"And he said what to that?" Mitch asked.

"Nothing. He paled a bit, but he said nothing."

"I'm assuming you confronted him about the affair with Olivia," Annie said.

"Oh, yeah. He admitted that. Somewhat reluctantly, but he didn't try to deny it. He also admitted that Olivia knew about her husband's affairs but he says he didn't think she knew with whom."

"Which could be speculation or a flat-out lie." Mitch nodded.

"I'm thinking lie," Wes told him. "But here's one thing I thought was strange. He seemed willing to talk about his affair with Olivia, but as soon as I brought up the fact that he'd taken Madden's place in the department, he made it clear the conversation had run its course."

"Touchy?" Regan asked.

"Very," Wes replied. "But he admitted that he'd been in love with Olivia. Which gives him a double motive for getting rid of Stephen. He wanted Madden's wife and his job."

"That's pretty strong motivation," Annie acknowledged. "And if he'd coveted those two things, it would certainly have given him great satisfaction to have set up Dr. Madden."

"That power thing you talked about," Nina said.

"Exactly," Annie told her. "It's just a few steps away from cannibals eating their enemies."

"There's a fun analogy," Mitch said.

"Man has a tendency to want to destroy what he wants to conquer. Once he's destroyed and made the vanquished part of him, then he has their power. He's taken their essence, all they have to give. That's what our killer wanted to do, I believe, though in a manner that's only slightly more civilized." Annie turned to Wes. "I'd say Dr. Overbeck makes a fine suspect. What did your gut tell you?"

"He's very cool on the outside, but like I said, I could see him becoming more agitated as the interview progressed."

"He wanted the wife, he wanted the job. Doesn't quite add up to the level of anger, the depth of emotion I was looking for. Overbeck already had the wife, right? Coveting the job . . . " Annie stopped to consider. "I was looking for something more deeply personal."

"I always had the impression that there was no love lost between my father and Dr. Overbeck, but I never knew why."

"Well, it's a relatively small academic arena. There could have been more there than simply wanting Madden's job," Annie explained. "Perhaps he felt more qualified for the position, or thought that somehow Madden was unjustifiably favored by the head of the department, or the dean. If Overbeck was convinced of his own superiority, losing out on a plum position to someone he felt to be his inferior would rankle, and over time fester."

"I have a question," Nina asked Annie. "Wouldn't my father have figured out that it was his girlfriends who were being targeted? The first one, he was probably really upset, but he wouldn't have suspected it was anything personal. But surely after the second girl was murdered he would have started to wonder. Why did he keep on having affairs with these girls if he knew someone was killing them?"

"Good question," Wes said.

"I have a theory on that." Annie reached over to squeeze Nina's arm gently. "I hope this doesn't upset you too greatly, Nina, but I've read all the psychological reports on your father. By all accounts, he was what we now recognize as having a sexually addictive personality. We've always known there were certain people who, in order to engage in sexual activity, would take risks or go to lengths that to many of us might seem ridiculous, even dangerous. The woman who's repeatedly driven to pick up strange men and take them home. The man who can't help but get involved in office affairs. We've only recently recognized that this type of behavior exhibits similar symptoms to those with drug or alcohol addiction. Starting with the inability to control the addiction."

Annie stopped to drink some of her tea, then continued.

"So while after the second murder Dr. Madden may have begun to wonder if the murders were not coincidental, in the long run, it wouldn't have stopped him from pursuing what he was addicted to."

"Between the first and second murders, seven

months had passed," Wes interjected. "Between the second and the third, there'd been four months. Between the third and the fourth, there'd been seven. Eighteen months in all."

"I noticed that, Wes," Annie replied. "The time frame seems off to me. I can understand the long stretch between the first and the second killings. If killing was new to him, it may have taken him a while to sort out his feelings, the guilt, whatever. Now, the shorter period between the second and the third is more telling—it tells me he liked it enough to kill again. Which makes the longer stretch between the third and fourth victims a little puzzling."

She drummed on the mug again.

"You mean, he wouldn't have waited as long to kill again, if he liked it so much," Regan said.

"Exactly. I'd have expected him to have looked for another victim sooner rather than later."

Mitch leaned forward and rested his arms on the table. "Of course, Stephen could have gotten spooked, and maybe didn't jump right into another affair as quickly."

"That's possible. Of course, it's also possible that the killer simply took the show out of town," Wes told him. "I can guarantee, reports of similar murders would have gotten my attention."

"Which means he went far enough away that they wouldn't have hit your radar, or he hid the crimes well enough that by the time the victims were found, it was hard to tell exactly what had happened to them."

"He was doing something during all that time," Annie murmured. "By the time he'd killed his third victim, I think he was as much addicted to killing as Madden was to sex."

"I'll go into the Bureau computers and see what I can find," Mitch told them. "I'm guessing once we start looking, we're going to find a few bodies somewhere between here, Delaware, and Maryland."

"What about the priest?" Annie asked Wes. "What was your impression of him?"

"He cared very much for Olivia, too. As a matter of fact, he admitted to having been in love with Olivia, but he more or less tossed it off as, every man who ever met Olivia was in love with her," Wes said. "And he, too, was definitely not happy when I brought up Stephen's name and the old cases."

"So you didn't really learn anything new," Regan noted.

"Actually, I did learn something." Wes turned to her. "I learned that he knows something he can't tell us."

"What's that supposed to mean?" Nina frowned. "If Father Whelan knew something about the murders, why wouldn't he tell you?"

"Because I think whatever he knows, he learned from Olivia. In confession."

He paused to let the words sink in.

Almost everyone at the table groaned.

"So even if she had known who was behind the killings, and she told Father Whelan, he wouldn't be able to tell anyone," Regan said flatly.

"Exactly," Wes replied.

"Well, damn." Mitch frowned.

"How would Olivia have known who the killer was?" Nina asked.

"Maybe he told her, bragged about it, even. 'Look what I did for you. See how much I love you,'" Mitch said.

"Does anyone else think it's creepy that Olivia could have known who the killer was, but didn't tell anyone?" Regan frowned. "That she'd let her husband go to trial—face the death penalty or, at the least, life in prison—for crimes he did not commit?"

"If he'd been cheating on her for all those years, yes, she could have built up some big-time resentment," Annie noted.

"She must have hated him a lot to have done that," Nina murmured. "Funny, I never got a sense of that."

"Maybe she didn't hate him as much as she loved someone else," Wes observed.

"Did she love her son, or her lover, enough to have sacrificed her husband?" Mitch asked.

"Well, here's something else. When I told him that we were taking a second look at the Madden case because there were similarities between this latest murder and the earlier ones, he looked stunned. And he said, 'Why would . . .'—then stopped and pretty much ended the interview by saying he had a meeting across campus."

"Now, that's an odd thing to say," Annie said. "You would have expected him to say, 'How could that be, Stephen died years ago,' or something along those lines."

Annie toyed with the ring on her finger.

"But instead, he said, 'Why would . . .'"

"As in, why would someone do something?" Mitch suggested.

"Yeah, that was sort of what I expected to hear," Wes nodded. "But whatever he knows, there's no way we're going to get him to tell."

"Okay, so what do we have?" Annie said. "We have a killer who was close to Olivia, someone close enough that she'd let her husband go to prison to protect him. Someone was punishing Stephen for having hurt her. We've already talked about the killer's need to take what was Stephen's, to have power over him. The question is, who would have most wanted to kill Stephen's women, then watch him go to prison for it?"

"The son, the priest, or the rival for his wife's affections?" Mitch said.

"Why would he have killed this latest girl?" Nina asked. "If the whole purpose of killing the others was to destroy my father, why start killing again now?"

"I spoke earlier of how our killer may have developed a taste for murder. He could have gone outside the area to find victims, or he may have managed to keep it in check and control that urge for a long time. Others have done it. I worked a case recently where a man had gone on a killing spree seven years ago, killed nine women in nine different states over the course of a year, then just stopped. He was never caught."

"How did they finally know he was a killer?" Nina asked.

"After he died, his son was cleaning out his truck to sell it, and found the souvenirs his father had kept of all his victims. Photographs, driver's licenses. Locks of hair." Annie sighed. "If the son hadn't had the guts to call the police, we never would have known who killed those women."

"So maybe this killer did stop . . . " Nina said. "But why would he have started again?"

"There would have had to have been a trigger, something that set him off again," Annie told her. "My guess is that Olivia's death was the trigger."

"That could have set off any one of the three. Emotionally, I'm sure each of them was affected," Regan commented.

"If that's true, then we need to work fast," Wes told them, "or we're going to have another murder on our hands."

"I'm on my way back to the office." Mitch stood. "I'll get on this right away, see what I can come up with on Kyle's background, and I'll look for any other similar murders over the past fifteen, sixteen years."

"While you're using those amazing computer skills, maybe you could check into something for me." Regan looked up at him.

"Sure. What do you need?" He reached down to her and pulled her out of her seat. "Some suggestions for a romantic weekend away?"

"Well, actually, I was hoping for a little something more on Eddie Kroll." She smiled.

"Damn that Eddie." Mitch shook his head.

Regan laughed. "I was trying to pull up more on his family but I'm afraid I haven't been successful. I know he had an older brother named Carl, and a brother named Harry, but I was wondering if he had other siblings."

"That should be a snap." Mitch then turned to Annie. "Are you ready for the ride back?"

"I am." Annie pushed her chair back. As she stood, she asked Wes, "What's your next step going to be?"

"I'd like to explore the relationship between Madden and Overbeck a bit more, but it's been hard to find someone who knew them both. The priest who'd pegged Madden to take over the department died some years ago, and except for Overbeck, there are only a few other professors who knew both of the men well. I've already spoken with those who did, but I didn't hear anything I didn't already know."

"Were they aware that Overbeck was having an affair with Madden's wife?"

"They didn't seem to be aware of it." Wes shook his head. "I haven't been able to find anyone who claimed to have known Madden very well."

"Did you speak with Mrs. Owens?" Nina asked.

"Who is Mrs. Owens?" Wes turned to her.

"She was the secretary Dad shared with Dr. Overbeck. Her office was between theirs. It was sort of a neutral area between the two."

"I'll see if she's still at St. Ansel's."

"Father Whelan would know," Nina offered.

"I'll check with him," Wes said. "It'll give me an excuse to talk to him again."

The entire group filed out the back door, and stood on the deck for a moment, saying their good-byes, before Mitch, Annie, and Regan walked toward his car, and Nina walked Wes to his.

"By the way, did you ever read the letter your father left for you?" he asked.

"Yes." Nina nodded. "Unfortunately, there wasn't really anything of any use to you on this case, other than the fact that he did say he was innocent."

"Do you think he would have said otherwise?"

"I think if he'd been guilty, he'd not have said anything at all."

"Maybe."

When they reached the stairs, Wes went down the steps, while Nina remained on the end of the deck.

"Wes," she called to him, and he turned back to her.

"I've been meaning to ask—what was the name of the book that was left at the scene of that last murder?"

"I don't remember. Why?"

"Just curious."

"Check the evidence list in the Maureen Thomas file. It should be noted there."

"I don't remember seeing it, but I'll take another look."

"Let me know if you can't find it. I'll look it up for you." He could have gotten in the car then, but didn't open the door. Instead, he said, "I wasn't kidding when I said I thought you should steer clear of your stepbrother. I know you're having a hard time accepting it, but he could very well be the killer."

"I am having a hard time with that," she admitted. "I still don't think he's the man you're after."

"When I met you the first time, I said something to you about hoping that you weren't looking into the case to prove your father's innocence, and you said you never doubted that he was the killer." Wes opened his car door. "Why would you readily accept that your father was a killer, but not your stepbrother?"

"I guess I had never questioned my father's guilt because I was so angry with him, so humiliated by his arrest." She smiled grimly. "Yes, I know how childish that sounds, but I was just nineteen when all that happened, still angry with him for what I'd felt was his abandonment of my mother and me. I was angrier still when he married Olivia. That had come without warning, and it took me years to forgive him for that. So while I may be questioning it now, I didn't question it then. We'd had an odd relationship, with the divorce, then the remarriage, then the arrest. I never felt I knew him very well, and most of my emotions as far as he was concerned revolved around anger. There's a lot that we were never able to resolve between us."

"Well, if you manage to help prove his innocence now, would that help?"

"It won't replace what we never were able to have, but it would bring him justice, and yes, that would go a long way in helping me to forgive both of us."

"Well, let's see what we can do about that." He got into his car and rolled his window down. "Are you going to be here through the weekend?"

"Yes." She leaned over the deck railing. "At least through Sunday, then we'll see."

"Don't forget to call me if you can't find that evidence list," he said as he pulled away.

She nodded and watched him drive off. When he reached the end of the lane and turned onto the road, she called to Regan. "Where did we leave the Maureen Thomas file . . . ?"

Twenty

Less than two hours later, Wes's cell phone rang. Nina had looked through all four boxes, but the evidence list wasn't there.

"Could I drive over to the police station and pick up a copy?" she asked.

"Sure. I'll be here for another hour or so."

"I'll be there in less than that."

Wes was in the storage room looking through the files he'd just sent back a week or so ago when his cell phone rang again.

"It's Mayfield. The chief is looking all over the station for you. Where the hell are you?" his partner all but yelled through the phone.

"I'm in the storage room," he told her.

"Only place in the entire building we didn't look."

"So what's the big deal?" He found the box he was looking for and knelt down to open it.

"Chief Raymond needs a briefing on the Mulroney case. The DA's office wanted to know if there were any leads."

"Sort of."

"You tell him. I'm not even going to try to guess what a *sort of* lead is." She hung up without saying good-bye.

Wes finished going through the box, and having found the file he was looking for, returned the box to the stack on which he'd found it, turned off the light, and closed the door behind him.

He rapped on the chief's door with his knuckles, then pushed the door open. Chief Milt Raymond sat behind his desk, the phone in his right hand, a cigar in his left. He finished his call and hung up.

"Better not let anyone from the town council see that cigar," Wes told him. "They voted us a no-smoking zone just two weeks ago."

"I will wrestle to the ground anyone who tries to take my cigars away from me." The portly man rested against the back of the chair. "What do you have for me on the Mulroney girl?"

"Practically nothing." Wes leaned on the back of the chair that stood to the left of the chief's desk. "No suspects. No witnesses. Nothing back from the lab yet."

"What the hell have you been doing all week? Chasing your tail?"

"Interviewing people at the college, but no one saw anything, or heard anything."

Wes was about to bring up the connection to the Madden case when the chief asked, "What's in the file?"

"It's the evidence list from the Maureen Thomas file." As soon as the words were out of Wes's mouth, he regretted them.

"Maureen Thomas?" Raymond frowned. "Maureen Thomas? From, what was that, 1989?" Without waiting for a reply, he asked, "What the hell are you doing with that?"

Wes began to explain the current interest in the old case, but midway through, the chief held up both hands and ordered, "Stop. I've heard enough."

Chief Raymond stood, his eyes narrowed to slits, and Wes remembered why he shouldn't have mentioned Madden's name.

"Powell, you listen, and you listen good. I do not want one more second spent on this, you hear me? I personally led the investigation in the Madden case, and I know that sonofabitch was guilty as sin."

"Chief, I felt the same way, but . . ."

"There are no buts here, Detective. That is a closed case, and it's going to stay closed."

"Sir, we have reason to believe that—"

"Who is *we*? What *we*? Who else is involved in this? Mayfield?"

"No, sir, actually, I haven't even had time to discuss it with her. As I started to tell you, Regan Landry was the one who wanted us to take a second look. I remembered how you were such a big fan of her dad's, so of course I pulled the files out for her."

"Shit. Josh's daughter?"

Wes nodded.

"She thinks there's something worth looking into, so I figured I'd give her the files, and she'd see there was nothing there. No smoke, no fire." Wes knew he was walking the line, but there was no turning back. "After looking into it, though, it appears there may be something there. She has a friend in the FBI who's looking into it as well, so I knew we were going to have to stay involved. I'd hate to be reading about this in the *Washington Post*."

The chief stared at him, and for a long moment, Wes thought the man was going to explode.

Finally, he said, "Christ. Now I'm not only looking for a killer, I'm playing nice with the feds and with Landry's daughter." He ran thick fingers through his thinning salt-and-pepper hair. "You keep an eye on them. Do what you have to do, but honest to God, Powell, I do not want one word of this to leak to the press, you hear me? I do not care what you have to do, but so help me God, if I get one phone call, or see one word written anywhere, or if I so much as hear Madden's name, you're out of here. You can get Landry's daughter's FBI friend to hire you, 'cause you won't be working here."

"Got it." Wes nodded. "No leaks. No press. No mention of Madden's name."

"And I want this other case solved, hear? You play nice with Landry, but I don't want any time taken from the Mulroney case."

"Yes, sir." Wes all but backed out of the room.

"Powell."

"Yes, sir?"

"Why did you pull the Thomas file?"

"Someone asked for the name of the book that Stephen Madden had left in Maureen Thomas's apartment."

"Why?" The chief stood up and appeared to be getting ready to leave. "Who?"

"Madden's daughter, sir. She just wanted to know what the title was."

"Why?" he repeated with a heavy sigh.

"I have no idea."

"Well, forget it. That's just the kind of stupid stuff I don't want going on. Takes you away from what you're supposed to be doing. Tell her you can't find it."

"Too late. I already told her I had it."

"Then put it in the mail to her and get back to work on the Mulroney case, would you?"

"She's on her way to pick it up."

"Fine. Make a copy of it and leave it at the front desk. I want a report on every interview you've conducted on Mulroney on my desk by eight tomorrow morning." The chief opened the center drawer of his desk, grabbed his car keys, and followed Wes into the hall. He closed his office door behind him. "Eight A.M., Powell."

"Sure thing, Chief."

Wes stepped out of the man's way and let him pass.

There was a joke around the station that the extent of the chief's agitation was always in direct proportion to the length of his stride. This afternoon, he was at the front door in less than six strides.

Wes held his breath as Nina walked through the front door. She smiled pleasantly at the chief and held the door for him. He touched his fingers to the side of his cap in a modified salute, his usual response to a pretty woman. Wes shook his head and tried not to laugh.

Nina came into the lobby and started to ask for him when she saw him in the hall. She smiled and waved.

Wes walked toward her, the file in his hand.

"Thanks so much for finding that for me, Detective." She met him halfway.

"I thought we were doing first names," he said.

"Right. Wes," she corrected herself. "Is that the file?"

"Yes, but it's the original. I'm going to have to make a copy. Want to come on into the back?"

"Sure. Thanks. I'm sorry to make you go through the trouble, but I couldn't find the list anywhere."

"It's no trouble." He held open the door to the small room that held the copy machine, the fax machine, and a bank of filing cabinets. He made the copy and handed it to her.

She skimmed the list until she found what she was looking for.

"This is the book?" Her jaw all but dropped. *"Hansen's Guide to Literary Critiques?"*

He looked over her shoulder.

"Yeah, that's the one. It's still in the box. I just saw it."

"Well, that makes no sense at all." She shook her head. "Here I was thinking that he'd taken some book of poetry or something to her apartment. You know, to read love poems or whatever. Even some classy prose, but a reference book?"

"That's what we found there."

"If you were going to see your girlfriend, would you take a reference book along?"

"Depends. Maybe she needed to look something up. Or maybe he was loaning it to her."

"She was a senior biology major. It said so in the file. There's no way she would have been using that book. That was for his freshman class for English majors, the kids who tested out of the standard required freshman English course. Maureen Thomas would not have asked to borrow that book."

"Then maybe he was taking it home with him."

"Sorry, but no. For one thing, why take it out of the car? For another, he had a copy of this book in his office at home. I know, because I took that course from another professor, and I used his book." She crossed her arms over her chest. "This just doesn't make sense."

"That's the book we found there, Nina."

"May I see it?"

"I don't see why not." He picked up his file and held the door for her, and then led the way back to the storage room.

He turned the light on and pointed to the box on the middle shelf.

"It's right in here," he told her as he opened the box. He took out the book and handed it to her.

She paged through it carefully, then stopped inside the front cover, to the place where Stephen Madden had written his name.

Nina stared at the signature, then looked up at Wes and said, "I can't think of one good reason why this book would have been in that girl's apartment, unless someone else put it there."

"Who would have had access to his things?" Wes asked, then answered his own question. "At home, Kyle would have. At school, Dr. Overbeck."

She nodded.

"I didn't go into my father's study when I was at the house. I wish now that I had." She thought it over for a minute, then told Wes, "I can still do that. I'll stop at the house on my way home and see if Kyle is there. I'll tell him I changed my mind, and that I decided I do want to look over—"

"Uh-uh." Wes shook his head. "There's no way

you're going into that house alone. Not with Stillman a top number on our hot list."

"Well, how about if I stop over now? I still have a key; if he's not there, I'll just go in. He'll never know I was there."

"And if he's at home?"

She stared at him for a long moment. "Okay, how about if we do this. You follow me. I'll stop at the house. If he's not there, I'll go in. If he is, you'll see me go inside, and three minutes later, you ring the doorbell. If no one answers, break the door down."

"I don't like it, but I can't stop you," Wes told her. "Fine. I'll follow you."

"Good." Nina looked down at the box. "What other sort of evidence is in there?"

"Everything from the clothes the victim wore that night to her personal phone book."

She thought about that for a minute, then said, "Did you ever think of testing some of it for DNA and that sort of thing?"

"Frankly, no. And since we don't have anything to compare it to, what's the point?" He returned the box to the shelf.

"On TV, you always see the detectives using those little sticky rollers, the kind you use to remove lint from your clothing."

Wes started toward the door, but Nina didn't move.

"What if you rolled one of those over the clothing in the boxes now?"

"For what purpose?" He stopped in the doorway.

"To see what trace evidence is there. Hair, maybe. On TV, they always find hair on the rollers." She stared at him, and he could have sworn he saw wheels turning behind her eyes. "Supposing we rolled the clothes from all four girls. Supposing we took the hairs we found there, and compared them to hair from the victims—you probably have something that has their DNA, right?—and from my father. Then we see if someone else's hair is there."

"First of all, we have no way of getting any of your father's hair. Second of all, even if we found hair or let's say even semen that doesn't match your dad, how do we match that to someone else?" Wes let that sink in, then added, "We can't force either Kyle or Overbeck to give samples, we have no probable cause."

"We suspect that Dr. Overbeck—"

"Not good enough. We have a theory. That's all." He watched the disappointment on her face. "It's a good idea, Nina, but I don't know that we'd find anything."

"You don't know that we wouldn't. And just FYI, the box of stuff that came from the prison had my dad's comb in it. So we probably have his DNA, if anyone's interested in testing it."

Wes considered the possibility.

"We'd still have to get it analyzed. As backed up as

the county lab is, there's no way I could get this around the chief."

"Mitch said if you needed help from the FBI lab, to just say the word."

Wes was still thinking.

"What do we have to lose?" she whispered.

Only my job, he could have said, but decided against it. It had been a long time since anyone had appealed to him as much as Nina did, and an even longer time since he'd gotten to play hero to anyone.

"I'll be right back," he told her.

"Where are you going?"

"To see if I have any of those lint rollers in my desk."

Two hours and forty minutes and three sticky rollers later, Wes was still working on the evidence from Maureen Thomas's case. He'd already rolled her clothing and bagged every sheet of sticky paper separately and was starting on the pillowcase and the bedsheet. They'd need more rollers and plastic bags in order to collect the traces from the other three case evidence boxes.

"We're done for today," Wes told her. "We can't do any more until I get some more supplies. We've gone through every roller in the building."

"So what now?"

"So tomorrow I'll pick up some more lint rollers

and a few more boxes of sandwich bags and I'll finish the job."

She watched him load the samples into several brown evidence envelopes.

"What about the sheet?" she asked.

He folded it carefully. "We're going to have it tested, too. There are three stains still visible. They may or may not give us anything, but you're right. Let's test it all."

Wes found a box to carry it all in.

"Ready?" he asked before turning out the light.

She nodded and followed him into the hall.

"Why not give that stuff to me, and I'll ask Regan to get it to Mitch. I think she'll be seeing him tomorrow night."

"I'd rather hand it over myself. Let's not compromise the chain of possession." He thought aloud as they walked toward the lobby. "Supposing we do find something that points to someone else. It isn't going to look good if it comes out that the evidence was temporarily in the hands of the daughter of the man who'd been convicted of the murders."

"Good point." She paused outside the door.

"Do you still have time to stop at Kyle's? It's after six."

"Only if we can stop for dinner first," Wes told her. "I'm starving."

"I could eat," she admitted.

"There's a really good Italian restaurant about three blocks from here."

"Great. I love Italian." She smiled and walked toward the Land Rover, which was parked in the visitor's spot near the front door. "I'll follow you."

The drive to the restaurant took less than five minutes. Wes parked his car out front and got out to wait for Nina while she tried to parallel park the Land Rover.

"Sorry it took me so long," she said when she finally got out of the vehicle after the fourth attempt to park was successful. "I was never very good at parallel parking, and since I don't have a car in New York, I hardly ever drive anymore. It takes me a while to get the hang of it."

She locked the vehicle and stopped when she realized what she'd said.

"Probably not what you want to say to a cop."

"I didn't hear a word." Wes grinned and opened the door to the restaurant.

There were fewer than twenty tables in the small storefront, and all but three were occupied.

"This looks like a popular place," Nina observed.

"Best Italian food in Stone River." Wes nodded.

A woman in a dark dress and silvery gray hair waved to Wes from the back of the restaurant.

"Oh, Detective, I almost didn't recognize you," she told him as she approached.

"What do you mean? I was here just last weekend."

"Yes, but it's been so long since I've seen you with a date, I didn't believe my eyes." She winked at Nina and picked up menus from the table that stood near the front door. "This way, Detective . . . and your lovely date."

Wes decided it would be more trouble than it was worth to try to explain to Dellarosa, who owned the restaurant with her husband, that Nina was not his date. Besides, Nina had shrugged good-naturedly, so he let it ride.

"This is a good table, Benny will wait on you tonight," Dellarosa told them as she seated them at a table near the back of the restaurant. "I'll have him bring you a glass of wine in just a minute. Does the lady like the red that you favor?"

Wes looked at Nina for help.

"Red is fine, thank you."

After Dellarosa walked away, Nina asked, "Didn't this used to be Caramuzzi's?"

"Yeah, you remember that?"

"I do. I used to have dinner here with my friends from school. I loved their spaghetti sauce."

"Whose spaghetti sauce you love?" Dellarosa appeared as if out of thin air.

"Nina was just saying that she used to eat here when she was in college, and she liked the sauce," Wes explained.

"Ah, Caramuzzi's. My sister and her husband." Dellarosa nodded. "We bought from them twelve years ago. How long it's been since you were here?"

"Sixteen years," Nina told her.

"You liked my sister's sauce, you'll love mine." Dellarosa winked again and patted Nina on the back as she went into the kitchen.

"The decor is pretty much the same." Nina looked around the restaurant.

"Same paintings, I think. Same music. Same menu. Not a lot has changed around here since you left."

"So it would seem." Nina glanced at the menu before closing it and setting it aside. "I did notice there were a few more shops out there on Main Street, some nice boutiques and a coffee shop. The bookstore is new, and I think there used to be a grocery store on the corner across the street. And there was a drugstore here somewhere, wasn't there?"

"Yeah, Kimmel's Drugstore was at the far end of the street. They sold out a few years back, when one of the chains built a store in that new mall right outside of town. There's a big grocery store out there, too."

"The streetscape looks pretty much the same, though. The store facades haven't changed."

"I think the local historical group is trying to keep the original architecture." Wes looked up as the waiter approached. "Ahhhhh, here's Benny with our wine. Thanks, pal."

"Here's your red, from Dellarosa's private stock.

She said to ask the lady how she likes it." Benny poured from the bottle into one of the two glasses he carried in his left hand, and passed the glass to Nina.

"The lady likes it just fine," Nina told him after tasting it, and Benny topped off her glass, then poured a glass for Wes. "Now, do we know what we're having?"

"Depends on who's in the kitchen," Wes deadpanned.

"Tonight, Frankie's sister Elle."

"She makes the chicken piccata?"

Benny just smiled. "Will that be for two?"

"Nina?" Wes asked.

"Sure. I love chicken piccata."

Benny gathered the menus. "She never had it like Elle's, right, Detective?"

Wes tipped his wineglass in the direction of the kitchen before taking a sip. "She's the best cook in the family."

"I won't tell her you said so," Benny whispered, "because then Frankie would want to hurt you."

He walked away as quietly as he'd appeared.

"Some place," Nina said.

"The best in town," Wes agreed.

They seemed to run out of things to say, so they each sipped their wine and pretended to watch the other diners.

"Were you able to locate Mrs. Owens?" Nina asked after the passage of a few too many minutes of silence.

"I haven't had a chance to look."

"I think she's a good person for you to talk to. I'm surprised I didn't think of her sooner. She knew everyone on the faculty."

"I thought she was the English department secretary."

"She was, that year. And for a few years before," Nina explained, "but before that she'd been with the math department. And I seem to remember her telling me once that before that she'd worked for the history department."

"So she really did know everyone."

"I'm surprised that wasn't reflected in the interview that was in the file."

"I don't remember an interview with her." Wes frowned.

"Probably because it wasn't you who spoke with her. It was someone named Raymond. He didn't ask her very many questions." She lifted her glass so her salad could be served. "It didn't seem like he did a very good job."

"Well, don't say that too loud." Wes grimaced. "Detective Raymond is now Chief Raymond. You passed him on the way into the station today."

"Heavyset guy, all spit and polish. All uniformed up?"

"That was him."

"He worked the investigation with you, back then?"

"He was the lead detective."

"Hmmmm" was all Nina said.

"I take it you weren't impressed?"

"Let's just say they don't do things that way on *CSI*."

"Here's a tip." He leaned toward her and lowered his voice as if sharing a secret. "No one really does things the way they do on *CSI*. That's television. This is reality."

"I like the TV way much better," Nina said as she speared a sliver of cucumber. "It always ends up so neat and tidy."

"It rarely does in real life, I'm afraid. With some cases, it seems like everything that can go wrong, does."

"Do you think my dad's case was like that?"

When Wes didn't respond right away, Nina said, "I'm sorry. I guess that wasn't a very good question."

"It isn't that it's a bad question, it's simply one I can't answer. Back then, we didn't have the benefit of technology that we have now. And yes, now we do have DNA and all kinds of tests that we can run, but it doesn't always happen. And when it does, it isn't always done right. There are labs that for years did DNA testing that were recently shut down due to irregularities in their testing procedures. So sometimes, even when you have the benefit of the technology, you get screwed over by human error." Wes ate his salad for a minute, then told her, "Sixteen years ago, we really believed we had a lock on that case. We had the offender in cuffs within three days of finding the last victim. We'd looked at the evidence we had and we followed the trail right to your father."

He put his fork down and looked across the table at Nina. "Now, in light of everything that's come up these past few weeks, I have to wonder if we weren't led to him by the real killer."

"That upsets you." She'd watched his face, and saw the conflicting emotions.

"Upsets me?" He considered the word. "I'm going to be more than upset if it turns out that someone concocted this scheme and led us through it. I'm going to be really pissed off. I don't like being manipulated."

"I don't blame you." She finished her salad and played with a rejected piece of tomato. "So that's why you're willing to see this through? Because you feel as if you were manipulated?"

"It's one reason, but not the only one. If your father was unjustly accused, unjustly convicted, I will have that on my conscience for the rest of my life. He died a convicted murderer. There's no way anyone could make that up to him, or to you. But oh, yeah, if someone set him up?" Wes's jaw set squarely. "Will I find him? What do you think?"

"I think I'm glad I'm not the person who set him up." Nina tilted her glass in Wes's direction. "To justice, Detective."

He was more than willing to drink to that.

Twenty-one

It was dark by the time Wes and Nina left Dellarosa's.

"Maybe you should wait until tomorrow to stop at the house," Wes suggested.

"I might as well go now," Nina said. "I'm really not afraid of Kyle. I still think you're all wrong about him. And besides, I'm already here in Stone River."

"All right. But here's the way it's going to be. I'm going to follow you and park in front of the neighbor's house. I will watch you ring the doorbell. If you are convinced there's no one inside, you will wave to me and use your key to go in. I will wait, cell phone in hand, for you to call me and tell me that no one is in there. If my cell doesn't ring within a minute of you going through that door, I'm right behind you."

"If you're so concerned, why don't you just come in with me?"

"Because you no longer own the house, and I

would be entering unlawfully. And on the outside chance that you find something that could be used as evidence, my being there could cause it to be tossed later as part of an improper search. Let's not take silly chances."

"Aren't I entering unlawfully?"

"Debatable. You're a relative, and you have a key. You could make a case that you're allowed to enter when the owner isn't home, because he knows you have the key and permitted you to keep it. I'm a cop. I get no such slack."

She nodded and walked to the Land Rover. "I'll see you there, then."

The drive to the Madden house—now Kyle Stillman's house—took less than ten minutes. Nina parked right at the curb near the front door, while Wes drove past her and parked two houses up the street, in the shadow of some large trees. Nina got out of the car and walked up to the front door and rang the bell. She peered through the sidelights, then rang the bell again. After several tries, she took the key from her purse and opened the door. She turned to wave at Wes, then disappeared into the house.

The door had barely been closed behind her when Wes took his cell phone out of his pocket and began the countdown. He'd reached fifty-two when the phone finally rang.

"All clear here," Nina told him.

"Are you sure?"

"Unless someone's hiding upstairs."

"Not funny." He frowned. "Did you leave the front door unlocked?"

"I think so." She paused. "Want me to go check?"

"No. I want you to get what you went in for and get the hell out."

"What did I come in here for?" He could hear her shuffling papers around, and a moment later, he heard a file drawer close. "Oh, yes. I'm looking for Dad's copy of *Hansen's*. Which should be right about . . . here."

"Is it?" Wes asked. "Is it there?"

"No, but that doesn't mean it's not on another shelf."

He listened as she moved books around, knocked a few off the shelf and onto the floor.

"Oops."

He heard her breathing into the phone, heard another drawer open and close. Heard her footsteps on the hardwood floor.

Heard a car in the driveway.

"Nina, you have to get out. Go out through the back. Kyle just pulled in the driveway."

"If he pulled in the driveway, he's already seen the lights on in the study. If I leave before he gets here, he'll probably call in a burglary," she told him calmly. "I'm going to stay here, he'll come in, I'll act very normal and very natural. I'll tell him I decided I wanted to go through Dad's books, and maybe take something back to New York with me. No big deal."

"And it won't be a big deal when I ring the doorbell about thirty seconds after he comes inside, so you'd better act surprised to see me."

She hung up and he slipped his phone back into his pocket. He watched as the house lights went on from the kitchen through the hall. He walked around the side of the house until he could see into the study window. Nina stood behind her father's desk, her cell phone in her hand. Apparently, in spite of her proclamations to the contrary, she wasn't one hundred percent sure of Kyle, either.

Kyle stood in the door, lighting a cigarette, and through reading body language and facial expressions, Wes could follow the conversation. Kyle had been surprised to see Nina. Nina was explaining how she'd decided that perhaps she might want a few of her father's things after all. Why didn't you call and let me know you were coming, we could have had dinner? It was a whim, spur of the moment. I did call the house phone earlier, there was no answer.

There appeared to be a lull, and suddenly Wes was unable to read Kyle's expression.

That's it. Time's up. Wes walked back to the front of the house and rang the bell.

He was just about to ring it for the third time when he heard footsteps in the hall.

"Detective Powell." Kyle opened the door. "You're working late tonight."

"I was on my way home, and I saw the lights on. I had a few questions and thought if you weren't busy, now might be a good time to ask them."

"Well, it isn't a good time for me," Kyle told him. "So if you'd like to stop by tomorrow, or the next day, that would be fine. Give me a call and we'll make an appointment."

"Actually, it will only take a few minutes."

"Sorry, Detective. I have company, and I don't have time to chat right now. If you'd like to come back tomorrow, I'll be home all day. But tonight is not good." Kyle started to close the door, and Wes was debating whether or not to stick out his foot to prevent the door from closing, when he saw Nina move into the hall behind Kyle.

"Kyle, I'm going to have to get going now, I'm staying with a friend and she expected me back hours ago and . . . " She paused and peered around her stepbrother. "Is that Detective Powell I see?"

"Ms. Madden, nice to see you again." Wes breathed a sigh of relief. He really hadn't wanted to alert Kyle that he was a suspect at this stage of the investigation.

"Nice to see you, too." She had a stack of books in her hands. To Kyle, she said, "I found a few old books of Dad's that I'd like to take, if it's okay with you."

"They're your books. I told you before, anything

you want from this house, it's yours. Just say the word." He patted her on the back. "Next time, you might want to call first. Not that I mind you coming and going, I certainly don't. But I'd like to be here when you're here, so we can visit."

"I'll call first next time. Thanks again." Nina scooted out past him and nodded to Wes as she went down the steps. "Detective."

Wes nodded in return, and took a few steps backward. Kyle stood in the door, watching Nina get into her car. He continued to stare as she drove off. Wes couldn't read the expression that crossed Kyle's face, and it made him uneasy.

"I'm sorry to have disturbed you," Wes said as he went down the steps. "I'll give you a call and you can let me know when's a good time to stop by."

"Well, you might as well come in, now that you've scared away my stepsister." Kyle stepped back from the door and gestured for Wes to enter.

What the hell, Wes thought as he stepped through the door.

"What was it you wanted to talk about this time?" Kyle asked, not nearly as hospitable as he had been the last time Wes had been there.

"Just a quick question or two. When I was here the other day, why didn't you tell me that you'd gone through the police academy? That you'd been a Maryland state cop for several years?"

Kyle's eyes narrowed. "I didn't think of it, actually. That was years ago, and since you checked into my background, you know that my leaving MSP was not exactly on friendly terms. I just don't think about that time anymore. Sorry if that made you feel suspicious toward me—apparently it has, or you wouldn't be back here asking about it. There was no big mystery, though. Maybe if you'd asked me for my employment background instead of what I did for a living, it might have come to mind." Kyle stood with his arms folded over his chest. "Was that all? Did you drive out here just to ask me about that?"

"I did want to ask you about your stepfather's affairs."

"What about them?"

"Were you aware that he was cheating on your mother?"

"Only after my mother told me."

"When was that?"

"I really don't recall."

"Before or after the murders?"

"I don't recall when they were, sorry."

"The last one was in 1989. Surely you remember that."

"I think maybe she didn't mention it until after he was arrested, and it came out that he'd had all those girlfriends over the years. Yes, I'd have to say that was when I found out."

"What was her demeanor?"

"She was devastated, of course. She loved Stephen."

"The last time we talked, you said you knew about her affair with Overbeck."

"Yes."

"So did you know about your mother's affair with him before you knew about Stephen's affairs?"

"What difference does it make?"

"Just wondering which one she mentioned first."

"I really don't remember." Kyle closed the door slightly. "Now, unless there's something else . . . ?"

"That'll do it for tonight."

"Good night then." Kyle stepped back, then said as he closed the door all the way, "And next time, call for an appointment."

"I'll be sure to do that," Wes said as he went down the steps and onto the walk.

On his way back to the car, he dialed Nina's cell phone. It occurred to him that he'd memorized it.

"Hi," she answered.

"Hi, yourself." Wes unlocked the car door and got in.

"You and Kyle have a nice chat?"

"Sure. He couldn't wait to get me out of there."

"I think he wanted to go back into the office and see what I'd taken."

"You do?"

"Yes. He seemed really concerned that I was there, although he was certainly gracious." She paused, then said, "I'm glad you were there. Something about him tonight put me on edge. I still don't see him as a murderer, but thanks for being there."

"Any time." Wes turned the key in the ignition and drove away from the curb. "So, what did you find?"

"Just a few books that I did want to read again. I didn't have time to find the *Hansen's,* but I can go back again and look."

"Not alone, okay?"

"I'll take Regan with me next time. She has a black belt and is a crack shot. She has several handguns."

"You're kidding."

"Uh-uh. She is armed and dangerous."

"Who'd have thought it?"

"Well, she's careful with her guns, but I guess living out on the bay, all alone, on that windy dark road with precious few neighbors, she needs to be able to protect herself."

"As long as she knows what she's doing."

"She took lessons for years, and she still goes to a firing range at least once a month. She said she's never had to shoot at anyone, but if the need ever arose, she wanted to know how to do it right."

When he didn't respond, she said, "Wes? You still there?"

"I'm here. I was just thinking, it's too bad you couldn't have gotten something with Kyle's DNA on it."

"Who said I didn't?"

"What?" He came to a stop sign and slammed on the brakes. "You found something?"

"Right under my nose." He could all but hear the smile in her voice. "Kyle smokes cigarettes. He lit one up when he came into the study."

"I saw through the window. So?"

"So when he went out to answer the door, he stubbed it out in the ashtray."

"And you swiped it?"

"It's wrapped in a tissue in my purse. I was so afraid it would start smoking while I was standing there next to him, I couldn't wait to leave."

"Where are you? Slow down and let me catch up."

"I've been waiting for you. See the car stopped at the side of the road about one hundred yards up from the stop sign you just passed? Pull up alongside and roll down your window, and I'll toss it to you."

"You are one smart woman," he told her as he slowed down and eased as close to the Land Rover as he could without sideswiping it.

"You betcha," she said, and tossed the rolled-up tissue into the front seat of his car.

"Was this the only butt in the ashtray?"

"Not the only one, but the only one I knew for sure was his."

"You might be in the wrong business."

She laughed softly.

"'Night, Wes."

"'Night, Nina," he said as he put the evidence into his pocket, and watched her drive off into the night.

Twenty-two

"So, what do you have for me?" Regan propped the phone between her shoulder and her chin so she could talk and take a cobbler out of the oven at the same time.

"I have a little bit of information," Mitch told her. "You gonna make it worth my while?"

"Don't I always?"

"Amen." He chuckled. "In addition to the two brothers you already know about, Eddie Kroll had two sisters. Dorothea and Catherine. Catherine died in 1993—cause unknown—but Dorothea is the widow of Joseph Brown and the mother of three grown daughters."

"Dorothea Brown," Regan murmured. "Dorothea Brown . . ."

"Yeah. Unfortunately, I didn't have time to look up anything else because—believe it or not—I actually had to work today. And I had to sort through all the hits I got on the stuff I was looking up for Wes. Do you know how many—"

"Dolly Brown," Regan all but shouted into the phone. "That sneaky little . . . "

"Whoa, who's Dolly Brown?"

"Dolly Brown is the woman I've been talking to in Sayreville, Illinois. She's the woman I spent several days with a few weeks ago, and never once did she let it drop that she was Eddie's sister. That explains why she didn't want me to talk to Carl, why she was so protective of him."

"Want to explain to me what you're talking about?"

"I will call you back in fifteen minutes or less."

"Let me guess. You're going to call Dolly Brown and give her what-for for not coming clean."

"I'm going to do better than that. I'm going to book myself on the first flight I can get out there, and then I'm going to do a little investigative work of my own. I'll call you back. And thanks, Mitch. Your hard work will be rewarded."

"I'm counting on it," he said as she hung up.

Regan called the airlines and made arrangements for a morning flight to Chicago, then shuffled through her purse in search of the small phone book she took with her everywhere. She found the number she wanted, dialed it, and leaned on the kitchen counter while waiting for the familiar voice to pick up.

"Hello?"

"Hello, I'd like to speak with Dorothea Brown, please."

"This is Dorothea Brown."

"Dorothea Kroll Brown?"

"Yes. Who is this?"

"This," she said, grinning from ear to ear, "is Regan Landry."

A long silence followed, and for a moment, Regan was afraid Dolly was going to hang up on her.

"Dammit." Dorothea Kroll Brown cursed softly. "I knew I shoulda got that caller ID thing . . . "

"Why didn't you tell me you're Eddie's sister?" Regan asked.

"You wouldn't understand."

"Try me."

"I don't feel like talking about it right now."

"Well, maybe you'll feel like talking about it tomorrow."

"Maybe not."

"Well, I'd like to see some photos of Eddie." Regan decided to ignore Dolly's remarks. She'd made her point. "I realized this morning I've never seen a picture of him, except the one in the newspaper, and that wasn't very good. Eighth-grade graduation or something, right?"

"Something like that."

"I'm sure you and Carl have pictures of him. I'd like to come and see, if you'll show me."

"I'll have to think about it and call you back in the morning."

"Well, you're going to have to call me on my cell

phone, because by then I'll be on my way to Chicago."

"You ever take no for an answer?"

"Not that I can recall."

"You know where to find me when you get here." Dolly hung up.

Regan danced around the kitchen while she speed-dialed Mitch. Disappointed to have to leave voice mail, she ran up the steps to the second floor to pack. She hoped Nina wouldn't object to her leaving for the weekend, but she was excited over the prospect of seeing what Eddie Kroll really looked like.

"Thanks for inviting me to tag along," Nina said as she got into the front seat of Wes's car. "I haven't seen Mrs. Owens since I left Stone River. I hope she remembers me."

"So do I." Wes nodded. "Otherwise, I won't stand a chance of talking to her. She wouldn't give me the time of day when I called. I thought maybe if I showed up with you, she might reconsider."

"Well, we'll soon find out. Porter Street is only two blocks off campus." Nina pointed to the stop sign up ahead. "You want to go left here."

"I called Mitch this morning. He told me to express mail the samples we collected yesterday. He's going to try to rush them through the lab."

"I heard." She turned to look at him. "He drove

Regan to the airport this morning. She's going back to Chicago."

"She's investigating someone for a book?"

"I think it'll turn out to be a book. Right now she's just curious about this guy Eddie Kroll." Nina filled Wes in on the parts he hadn't heard.

"It might turn out to be nothing at all," Wes noted.

"Or it could be something really good. Regan has good instincts when it comes to subject matter. She'll know if it will work." Nina looked out the window.

"When is she coming back?"

"She wasn't sure. She thought maybe Sunday or Monday."

"Maybe we could have dinner again tonight. I enjoyed being with you the other night." He stared straight ahead, as if afraid of what he'd see if he looked at her.

"What a coincidence." She turned back to him. "I'd love to go to dinner tonight."

"Great." He nodded. "Let's see what time we finish up with Mrs. Owens. Maybe we'll go right from there."

"I'd probably like to change for dinner." She looked down at her khakis and button-down shirt.

"You look pretty good to me," he told her.

"Thanks, but I'd really like to go home and change if we're going out. We should have time."

"We would have had more time if I hadn't had so damned many reports to turn in this morning. The chief has a bug up his butt, wanted a copy of every report and every interview on the Mulroney case."

"How many interviews?"

"Twenty-seven."

"That's a lot of typing."

"You're telling me. Fortunately, I didn't have to type them all this morning. I've been doing them as I go along, so all I had to do was finish up the reports from yesterday."

"You keep a daily log?"

"Yes. It's easier to keep track of what's gone on, and it's a lot easier and faster to type up a couple of reports at the end of the day than it is to type up a couple dozen at the end of the case."

"The Owens house is the white one with the blue shutters on your side of the street," Nina told him.

He parked across the street and turned off the ignition.

"Ready?"

"Sure." She opened the passenger door and got out. She walked around to the front of the car and waited while a trash truck rolled past, then crossed the street with Wes.

From the end of her driveway, they could see Mrs. Owens raking the leaves in her backyard. Halfway up the drive, Nina called to her, rather than startle the woman, who was in her early seventies. She wore tan slacks and a gray cardigan sweater that was at least four sizes too big for her.

"Mrs. Owens?"

The woman turned and squinted. "Who is there?"

"Nina Madden, Mrs. Owens."

"Nina . . . oh, for heaven's sakes." Mrs. Owens leaned her rake against the side of the house and walked toward her visitors. "Well, haven't you grown up nicely? I never would have recognized you."

The woman stopped ten feet from them and studied Nina, then said, "Well, maybe I might have known you. You've grown up, but now that I'm a little closer, I can see that you haven't changed all that much. You look wonderful, dear."

"So do you, Mrs. Owens. You haven't changed at all."

"Now, aren't you a smooth thing," she replied with a laugh. "But I appreciate the thought. And who's this here with you?"

"This is Detective Powell, from the Stone River Police Department," Nina told her. "He's looking into a murder case at the college, and had some questions about my father's case."

Mrs. Owens's face changed slightly as she appeared to evaluate Wes. "You the one who called me earlier today?"

"Yes, ma'am, I am."

"Why'd you drag Nina along?"

"Because I figured you wouldn't talk to me otherwise."

"Well, that's probably true enough. I really don't have much to say about any of that."

"Any of what?"

"Any of what goes on around the college. I can't see where you need to talk to me, anyway. I haven't worked at St. Ansel's since . . . well, in about fifteen years or so."

"Why'd you leave?" Nina asked.

"It was time to retire." Mrs. Owens grabbed the rake and started on the lawn again.

"Mrs. Owens, you loved that school. You loved working there," Nina said.

"I did, at one time. It just seemed that after . . . " She looked at Nina apologetically. "After your father was arrested, and there was that trial and everything, things changed. It just wasn't the same anymore. That was such a terrible time for everyone. The school. The kids. The whole faculty. And of course, it must have been horrible for you."

Nina nodded.

"I will never forget that day they came and arrested your father, took him right out of his office. I was at my desk, right there in that small office between Dr. Madden's and Dr. Overbeck's, and all of a sudden that small space was filled, wall to wall, with police officers. They all had their hands on their guns, the holsters unsnapped so you could see what they had there. As if they were going into some den of thieves instead of an academic environment." She shook her head. "Dr. Madden had his faults, but he wasn't a violent man."

"And yet he was convicted of four murders," Wes reminded her.

"Yes, well, I have my own theory on that," she told him.

"I'd like to hear it."

"I just don't think he was guilty, that's all. Dr. Madden was no saint—good Lord, the things that came out about him and those young girls at the trial! But he wasn't the only sinner in the department, and that's all I have to say about that."

"I have the feeling there's plenty more you could say." Wes took off his sunglasses and put them in his jacket pocket. "And we've got all day."

"We might as well sit over there at the picnic table, then." Mrs. Owens led the way. "The arthritis in my knee is acting up today."

"So who were the other sinners in the department, besides Dr. Madden? Oh, and Dr. Overbeck, of course," Wes said as they took seats on the benches that were attached to the old wooden table.

"Oh, that one." Mrs. Owens waved her hand as if to dismiss him.

"You left the college right around the time he became head of the department, didn't you?" Nina asked.

Mrs. Owens nodded.

"Any particular reason?" Wes rested his arms on the table.

"I just wasn't going to work for that man. He just annoyed me so bad." She shook her head. "Always acted so pious and righteous, and all the while he was . . . " She stopped in midsentence.

"It's okay, Mrs. Owens. I know he was having an affair with my stepmother," Nina told her.

"Well, that man just couldn't get enough of what your father had. If Dr. Madden had it, Dr. Overbeck wanted it. That's how I saw it."

"That's an interesting observation, Mrs. Owens. Can you be more specific?"

"I think I've been specific enough. If Dr. Madden taught the class on Poe, Overbeck had to teach it the following year. Dr. Madden set up a discussion group on Thoreau, Overbeck had to take it over after Madden left."

She turned to Nina. "Your father was a fine teacher. He was well respected by his peers. Some of the younger faculty members used to attend his lectures; were you aware of that?"

Nina shook her head, unable to speak suddenly as an unexpected lump formed in her throat.

"He was widely published—the most published member of the faculty—and was in demand as a guest instructor at foreign colleges and universities. The offers started coming in by November every year for him to teach the following summer. And his students loved him." She added drily, "Some apparently more than others."

"I remember that he did go away every summer," Nina said.

"Just a week or two before he was arrested, he'd received requests to lecture at two very well known English universities." Mrs. Owens's smile turned sly. "It drove Dr. Overbeck crazy."

"What do you mean?" Wes asked.

"He'd been applying at one of those schools for years and he'd been passed over every time. And here his rival is being courted by the same dean who'd been turning him down. He was furious."

"Really." Wes exchanged a long look with Nina. "And you're sure this was just a few weeks before Dr. Madden was arrested."

"Positive. I remember because the dean from England who'd made the offer to Dr. Madden called when he hadn't heard back, and it was left to me to explain that Dr. Madden wouldn't be guest lecturing anywhere that year."

"So you'd say that there was no love lost between the two."

"None at all, Detective. Though I would say it was more on Dr. Overbeck's part than on Dr. Madden's. He seemed more amused by it than anything else."

"How many years did you work in the English department, Mrs. Owens?" Wes asked.

"Oh, eight or nine. Father Candelori hired me, and I stayed on until he retired." She pulled the oversize cardigan closed in the front as a cool breeze blew through the yard. The fingers of her left hand worried the buttons, and the fingers of her right traced the pattern of the ribbing that edged the sleeves. "My husband died right after Father Candelori left, and I would have stayed on if Dr. Madden had been here. But I wasn't about to work for Dr. Overbeck."

"I heard somewhere that Dr. Madden was Father Candelori's first choice to take over the department," Wes recalled.

Mrs. Owens nodded. "He was. That's another thing that drove Overbeck nuts. He tried everything he could think of to curry favor with Father Candelori, but Father wouldn't have none of it. He actually stayed for another year after Dr. Madden left, because he didn't want to turn over the department to Dr. Overbeck. But finally, he'd gotten so sick, he couldn't go on anymore."

"Why didn't they give the position to someone else, if everyone disliked Dr. Overbeck so much?" Nina asked.

"Because he had tenure, and he had seniority, after Dr. Madden. And them being about the same age, there was no way he—Dr. Overbeck—was ever going to get that job once Dr. Madden took over. He wasn't going anywhere, he'd made that plain enough. He liked St. Ansel's, always said he'd retire here."

"So just another reason for Overbeck to resent Madden," Wes observed. "Sounds like a lot of professional jealousy."

"On Dr. Overbeck's part, certainly. As I said, the whole thing seemed to amuse Dr. Madden."

"Mrs. Owens, earlier you referred to Dr. Madden as Dr. Overbeck's rival."

"I don't know what else you'd call it, Detective. Like I said before, if Dr. Madden had it, Dr. Overbeck wanted it. Pure and simple. Just like a child."

"I think you said you were aware that Dr. Overbeck was having an affair with Dr. Madden's wife. How did you know?"

"She'd come in, supposedly to see her husband when she had to know he'd be in class, then go behind closed doors with Overbeck. I'm not stupid."

"How often did that happen?"

"At least once a week."

"Before or after the killings on campus started, do you remember?"

"Before." She nodded. "Definitely before. And it continued on for a while, too. They were still seeing each other right up until the time Dr. Madden died, and for a time after."

"You said something earlier that gave me the impression that you were unaware of Dr. Madden's involvements with several of his students."

"Never suspected a thing." She shook her head adamantly. "I never would have stood for that. Disgusting, to take advantage of those girls like that. It was a big shock to all of us there when that news came out, I can tell you that. No one I knew had an inkling. He was discreet, I'll give him that much."

"One other thing. Did Dr. Madden leave his office unlocked?"

"He never locked that door. He'd have students coming and going all the time."

"Did you ever see Dr. Overbeck going in or coming out of Madden's office?"

"Every chance he got, if he thought I wasn't looking." She nodded.

"Thank you so much for speaking with us frankly, Mrs. Owens." Wes rose. "We won't take any more of your time."

"Time is one thing I have a lot of these days."

"It was good to see you again, Mrs. Owens." Nina hugged the woman. "Thank you for . . . for reminding me that my father did have his good points."

"Your father was a good man in many respects. But he had one serious flaw, and it was his downfall."

Mrs. Owens walked with them to the end of the drive, and stood there until they drove away.

"She certainly had a lot to say," Wes said when they reached the stop sign at the end of the street. "And none of it flattering, as far as Overbeck is concerned. I'm liking him more and more. Motivewise, he's got it over everyone else."

"So my stepbrother is no longer at the top of your list?"

"He's still right up there."

"She misses her husband so much," Nina said. "Did you see the way she kept touching the sweater? I'll bet it was his."

"I didn't notice," he admitted.

"They were married when they were eighteen, she told me once. She said they'd gone all through school together, from third grade on, and they'd always known they'd be together," she told him. "I always thought that was the most romantic story I ever heard. Coming from a broken home, it seemed like fiction to me. Like an unattainable ideal."

"Not completely. My parents are still married after almost fifty years. And they're still talking to each other."

"They're lucky." She turned to him. "You're lucky that you have that experience in your background. You understand relationships that work."

"Excuse me, you're talking to a man whose marriage lasted exactly twenty-two months. And most of them weren't particularly happy ones."

"But you've seen close up what it's like when it works."

"Which is how I knew it wasn't working for me."

They rode in silence for a few minutes, then he asked, "Were you ever married?"

"No."

"Ever come close?"

"No. Not really. Once or twice I thought maybe . . . but no."

"Still looking for Mr. Right?"

"As opposed to Mr. Right Now, as they say?"

"What's wrong with right now?"

"It smacks of settling for something less." She stared out the window. "I'm afraid I'm not very good at settling."

His cell rang.

"Powell."

He listened without comment for several long minutes, then said, "It's going to take me about an hour. Secure the scene and I'll get there as soon as I can."

He hung up and dropped the phone into the empty cup holder.

"Earlier this morning, a student taking a shortcut from the parking lot behind the maintenance building at St. Ansel's stumbled—literally—over a body that was left near the Dumpster."

"Oh, my God . . . "

"Yeah." His eyes were on the road and he hit the accelerator. "Dinner might be a little late tonight . . . "

Twenty-three

Nina stood on the deck off Regan's kitchen, snipping the dead blooms off the few hardy geraniums that managed to survive this far into the fall. The first real frost would do them in, but for now, all-day sun and regular watering would keep them going. She'd just finished watering all the big pots, and had to remind herself to avoid the overflow from the pots she'd overfilled.

It was almost dark, and the light-sensitive lamps on the posts around the deck would be coming on automatically any time now. She was dressed for dinner, in heels and a short skirt topped with a light jacket, and was hoping Wes wouldn't be too much longer. She'd been disappointed when their Friday-night dinner plans had to be postponed, but was happy to be seeing him tonight instead. He'd called late on Friday afternoon, all apologies, but he just wasn't going to make it. She'd understood, certainly. A young woman was dead. That took precedence over a dinner date any day.

"Thanks for not making me jump through hoops," he'd told her.

"Why would I do that?"

"Most women don't like it when you break a date because of work."

"This isn't like normal overtime."

"You're telling me. Thanks for being so understanding."

He'd called two hours ago to tell her that he'd be a few minutes later than he'd hoped, but he'd be there.

"And I do have some news you might be interested in."

"What's that?"

"A package was delivered from the FBI this morning, but I wasn't here to pick it up. When I came in this afternoon, it was on my desk." He cleared his throat. "Mitch was able to uncover eight more murders over the past sixteen years in the Delaware-Pennsylvania area. All young women, all stabbed. Raped. The bodies all posed the same way."

"Eight . . . " she whispered.

"There could be more. He's still looking. And I also had a message from the Maryland State Police, on my inquiry regarding Kyle. I tried calling back the trooper who called, but he'd left for the day. I probably won't get him until Monday."

"You must be exhausted. Are you sure you want to drive down here? Why don't you let me drive up to meet you halfway?"

"I appreciate it, but I've already made reservations at the Clam House. I've been looking forward to some tasty seafood and listening to a great jazz band in the company of a pretty woman. I could really use a little R and R right about now."

"If you're sure . . . "

"I'm positive."

"Wes, do you think this murder is connected to the others?"

"Right now, it's tough to tell. Allison Mulroney was found in her apartment, and as you know, the similarities were striking to the earlier four cases. Could that have been the work of a copycat? Sure. But this girl yesterday—Lanie Jacobs—lived in a dorm on the opposite side of the campus, not an apartment as the others all had, and she wasn't posed at all."

"So you think this is a different killer?"

"I honestly don't know. There's nothing to tie it to the others, but it feels like there should be. This crime scene is totally different from the others. The only things these girls have in common is that they were both students at St. Ansel's and they were both stabbed."

"But as you just said, last week's case fit right in with the others. What are the chances there are two killers in Stone River?"

"It's hard to believe there could be, and I'm a bit baffled, frankly. I was hoping there'd be something at the scene we could use to tie this to someone, but so far we haven't found a thing, except for one footprint leading away from the body. Our crime scene people are still working on that; they think they'll be able to match the size and make real soon. But there was trash around and in the Dumpster, so all that has to be sorted through."

"Are you still thinking that Dr. Overbeck is involved?"

"Maybe, if we're talking about the Mulroney case, but not Jacobs. I did try to talk to the chief about putting both Overbeck and your stepbrother under surveillance, but he hit the ceiling. As far as he's concerned, that case was then and this case is now. I even tried to talk to someone in the DA's office, but he all but laughed in my face. No one wants to make that connection. Especially with this new one being so different."

After the call, Nina'd hung up the phone and showered and dressed, and was now finding ways to pass the time until he got there. She figured deadheading the flowers in the pots on Regan's deck could take a while.

The lights from a car appeared at the end of the drive as she snipped the last of the seed heads from the coleus. The car had already stopped and the driver had gotten out when she realized it wasn't Wes.

Instinct caused her to hide the small garden snips in the pocket of her jacket.

"Kyle." She watched him climb the steps to the deck.

"Surprise, Nina." He looked her over. "You look lovely. Are you on your way out?"

"Yes, I am. Actually, I thought you were my date."

"Well, I probably should have called first."

He looked around the parking area and nodded in the direction of the Land Rover. "Oh, good. I see Regan Landry's car is here. I'll finally get to meet her. I was such a fan of her father's."

He looked back at Nina and said, "That is her car, isn't it? The white one, the one she lets you drive?"

"Yes."

"Good." He held out a package. "I really just stopped in to bring you some things."

"What's in here?"

"The photographs I told you about, pictures of your dad's family. And a few pieces of Mom's jewelry. Some things I thought she'd want you to have."

"Thank you, Kyle," Nina replied, feeling just a little confused. "But don't you think your mother's things should go to Marcy?"

"Marcy has taken the kids and gone to New Jersey to live with her mother." His eyes darkened. "I don't think Mom would approve of any of her things going to Marcy."

"I take it there's no chance of reconciliation?"

"Not in this lifetime." He forced a smile. "So. Do I get to meet your friend?"

"Ah, well, Regan isn't here right now."

"So, are we all alone here, Nina?"

A chill went up her spine.

When she didn't answer, he nodded. "Apparently so."

He reached down and broke a stem off one of the geraniums.

"Nina, Nina, Nina. Why'd you do it?" he asked softly.

"Why'd I do what?"

"Why'd you take the cigarette from the ashtray?" His eyes had gone dark again. "Who'd you give it to? Powell? Hoping to find a little DNA that might match something?"

He snapped the geranium's stem and let it fall to the deck. "Stupid, stupid, stupid . . . "

She took a step backward, her hand in her pocket gripping the shears.

"Why did you do that, Nina?" His voice dropped, and he appeared to be close to tears. "I did not want to hurt you. I told Mother, I won't hurt Nina." His bottom lip was trembling. "You're the little sister. I'm supposed to protect you. Big brothers protect the little sisters. I told her that."

"When did you tell her that, Kyle?" *Keep him talking until Wes gets here,* she told herself. *Make him keep talking.*

He seemed not to hear her.

"Your detective friend can test and test away at

that old DNA, but he'll never match it to me." His demeanor changed. "You think I killed those girls, but nope. Wasn't me. Not that I didn't want to. I told her I wanted to, but she wouldn't let me."

"Did Olivia kill them? Was my father right about that?"

"Your father." His laughter was derisive and brittle. "I told Mom, let me take care of him for you, he's hurt you so much. I wanted to kill him. But she said no, that he needed to suffer. She wanted him to suffer. She wanted him destroyed."

"So she wanted his girlfriends to die."

"That was my idea. I said, fine, you won't let me kill Stephen, let me take away his little toys. Maybe if all his little girlies die, maybe he'll stop. Maybe he'll come back to you." He shook his head. "But she wouldn't let me do it. She said it was too dangerous for me. She was afraid I might be caught and go to prison. She wanted prison for Stephen."

"Did she do it herself, then?" *Dear God,* Nina thought. *Did I not know this woman at all? Did I not know either of them?*

"Of course not. There was someone else."

"Dr. Overbeck," Nina said flatly.

"He'd have done anything for her, anything to keep her happy."

"He told me he'd been in love with her."

"Maybe. Actually, I thought he'd hated Stephen as much as he loved her. Maybe more." Kyle shrugged.

"Doesn't really matter, though, the end result was still the same."

"Why didn't she just divorce my father if she was so unhappy, Kyle?"

"Where's the fun in that?" He laughed again. "Of course, Overbeck had all the fun. And who knew he'd enjoy it so much? I don't think him having sex with those girls was part of Mom's plan, and I can tell you, she didn't like that one bit. But what was she going to do? She'd created a Frankenstein monster, and couldn't control it."

"So what now, Kyle?" she asked softly.

"Now, we take a boat ride." He nodded in the direction of the bay. "I see your friend has a real nice-looking boat out there. What kind of boat is that?"

"I have no idea."

"Well, it doesn't matter. I'll bet it's nicely equipped, and it looks big enough for a sea cruise. What do you think, Nina? Shall we take her for a spin? I'm wondering if maybe we can't go right on up the bay and through that canal up near Chestertown, right on out to the ocean. Wouldn't that be fun?" he smirked.

She couldn't bring herself to respond. He knew she'd always hated deep water.

"So, Nina—you ever learn how to swim?"

Her answer froze in her throat.

"Well, let's go see." He took a small handgun from his pocket and waved it in the direction of the dock. "After you."

"Kyle . . . " She tried to think of something to say, but her mind felt frozen.

"Too late to play the helpless little sister card. I can't protect you now. You should have protected me the way I protected you."

"Kyle, look, you haven't done anything." Her mind began to race. "You didn't kill anyone, you didn't hurt anyone. They can't arrest you for what you haven't done . . . "

She glanced down at the deck, and noticed the pale red stains on the wood, the footprints he'd made after he'd walked through the water that had spilled out of the pots.

He followed her gaze.

"What can I say? It was my turn." He smiled. "Why should Overbeck have all the fun?"

"You killed those two girls. Allison Mulroney and Lanie Jacobs."

"Was that her name? Lanie Jacobs? I didn't know."

He waved the gun again.

"Let's go, Nina."

It's going to be okay, she tried to reassure herself, thinking calm and rational was preferable to panic under the circumstances. *This is where the hero is supposed to show up and save the day. Wes is going to pull up any minute now.*

And if he doesn't?

Her fingers clutched the garden snips. They weren't very sharp, and they weren't very big, but they were all she had. She'd have to pick her moment, though. She was definitely outmanned when it came to weapons.

She walked ahead of him along the path through the marsh toward the dock, then down the long wooden walk to the very end where the boat was tied, all the while trying to will away the image that popped into her mind of a pirate walking the plank.

She paused at the end of the dock. The boat had drifted to the end of its rope, too far from the dock for her to board, so Kyle grabbed a line and pulled it toward them, keeping one hand on her arm. She racked her brain for something to say, something that would distract him, but she couldn't work through the fog of fear.

"Come on, step up," he instructed her.

She did, and the boat rocked slightly under her feet. She spaced them apart so she could get her balance. He held the gun to her back and directed her toward the cabin.

"I don't suppose you know where she keeps the key for this thing," he said.

"Sorry, but no."

"You're not sorry. You're not sorry at all." He started looking around the cabin, over and under everything that moved, his frustration growing. "But you will be . . . "

* * *

On the way out of Stone River, Wes tried Nina's cell phone three times and Regan's house phone twice. *She's probably in the shower,* he told himself after the first attempt.

If she took a shower, she might have the hair dryer on now, he rationalized after the second. Not knowing how long it took to dry her hair, he gave her ten minutes before trying a third time. When there was still no answer, he pulled over to the side of the road and looked through his wallet for Regan's number. When he found it, he dialed and pulled back into traffic while listening to it ring and ring. He might have dialed wrong, he told himself. He pulled over and checked the number again. Maybe that one was really a seven. He redialed, but still there was no answer.

I'll bet Nina's outside, he reasoned. *Maybe she's even outside waiting for me.* He increased his speed and glanced at the clock on the dashboard. He could make it in ten minutes, and he'd actually be on time. He'd told her he'd be there around seven-thirty. It was now sixteen after.

He tried not to think about the body they'd found yesterday, and the family he'd spoken with last night. It had tied him in knots, facing Lanie Jacobs's mother and father in the station last night. Because they lived in Newark, Delaware, the chief had made the call. When they arrived a few hours later, Wes was just leaving for the night. But he'd passed them in the lobby, and known them by their grief even before they identified themselves to the desk sergeant. In spite of his fatigue, he couldn't walk by and out of the building, knowing what they were going to be facing over the next several hours. So he turned around, and went back in, and talked with them.

There'd been no consolation for the grieving parents, but he'd stayed with them and offered what support he could. When it was time for them to identify their daughter, he drove them to the medical examiner's office, and stayed with them through what surely had been the worst night of their lives.

Wes tried not to think about the butchered young body that had been waiting on that cold steel table.

He'd promised the parents he'd find the man who'd taken their daughter, but it was a promise he'd made before. And that time—the last time he'd been so bold—he'd arrested and helped to convict an innocent man.

Of course, as far as the rest of the world was concerned, Stephen Madden had been rightfully convicted. It had been the greatest shock of his life to discover how wrong they'd all been. And he'd still have to prove that to the chief, who wasn't willing to hear a damned thing where the possibility of Madden's innocence was concerned. Well, it was a talk they'd have to have first thing Monday morning.

He turned into Regan's drive, and wondered why Nina hadn't turned on the lights that illuminated the parking area. He parked next to an unfamiliar Buick, and walked across the darkened deck to the house, which was also dark.

An uneasy feeling spread through him. He went inside, and called Nina's name.

Silence.

He took the steps to the second floor two at a time.

"Nina? Are you up here?"

Nothing.

He raced back downstairs, and noted the handbag on the kitchen counter. It was one he hadn't seen before, so he searched through it for the wallet to look for identification. He found a New York driver's license in the name of Nina Madden.

Where the hell was she?

He went out the back door, calling, then around the front, but there was no answer.

Wes went back to take a closer look at the other car that was in the driveway. A 1987 Buick. He walked around it. The car was in mint condition for a vehicle its age. He took out his cell phone and called into the station.

"Tony, give me a rundown on this license plate, would you? I don't mind waiting . . . "

He read off the plate number, then waited while the dispatcher ran it through the computer.

"Got it, Detective." The dispatcher returned in minutes. "The car is registered to an Olivia S. Madden, Stone River."

"Thanks."

I should have seen that one coming, Wes told himself. *But where has he taken her?*

Wes stood in the driveway, acclimating himself to the sounds of the bay at night. There was not so much as a whisper from the direction of the house, but there, from the water, was the faintest . . . something.

He walked down the path through the tall reeds to the bay, his gun drawn, following the hushed lapping of water on wood. Twenty feet out from the end of the dock, a boat drifted on the water. There were lights on in the cabin and across the side and back of the boat, but the motor was off and the boat bobbed up and down ever so slightly with the tide.

On the deck stood Nina, Kyle directly behind her. Her posture was ramrod straight, her head tilted slightly back. Wes stared for several seconds before it dawned on him what was going on. Nina's arms were behind her back, and if Wes wasn't mistaken, Kyle was in the process of tying her hands together at the wrists.

Dear God, Wes realized, *he's going to toss her overboard.*

Twenty-four

"I suggest you step out of those shoes," Kyle said as he tugged Nina's arms behind her back. He added sarcastically, "Unless you think you can tread water better in high heels."

I'm not going in that water, Nina told herself firmly, her old terror of drowning rising up and threatening to make her faint. *I do something now, or I die.*

She felt herself begin to shake, and sweat trickled down between her shoulder blades. She willed the shaking to stop. This was no time to be weak. She had less than a minute to come up with something. The hero was not going to arrive to save the day. She was going to have to save herself.

Focus, she demanded. *Focus . . .*

Okay, he has a gun, I have garden snips. He has a rope, he's about to tie my wrists together, and I have high heels . . .

It occurred to her then that in order to tie her up, he'd have had to put the gun down.

She turned her head slightly to the right, and saw

the small handgun on the table. Instinctively, she turned her body to the left, feigning a loss of balance.

"Take the shoes off, Nina. You don't need to look hot where you're going."

She could feel him begin to tie the first knot.

Another feigned wobble to the left. Another step farther from the table, another step between him and his weapon.

"Damn it, hold still," he growled.

The knot tightened.

Now or not at all. Now or never . . .

She leaned forward momentarily, then thrust herself backward, head first, with all of her strength, smacking him square in the middle of his face with the back of her head.

"Ow! What the fuck . . . !" Kyle stumbled backward, then lunged for the table.

Twisting her wrists to slip off the untied rope, she slipped her hand into her pocket and pulled out the scissors. They weren't much, but she attacked with a fury, and went straight for the only place she knew was totally vulnerable.

She went for his eyes.

Wes had stripped off his shoes and his jacket and, with great reluctance, his gun. A water-logged handgun would be of no use. He dove off the dock and tried to ignore the chilly shock as he began to swim for the boat. The Chesapeake in November was choppy and cold and dark, but the sight of Nina about to be tied up and tossed into it had left him no choice. As he swam, he planned his game. If she was in the water by the time he reached the boat, he'd untie her, and get her to one of the ropes dangling from the side of the boat where she'd just have to hang on while he pulled himself on board and took care of Kyle. Exactly how he was going to manage to get onto the boat unseen, or what he was going to do once he got there, well, he was going to have to play that by ear. The important thing was to keep Nina from drowning.

The night was split by an ungodly scream.

Jesus God, Wes prayed, *what is he doing to her?*

He increased his speed, the screams echoing in his ears. When he reached the boat, he pulled himself up onto the narrow diving platform that ran across the back and lifted himself onto the deck.

Nina stood in the doorway to the cabin, wearing a short tight skirt and high heels, a gun in her right hand, and the microphone for the boat's radio in the other. On the deck, Kyle Stillman sobbed and writhed, blood pouring from between his hands, which were held to his face.

"What took you so long?" she said without turning around.

Without waiting for a response, she pointed to the radio. "You know how to use one of these? I'm trying to call the Coast Guard . . . "

"What the hell is going on here?" Regan cried when she got out of Mitch's car and saw the police cars and ambulances in her driveway.

"Regan?" Nina called to her from the deck chair where she was wrapped in Wes's jacket. "I thought you weren't coming back until tomorrow."

"Dolly ran out of things to say," Regan told her as she ran onto the deck. "Honey, what happened here?"

"Kyle decided to take her for a boat ride," Wes told Regan and Mitch. "She didn't want to go."

Regan's jaw all but dropped as she watched the paramedics load the stretcher holding Kyle onto the ambulance.

"What happened?" Regan repeated. "What happened to him? Wes . . . ?"

"Wasn't me." He nodded toward Nina. "She took care of him all by herself."

"Honey, what did you do?" Regan knelt in front of Nina's chair.

"He was going to throw me into the bay," she said solemnly, tears welling in her eyes. "I'm afraid of the water. I couldn't let him throw me in . . . "

"Okay, honey, let's take you inside where it's warm. You are positively shivering," Regan noted.

"Come on, Nina." Wes reached out to her. "Let me give you a hand."

He helped her out of the chair and pulled the jacket closed around her.

"And then I think someone had better fill me in on what went on here tonight," Regan said.

Wes did so as they went into the house.

"So your father was right," Regan said as she brought a tray holding four mugs and a pot of steaming tea into the sitting room. "Olivia was behind the whole thing."

"You know, when I first read his letter, I assumed he was accusing Olivia of having committed the murders herself," Nina said from the sofa where she was curled up in a cozy afghan. "Which of course made no sense if in fact the girls had been raped. And in the absence of DNA reports, it was something I felt we had to question, if for no other reason than to get the police to take another look at the file."

"I have to tell you the truth, I wasn't willing to do that," Wes told her. "And frankly, if you'd come in alone, without Regan, I probably wouldn't have given you the time of day."

"I never liked to play off my father's name," Regan admitted, "but I must say, it came in handy this time."

"Do you think your father realized exactly what Olivia had done?" Mitch asked Nina.

"I don't know if he'd understood just how treacherous this woman was," Nina replied. "God knows, I never did. I always thought she was cool, removed.

But then, talking to Kyle, I was starting to think that maybe I'd misjudged her all along. I'd never felt there was any love lost between us. But then Kyle was saying things like, my mother wanted you to be the daughter she never had, things like that, and I thought maybe I'd just been too wrapped up in myself to see how she really was."

"Well, that much is true. Apparently no one saw her for what she really was," Regan said.

"Except for her son, and he didn't seem to mind," Nina reminded her. "He really had me fooled. I still can't believe he killed those two girls this past week."

Her voice dropped. "And he was going to kill me. He knew I'd always been afraid of drowning. He was going to do that to me."

"And then there's Dr. Overbeck. She certainly had him wrapped around her little finger," Regan reminded them. "I can't believe he got away with murder for all those years."

"I can see looking to lay a dozen at his feet. Four in Stone River, eight more at the very least in other states," Mitch commented. "I hope you don't mind, buddy, but I'm going to have to take that one from here. I know I said I didn't want the case, but we've got multiple jurisdictions, and it looks as if at least one of the victims was taken across state lines. That brings it into the Bureau. I'll try not to step on your toes."

"He's all yours, as far as I'm concerned. The chief

isn't going to want to cough up the case, but in light of the fact that he was the lead detective at the time Stephen Madden was arrested, I think it should be in someone else's hands, to be honest. I want this thing done clean. I don't want to see it stalled anywhere along the way because Chief Raymond is in a snit." Wes added, "You need anything from me, you just say the word."

"I appreciate that," Mitch told him.

"How do you think Father Whelan is going to feel when he realizes what Olivia did?" Nina was hunkered down with her head on a pillow, her eyes at half-staff.

"I think Father Whelan knows exactly what Olivia did," Wes told them.

"You think Olivia confessed to him?" Nina asked.

Wes nodded. "I knew the entire time I was speaking with him that he was holding back something important. He all but admitted it to me when he said anything told to him in confession could never be revealed."

"Well, that would have just about killed him, if she'd told him what she'd done," Nina said. "All those years, he'd been very close to her, he'd been her friend. I'll bet he was as shocked as I was to find out what she really was, and how she'd manipulated everyone around her."

"Including him. By telling him in confession, he'd never be able to tell anyone," Wes reminded her.

"If she'd told him about Dr. Overbeck being the killer, it must have driven Father Whelan near crazy to see that man walking around the campus every day," Nina said sleepily. "Knowing Overbeck had gotten away with murder, knowing my father had been convicted of Overbeck's crimes . . ."

"And knowing there wasn't a damned thing he could do about it." Mitch said what the others were thinking.

Wes sat in thoughtful silence for a while, then patted Nina on the leg softly.

"Father Whelan says the seven o'clock mass at St. Benedict's on Sunday. Think you'll be up for an early ride into Stone River?"

Nina, out cold, never heard a word.

He tucked the blanket around her, and let her sleep. She'd more than earned it.

Twenty-five

"Father Whelan," Wes called to the priest who, having chatted with the last of that morning's worshipers, was crossing the lawn next to St. Benedict's Church on his way to his car.

The priest turned at the sound of his name.

"Good morning, Detective . . . Powell, was it? And Nina," he greeted them. "Good to see you both here."

"I was hoping to catch you before you saw it on the news," Wes said.

"Before I saw what on the news?"

"Kyle Stillman was arrested last night for the murders of Allison Mulroney and Lanie Jacobs," Wes told him.

"Kyle!" The priest appeared genuinely shocked.

"Were you expecting it to be someone else, Father?" Wes asked.

"I'm just . . . I'm just very surprised to hear this."

"Well, Kyle was just full of surprises last night," Nina said. "He told me about how his mother had convinced Dr. Overbeck to murder the girls my father'd been involved with. How she'd planned to have my father blamed. How she'd stood by and watched him arrested. Tried. Convicted. Sent to prison to serve a life sentence."

"But of course, you'd already heard that story, hadn't you, Father Whelan?"

Father Whelan's sigh seemed to come from his soul.

"I've already figured out that Olivia had confessed her involvement in the murders, and her scheme to have Stephen sent to prison for them. But as her priest—as her confessor—you were bound to silence. She really knew how to get the most out of her relationships, didn't she?" Wes jammed his hands in his jacket pockets. "She got Overbeck to kill for her, to punish her cheating husband—who once he figured out what she'd done, offered to take the blame for her—and then she got you to absolve her of her sins. What a woman."

"You cannot imagine the despair I felt when I realized what she'd done. The extent of her treachery astounded me." Father Whelan's face was etched with sadness. "And I was helpless to do anything about it. All those years, I'd believed, as had everyone else, that Stephen Madden had killed those girls. And, as far as absolution is concerned, I'd like to believe Olivia's confession was sincere, that she was truly contrite. But that's between her and God."

He appeared at a momentary loss for words. Finally, he said simply, "The truth has been a terrible burden on my soul, and on my heart, for the past several weeks."

"So I know you must be happy to have that burden lifted," Wes noted.

"I'm happy, yes, delighted, that the truth has finally been discovered." Father Whelan took Nina's hands in his. "You must be so relieved to have your father's name cleared, after all these years. It's truly a miracle."

"A miracle of your making, Father." She smiled up at him.

"Me?" His eyes darted from Nina to Wes and back again.

"If you hadn't remembered to give that letter to Nina—the one Stephen had sent to Olivia—no one would have ever thought to take another look at that case. Olivia's scheme would never have come to light. The real killer would never have been identified. And Stephen Madden would always have been known as the Stone River Rapist."

"Well, it was certainly a lucky break, wasn't it," Father Whelan said.

"Was it now?" Wes smiled. "I think there was more at play than a little luck."

Father Whelan looked away.

"I'll tell you what I think, Father." Wes lowered his voice as the altar boys raced around them to the parking lot. They called to the priest, and he waved to them absently before turning back to Wes.

"I think you planned all along for the truth to come out. I think once you realized what Olivia had done, your sense of justice tormented you. I think Olivia never looked in that box the prison sent her after Stephen died, so she'd never seen the letter, much less read it. If she'd read it, surely she'd have destroyed it."

"But you read it, Father," Nina said softly. "And once you did, you had to make sure it got into the hands of the one person you knew would do something about it. And that would be me."

"I really didn't know what else to do, Nina," the priest said wearily. "I knew what had happened, yes. Right before she died, Olivia told me everything. She asked for absolution for her sins, and as her priest, I had to assume she was contrite. But the knowledge of what she'd done, the injustice of it all, ate at me every day. I couldn't tell, and at the same time, I couldn't live with the secret."

"Why didn't you bring the letter to me, Father?" Wes asked.

"And what would you have done with it, Detective?" Father Whelan replied. "I was afraid it would have been disregarded. You'd investigated the case once, you'd had your trial and gotten your conviction. Why would you have wanted to revisit the case, especially on the basis of a letter from a dead man—a dead man who'd already been convicted of the crime. Tell me, Detective, what would you have done if I'd brought the letter to you?"

Wes thought it over, then said, "I'd like to say I'd have looked into it, but honestly, I'd have tossed it in my desk drawer or the trash."

"That's what I thought you'd do." He turned to Nina. "You were really the only hope to have the truth come out. I'm sorry I couldn't have done more to help you."

"Father, what would you have done if I hadn't read the letter?" Nina asked. "Or if I hadn't gone to the police with it once I had?"

"I suppose I would have had to go to Plan B." Father Whelan smiled weakly. "I'm not quite sure what Plan B would have been, but I'd have had to come up with something."

"I'm grateful for what you did." She shook his hand. "And I'm sure that my father is finally at peace."

"You know, ever since Olivia's confession, I've been haunted by that quote, that line about justice delayed being justice denied," Father Whelan told them as they started to walk toward the parking lot. "It's been a terrible weight on my soul."

"Then you can be at peace now, too, Father." Nina patted his arm. "In the end, justice delayed has been justice served."

Twenty-six

On their way out of the Branigan police station, where they'd spent the last four hours answering questions and signing statements, Wes took Nina by the elbow and said, "Well, maybe we'll get to have that dinner after all. I hear that the third time is supposed to be the charm."

"Actually, I'm going to have to take the train back to New York in a little while. I have to go back to work tomorrow."

He thought it over while they walked to his car.

"Do they still have dining cars on the trains?"

"Some of them do, yes."

"Well, if that's the best we can do . . . " He took her hand.

"You'd ride all the way to New York just to have dinner on the train?"

"Dinner on the train with you, yes, I would."

"Do you realize that means you'll be spending about six hours on the train? And then there's going to be waiting time in the station while you wait for a return train . . . "

"It'll be worth every minute," he told her. "Besides, if I can avoid Chief Raymond for a few more hours, I'm doubly happy. I gave him a heads-up report last night, but he's called me about six times already today. The press has been driving him crazy since Overbeck was arrested this morning. Did I mention that Mayfield said the professor cried like a girl and admitted everything?"

She laughed. "Twice."

When they got to the car, he unlocked it and opened the passenger door for her. "I'm not ready to let you go."

Nina put her arms around his neck and drew his face down to hers, and kissed him. She'd been wanting to do that all weekend long, from the minute she'd sat across the table from him at Dellarosa's and wondered if the wine would have tasted as good on his lips as it had in her glass. She wasn't disappointed.

"Actually," she said into the collar of his jacket, "I was thinking about asking if you'd like to come up to the city weekend after next."

"Not next weekend, but the one after that?"

"Right."

"I can do that. Next weekend I have Alec for Saturday and Sunday, but the following weekend I'll be free."

"Great. I have an awards thing to go to—the

Golden Leaf Awards, it's an industry thing, very big deal. They're giving a special achievement award to Regan's father, so she and Mitch will be there. It's going to be held at a very posh club and will be a very frou-frou event."

She leaned back and asked, "Do you have a tux?"

"I can get one." He smiled. "It's been a long time since I've done frou, but I can pull it off. I've been told I clean up real good."

"I'll just bet you do, Detective." She smiled. "I'll just bet you do . . . "

"Well, they had quite a weekend," Regan said as she and Mitch watched Wes's car disappear down the long drive from her house. "Who'd have thought my editor would have been capable of such a kick-ass performance? Singlehandedly taking down a cold-blooded killer? It defies comprehension."

"Hey, you never really know what someone is capable of until they're cornered. And he had her cornered, that's for sure. It was all on the line for her. She had to fight or die."

"True, but still, she surprised me. Nina's never been particularly athletic. Oh, I think she may have played sports in college, but that was some years ago." Regan grinned. "I'm so proud of her."

"You should be." Mitch draped an arm over her

shoulder and watched as the last of the crime scene technicians came off the boat. "Guess it's going to be a while before they let you use that boat."

"I never liked that boat much anyway," she told him. "It came with the property."

"I thought there was no house here before you built one."

"Some years ago there'd been an old fisherman's shack. He'd built the dock and had that boat tied up to it. When he died and the parcel was divided up, I got the part with the dock. The boat came with it."

"And the shack?"

"We tore that down. It stood right about where my garage is now, I think."

"You can always buy another boat, if you don't like that one."

"I'm thinking about it." She nodded. "Something big and fast, maybe. I'll have to see what they have up at the marina next time I'm there."

She tugged on him to follow her into the house. The sun was starting to set and the temperature was dropping. In another week, it would be Thanksgiving.

"Mitch, have you ever cooked a turkey?" she asked on their way inside.

"No. My mother does that." He glanced at his watch. "And I guess she'll be getting ready to do that soon enough."

"Do you go home for the holiday every year?"

"Sure. We all do. It's pandemonium. All my brothers

and sisters and their spouses or significant others and their kids, and my mother's sister and her family, my father's sister and hers . . . " He laughed. "You can barely find a place to sit when everyone finally arrives."

"And your mother has to cook for that crowd?"

"Everyone brings something. My mom just does the turkeys. Plural. Usually two of them. And a ham. It's quite a feast. It's noisy and people argue over politics and which football game to watch. Someone's kid always feeds a sock or something to the dog and then someone has to take the dog outside and make him throw up the sock. Someone always drinks too much wine and insults someone else." He smiled happily. "I can't wait."

Regan forced a smile and turned to the sink where she absently rinsed the coffee mugs they'd used earlier in the day. This was the tough part about not having family. She'd never experienced the kind of boisterous event that Mitch described. Her holidays with her father had always been fun, in their own staid way. But now, with him gone, the looming holiday season seemed to be a long black tunnel with nothing at the end for her. She felt the lack of any extended family most acutely this year.

She could go to England for Christmas with her cousins, she supposed. It would be better than being here alone, especially knowing that Mitch was celebrating with a loving cast of thousands.

"Regan?"

"What?"

"I asked you what you thought."

"I'm sorry, Mitch. I must have spaced out for a second." She turned off the faucet. "What do I think about what?"

"About making the trip to Maine with me next week. Do you think you could handle it? All those strange people doing strange things?" His eyes never left her face.

"Really? Seriously?" Her hands fluttered to her midsection.

"Sure." He put his arms around her. "My mom keeps asking me what's so special about this woman who occupies all my spare time. I think she needs to see for herself."

"What do you tell her?" Regan snuggled into him. "When she asks, what do you tell her?"

"I tell her you're quite wonderful and brilliant and beautiful, and that I don't mess with you because you're a better shot than I am, and you have a black belt and mine is only brown."

"I am quite good," she murmured.

"You are indeed." He smiled. "So, what do you think? A trip to Peyton-land over the long holiday weekend?"

"I'd love to go. Thank you so much for inviting me." She swayed with him for a long minute. "We should bring something, too, if everyone else does."

"I'll ask her what she still needs."

Regan closed her eyes, and began to count her blessings, a week early.

"Hey, what's up with Dolly Brown, anyway?" Mitch was asking. "There was so much going on here last night when I brought you home from the airport, I never got to ask you. What happened in Illinois?"

"Oh. Dolly is Eddie's sister, I figured that out, as you know. I still don't think I really understand why she felt she had to hide that from me." Regan frowned. "But, in any case, I did get her to show me some pictures of Eddie. She only had photos of him when he was younger, or so she claimed. And almost none of their younger sister, Catherine, which I thought was also very odd."

"Dolly sounds like a lady who is hiding something."

"You bet she is, and you can bet I'm going to find out."

"My money is always on you, Ace." Mitch laughed.

"Here's the strangest thing, though. As I'm getting ready to leave for the airport, the doorbell rings, and it's Stella, Carl's wife. She says she just stopped over to show me some of the pictures she had, and she whips out this pile of photos, mostly of the whole group when they were kids. Eddie, Carl, Harry—he's the brother who died—Dolly, and a few of

Catherine. She died in a car accident in the nineties, not so long ago that they wouldn't have had pictures of her, which I thought was another odd thing."

"Sounds like that Sayreville crowd is a puzzling bunch."

"It gets better. I spend a few hours with these two, and then I leave, figuring Dolly Brown is not going to tell me another damned thing. I get on the plane, and reach into my purse for some aspirin, and what do you suppose I found?"

"I have no idea."

She went to her purse and took out an envelope and handed it to him.

"Open it." She gestured, and he did.

"Photos." He thumbed through them. "Who are these people and why were they in your purse?"

"They are the Krolls, and they were in my bag because Stella slipped them in there."

"Why would she have done that?"

"I have no idea."

Regan leaned over his shoulder. "The boy on the left, the one in the cowboy hat, that's Eddie. Then there's Carl and Harry and I don't know who the other boy is."

She turned the photo over and read the names on the back. "Danny. Whoever he was."

She flipped the picture over again. "He was a cute little guy, don't you think? Eddie? I think he's probably around seven or eight in this picture." She shook her head. "Hard to imagine that five or six years after this was taken, he'd be arrested for his part in killing another young boy. A friend."

"Maybe that's why the family doesn't like to talk about him, Regan. It has to be very painful for them to look back on it. He was their brother. It's a small town. Besides the obvious, the family must have taken a lot of heat over this."

"They probably went through a lot of the same emotions that Nina did, after her father's arrest," Regan murmured. "Only she could leave town. She never really had to deal with what the locals were saying. The Krolls had to stay and face it all. It must have been hard to live with that."

"Who's this?" Mitch went on to the next picture.

"That's Dolly and Carl. Wasn't she a cute little bugger?" She laughed. "She's still a cute bugger, though I'd never say it to her face. She's some character. I wish you could meet her. She's given me headaches every step of the way, and yet I can't help but like her."

"Hey, who's this?" He held up a photo of a little girl with light auburn curls.

Regan stared at it, then turned it over for the name. "It's Catherine. The other sister."

She turned back to the photo. There was something eerily familiar about the girl in the picture.

"And this is . . . " Mitch had gone on to the next picture in the stack.

"This is who?" Regan asked, putting Catherine's picture aside.

"Well, if I didn't know better, I'd say it was you." Mitch held up the photograph.

Regan studied the face in the photo, then turned it over. *Catherine Kroll—1963.*

"Dolly said that Catherine died when she was in her mid-fifties, in the early nineteen-nineties. Ninety-three, maybe. If she was fifty-five in 1993, she would have been born in . . . " She paused to do the math.

"In 1938," Mitch said without hesitating. "So in 1963, she'd have been twenty-five."

He looked over Regan's shoulder. "She was beautiful, but babe, she looks a hell of a lot like you."

Regan sorted through the remaining pictures. Catherine appeared in six of the thirteen. The resemblance to Regan was striking, both as a child and as an adult. Regan felt almost dizzy looking at them.

"Dolly claimed to have no pictures of Catherine other than as a child. She was lying. If Stella, her sister-in-law, had these, Dolly had to have some, too."

"Why would Dolly hide them from you," Mitch asked, "while Stella clearly wanted you to see them?"

"I don't know," Regan told him, resolve settling into her face, "but you can bet your sweet ass I'm going to find out."

"Like I said, Ace, my money's always on you . . . "

CAN *YOU* HANDLE THE TRUTH?

Then get the *whole* Truth series by Mariah Stewart

More sizzling romance and nail-biting suspense await you.

COLD TRUTH
Book 1

HARD TRUTH
Book 2

DARK TRUTH
Book 3

And then:
FINAL TRUTH
The stunning hardcover conclusion